GLUE, BABY, GONE

BOOK #12 IN THE KIKI LOWENSTEIN MYSTERY SERIES

JOANNA CAMPBELL SLAN

spot on publishing

Glue, Baby, Gone: Book #12 in the Kiki Lowenstein Mystery Series

Joanna Campbell Slan

Spot On Publishing

9307 SE Olympus Street

Hobe Sound FL 33455 / USA

http://www.SpotOnPublishing.org

http://JoannaSlan.com

Publisher's Note: This is a work of fiction. Names, characters, places, and incidents are a product of the author's imagination. Locales and public names are sometimes used for atmospheric purposes. Any re-semblance to actual people, living or dead, or to businesses, companies, events, institutions, or locales is completely coincidental.

Revised 09/03/2020

Covers: http://www.WickedSmartDesigns.com

Glue, Baby, Gone: Book #12 in the Kiki Lowenstein Mystery Series by Joanna Campbell Slan. – 2nd ed.

CONTENTS

PART I

1

January 10, Friday
Five days before Kiki's due date

~Kiki~

Time slows to a crawl when you're nearly nine months pregnant. Every day is a struggle, because you feel like a klutz. A fat klutz at that. Your joints loosen up, your balance shifts, and your feet become a distant memory. With the first baby, you're excited and scared. With the second, you just want to get the delivery over with. My little passenger must have felt the same, because the baby struggled to get comfortable, turning and twisting and kicking against me as though my skin was a set of covers he could knock to the floor.

Added to our joint misery was the weather. I stayed indoors as much as possible, out of the brutal cold. A beautiful dusting of snow totally hid a mirror-slick frozen surface. With subzero temperatures the norm, even a short walk could prove hazardous.

Yes, January had slammed Missouri like a boxer dealing a knock-out blow. An overnight ice storm turned the bleak winter landscape into a crystal wonderland, broken by the fluff of snowflakes here and there. Light bounced and reflected off of every bush, branch, and broken blade of dead grass. The landscape twinkled as if it had been salted with a handful of diamonds. Although the world outside my window was breathtakingly beautiful, I knew that it was also very, very dangerous.

Shards of tan stuck out on one of the branches of our sugar maple. The crack proved that the limb was going to come down any minute. Tracing it with my eyes, I could see it would take a power line along with.

"We need to get out there and grab that thing before it takes out our power," I said, turning to my children's nanny, Bronwyn Macavity, affectionately called "Brawny."

"No, we don't," she said, in that deep voice of hers. Her Scottish accent always seemed heavier in the mornings, leaving me to wonder if she spent the night dreaming in her native Gaelic tongue. "You are going to stay right here. I can get that down in no time. If I hurry, I can get it done before your husband wakes up."

"I agree. The last thing we need is for Detweiler to get out there and pull out his stitches."

"*Aye,* and sure he would. He's not taking well to the doctor's orders to rest up and heal, is he? Do you really think he should be going back to work so soon?"

I turned away from her so she couldn't see how worried I was. "Of course I think it's too soon for him to be going back. He's still weak from all that blood loss, and he's not supposed to lift anything heavy. But with Robbie Holmes out on leave,

Prescott Gallaway is acting police chief, and Prescott hates Detweiler."

Brawny sipped her coffee. "I'll finish my cup and then take down that branch."

She drinks hers strong, black, and unsweetened. Mine is decaf mixed with almond milk and two packs of Truvia. I'm a big believer in trying to give my babies their best start in life, so I avoid caffeine, artificial sweeteners, and any food additives that might be harmful. That doesn't leave much.

A few sips later, Brawny was more awake. She asked me, "Why would Prescott hate Detweiler? That makes no sense. Detweiler's one of the best detectives on the force. His close rate is brilliant."

"Ah, but it does make sense in Prescott's pea-sized brain. Think of it this way: Detweiler is loyal to Robbie Holmes. Prescott knows that Detweiler has got his number. So he hates my husband, pure and simple."

"Got his number? What does that mean?"

Every once in a while, American slang confuses Brawny. So do references to popular culture. I'd considered saying, "Detweiler is Team Edward, and Prescott is Team Jacob," but that would have totally thrown Brawny for a loop. I doubt that she's heard of the Twilight series, much less Edward the Vampire and Jacob the Werewolf. Her choice of reading material seems to be strictly non-fiction, books on history and biographies. Each time I see one of her heavy tomes, I think, I really need to read material that's more educational. Then I pick up a cozy mystery, or a women's fiction title, and happily lose myself for hours. And guess what? I usually do learn a thing or two.

I explained, "Detweiler knows that Prescott is incompetent —and worse luck, Prescott knows that Detweiler doesn't think much of him."

"I see," she put her coffee mug in the sink, rinsed it, and

grabbed her boiled-wool jacket from the back of the kitchen chair. Pulling on a pair of scuffed suede gloves, she headed for the back door.

"You aren't going outside in that? You'll freeze." I stood up and stared out the window at the frozen, skeletal shapes of trees and shrubs.

We live on a prime piece of property in a charming community called Webster Groves. The lot is nine-tenths of an acre, complete with mature trees and a garden most people would give their eyeteeth to grow. My former landlord, Leighton Haversham, the author, sold us the property with the proviso that he be allowed to live in the garage he'd converted into a small cottage, when we moved into what was his former family home.

"Ach, this is more covering than most of my clan wear even when they're outside on the heather all day and all night. Don't be worrying your sweet self about me, Kiki. Sure and I'll warm up the car and drive you into the store later when you get yourself dressed and ready. There's no need for you to set your bahookie on a freezing leather car seat. A happy mum makes for a happy baby. You are feeling all right, aren't you?"

"Perfectly fine," I said. "I wish this baby would hurry up and come. I'm tired of being pregnant. I'm so uncomfortable that I barely get any sleep these days."

"Is that what's bothering ye?" asked Brawny. "You're certainly not your usual happy bunny self."

"That and the weather." I stopped myself from complaining about my mother-in-law. Thelma Detweiler, who'd once been my biggest fan, had turned against me. She thought I should have quit working at my store. According to Thelma, I was putting my baby in jeopardy.

Each time I thought about how she was carrying on, I fought the urge to snicker. Did it occur to Thelma that sitting at home would send me out of my pea-picking mind with boredom? Now that would definitely put my baby in danger. Working, not so much. At the store, all my employees treated me like a fragile blown glass vase.

But Thelma? She was treating me like I was her personal piñata.

My patience with her was wearing thin, while the ice outside was growing thicker and thicker.

The storm had added yet another coat of frozen wet stuff, a menace so undetectable on the roads that you think you're driving on dry pavement. One minute you're traveling along, and the next your car is spinning out of control, thanks to what we call "black ice." Despite the warmth in the house, I shivered violently. Ice storms scared me. When Anya was an infant, she came down with an ear infection the morning after a bad ice glazing. My first husband, the late George Lowenstein, was at a conference, so I had no choice but to pop her into her car seat and head for the pediatrician's office. I crept along, gaining speed as the car seemed to have good traction. Halfway there, on a busy stretch of Highway 40, my car spun out of control. The change of direction snapped my head left to right, disorienting me. For a second, I thought I was on a carnival ride. Then my car hit a guard rail. I remember thinking, "I've killed my baby!" I unbuckled my seat belt and climbed over the console, so hysterical that I couldn't even see for my tears. In fact, I tumbled onto the floor behind the passenger seat. The whiplash of the car had messed with my sense of balance, so I then had to do a somersault to right myself. When I did, Anya was staring at me, those denim blue eyes wide with surprise.

"Anya, honey, you okay?" I whimpered, sure that I'd hurt her so badly she was paralyzed.

Then, blessedly, she began to cry.

As I did now, just thinking back on it.

Brawny shook her head at me, setting that thick gray ponytail of hers swinging this way and that. "*Aye,* the dark and the gloom gets to some people more than others. Seasonal Affective Disorder, it's called. Or maybe it's the lack of sleep, but you certainly aren't yourself these days."

"No. No, I'm not," and I blew my nose on a paper napkin.

Kiki's story continues in ***Glue, Baby, Gone***, available here: https://amzn.to/2Ts16Wn

2

We'd gone over and over the work schedule, adding as many events as we could to our store's calendar. Clancy and Margit glowered at me.

"You're nuts," said Clancy. "Out of your mind. Kiki, what's the goal? To tire yourself out so badly that you have to be hauled off the sales floor in an ambulance?"

"Dummkopf," muttered Margit under her breath. Although I've never had a class in German, I was able to translate the word without any trouble. Margit's vehemence stunned me. She's never said anything so nasty to me. "This is too much for you to do! You will hurt your baby!"

That ticked me off. I pointed to my belly. "This baby will be fine. It's this baby—" and I made a circling motion with my index finger, "that I'm concerned about. I'd like to do as much as possible so I can take time off and not be stressed out about the store."

"The store will be fine," said Clancy.

"We are capable of handling whatever arises," agreed Margit.

"You're worrying about the wrong thing," continued Clancy.

"You should be thinking more of yourself, because a happy mommy makes for a happy baby."

They had been right. I had been wrong and bullheaded to boot. As the days on the January calendar flipped past, my energy dipped below sea level. To keep going, I'd slip away to the bathroom, sit on the toilet seat, lean my head on the toilet paper roll dispenser, and nap. When my backside hit the water, I'd wake up, dry my tushie, and head out the door for more fun and games.

Like this crop. We'd advertised it as "Baby Album Blast Off: We'll show you a speed scrapping technique that'll help you complete an entire album in an evening! Preparing for a blessed event has never been so fast or so fun."

Right.

Obviously, I'd lost my mind and with it any sense of dignity. To top it off (and I'm being intentionally ironic here), my feet had swollen to the point that none of my shoes fit. So I was padding around the back room in mukluks. Clancy had taken one look at my Franken-tootsies and said, "This is humiliating. I should walk right out the door and leave you to this. By yourself. Are you channeling a 'What Not to Wear' television program? Or is this a new low point? Hmm? Inquiring minds want to know."

"Stow it," I snarled, as I gathered up the bags of supplies and marched over to the teaching tables. There I faced twenty-two eager students who couldn't wait to put together their albums. Most of my guests were expecting their own bundles of joy. Two were grandmothers. But I was the only fool who looked like she'd swallowed an inner tube. Even my friend Bonnie Gossage looked less inflated than I did. That's saying a lot, because Bonnie typically gains a lot of weight when she gets pregnant. Watching her bump into the edge of the table, I realized how smart she'd been to take time away from her law firm. Try as she might to be professional, that belly bump screamed, "Mom to be! Hormones on the loose!"

I always start my sessions with a little light-hearted monologue designed to break the tension. I'd practiced my opening in front of the bathroom mirror, even planning my cheery tone of voice: "With my first baby, I was scared spitless about giving birth. Totally freaked out about the pain and the whole idea of labor. But now that I'm in my last trimester with my second child, the prospect of going into labor has become more and more appealing every day."

Most of the students giggled as I passed out supplies for making a baby album.

They'd been there, done that, and had the stretch marks to prove they were mothers. A couple others looked shocked at my bold admission. These were the younger women at the craft tables. They couldn't imagine themselves big as a beached whale, like I was.

"Your day will come," I said under my breath in a snarl.

Lee Alderton has been coming to my crops for years. Although there wasn't a baby in the Alderton family yet, I knew she had high hopes that her daughter-in-law Maggie and son Bradley would have a happy announcement soon. Because she overheard my nasty comment, Lee shook her head in amusement, but she was far too kind to rat me out.

Frankly, I didn't care. I was too tired, angry, and uncomfortable to worry about other people's opinions of me.

"I'm pregnant, too," said Jana Higgins. Everyone turned to stare at her. She sure didn't look like she was carrying a baby, but it was really hard to tell because she was a big girl. Her bump seemed to be barely hanging over her belt. Most of us had these hard, high mounds, but Jana's bulge seemed more jiggly. The way it moved seemed at odds with the rest of her. She wore her hair in a severe ponytail. Her dark-rimmed glasses would have been more appropriate on an accountant than a young woman. She sat in a very self-contained way, as though she was jammed into a small glass cubicle.

Three other women who were new to the store introduced themselves one by one. Deena Edmonds was as tall as Detweiler so she barely looked pregnant, since she had nearly six feet of height to disguise her weight gain. Deena's size could have made her intimidating, but there was an open quality to her face that offset the way she towered over people. She was a sprawler, like me. Within minutes of sitting down, she'd scattered materials in a half-circle around her.

The child-like expression in Marnie Sampson's blue eyes matched the toy-sized baby bump she had going. Marnie brought a neat pink toolbox. Inside were all the tools a crafter would need.

Amy Romanovski's belly was barely noticeable, not big. Her heart-shaped face suggested she was as sweet as a box of chocolates. Behind her, she pulled a collapsible bin with an apron of cloth pockets all around the outside walls. Obviously, this young woman was the veteran of numerous crafting adventures.

"When are you due?" I asked each of them. I was determined to be nice. Really nice. I heard a variety of dates as each woman responded in turn.

"Not until May. I'm glad because the weather will be nice, right?" Amy said, with an upward inflection of her voice.

Instead of answering, Jana ignored my question and parroted back, "Kiki, when are you due?"

Lee gave her a look that echoed my thoughts, What pregnant woman doesn't have her due date engraved on her heart? Hmmm?

"Not a moment too soon," I said, "and you?"

"Me, too. Not a moment too soon."

Was she making fun of me? I couldn't tell. Lee blinked in

surprise, but neither of us pursued the matter, because Jana then turned to Bonnie Gossage, who hadn't spoken yet. "When's your baby coming?"

"February 7th, three weeks from now. I think the doctor is wrong. I'm pretty sure I'm further along than that. I bet Kiki and I bump into each other at the hospital," said Bonnie, as she patted her belly.

"I'm thinking about a home birth," said Amy. "Did you hear that somebody tried to smuggle a baby out of the hospital in St. Peters? Fortunately they'd tagged the infant. A bunch of alarms went off. That is so scary, right?"

"They can tag a baby?" Deena's eyes went wide. "Like a dog tag? How does that work?"

"It's a radio frequency tag," I explained. "They attach it to the umbilical cord. Kind of like those anti-shoplifting tags at a clothing store."

"Home births are scary. If something goes wrong, you've got a problem. A big, big problem." Bonnie popped the top on a can of Vanilla Coke.

"Bonnie, how can you drink that when it's so cold outside?" I asked. I'd sworn off my favorite beverage, Diet Dr Pepper, in part because of the caffeine, but also because of the artificial sweeteners.

She grinned at me. "With the first two, I craved Sprite and Orange Crush. With this one, it's Vanilla Coke. What can I say?"

"You can say, 'Kiki, please hand me a drink holder so we're positive I won't spill any of it,'" and with that I grabbed a drink holder, clipped it onto the side of the table, and put the can inside the plastic container. Drink holders keep beverages lower than the work surface. An accidental bump won't dislodge the can. That way one dumped drink won't ruin everyone's work. It also clears more work space.

"Thanks," said Bonnie. "Kiki, you spoil us."

"I try to. Now would everybody open their kits?"

My students eagerly tore open the cellophane packages we'd bundled up for each individual. We'd asked participants to choose a color scheme ahead of time, so each person's pack had to be done separately. That made this class a total pain in the backside. That said, it was one of our more popular offerings. This class brought in more new customers than any other class we offered. New moms are eager to document each new experience, so scrapbooking is the perfect hobby for them. Marnie had opted for aqua. Amy wanted yellow. Deena pink. Aqua and yellow seemed safe bets if you didn't know your baby's sex.

"Another boy for you, Bonnie?"

"That's right. Jeremy had his heart set on a girl, but we'll take what we can get."

"Or what God gives you, to be more precise. Jana? You're having a boy?" I asked Jana, as I watched her open her package of carefully selected supplies for the baby album. Jana had requested all blue paper and embellishments.

"Yes," she said.

Lee had opted for two kits, one yellow and one aqua. "To keep our options open. Jeff and I don't care what sex the baby is. Or who has a baby first, Taylor and Ryan or Maggie and Bradley. Of course, we hope that Taylor might wait until after her wedding, but we'll take life as it comes."

Marnie nodded. "That's what my parents say, too." Her skin was so translucent that she reminded me of a slice of onion. Her eyes were the palest blue, the color of bleached out jeans. She looked like she'd swallowed a small exercise ball, the way her tummy stuck out. Except for that, she was rail-thin. Her auburn hair stood out from her head like a halo, thanks to all the static electricity in the air.

"I asked the tech to keep it a surprise because I was afraid I'd slip and tell our folks. Kiki, is your skin dry? I feel like mine is about to split open. It's like I'm wearing a corn husk," she lifted a pant leg to show me the flakes on her shin. She'd rubbed a carpet burn on one spot, trying to get the itching to stop.

"Use coconut oil. In fact, I've got some in the back on the bathroom counter. Feel free to help yourself."

She grinned at me, and suddenly I could see that she was actually a very pretty girl. "Thanks, I will. Since I know that I'll have to use the john ten minutes from now, that'll give me the perfect chance to try some."

"There are baggies in the kitchen. Grab a spoon and dig out a glob to take home with you."

"How much would I owe you?" she asked.

"Not one red cent. Girlfriend, we preggies have to stick together."

Jana had been listening intently to every word. She had this look on her face, like when a child watches its parents. "My skin's dry too."

"Then you can help yourself, too," I said. "Now let's get working on our interior pages."

3

Friday night

The class ended at nine thirty, dragging on a half an hour longer than we'd planned. I tried to get my students to finish up and leave, but everyone seemed incredibly chatty. Too chatty, according to my aching lower back.

"Don't forget, everybody," Clancy said. "We've also scheduled a crop where you can show off your baby's pictures. It's called 'A Star Is Born.' It's the second Friday in February. If you sign up for it tonight and let us add you to our email list, we'll give you a twenty-five percent discount off any purchases you make this evening."

Jana was trying to bond with Bonnie, sticking to her side like glue. But Bonnie and Lee were trying to get caught up. That left Jana making an awkward third wheel. Marnie tagged along behind them, acting more like an obedient puppy than a grown woman. It would have been amusing had it not been so socially inept. Here were Bonnie and Lee, trying to talk, and then

Marnie and Jana would insert some inane comment, just to get attention.

"I remember when we first met," Lee said with a chuckle. "Someone brought up Green Acres and you sang the theme song. Do you remember that?"

I laughed. "How could I forget?"

"Kiki, when you think of everything we've been through," Bonnie said, while pulling on her navy wool jacket, "it's divine justice that we'd be pregnant at the same time. Not much longer for us to go. If you need me for anything, you've got my number. Lee has it, too."

"I don't have your number." Jana nearly rear-ended Bonnie. The young woman was that close to my friend. Some people have no sense of personal space.

Bonnie had a look on her face that could only be interpreted as, "I don't want to share my phone number with this woman." Bonnie was a busy mom, a supportive wife, and a powerful attorney. I had her number, but I guarded it carefully. Bonnie had so little time to herself that I tried not to call her unless it was absolutely necessary.

"Your number?" Jana repeated her request.

Rather than make a scene, I called over to Lee. "Lee? Have you signed up for the 'A Star Is Born' class yet? Would you show Jana where we keep the sign-up sheet?"

Blocking Jana's access to my friend, I reached out and hugged Bonnie, as best I could, despite our burgeoning bellies. Pitching my voice low, I said, "You and me. Whenever I've needed help, you've been there for me. I'll do the same for you, Bonnie."

She knew immediately that I was referencing the time that my mother-in-law by my first marriage had me thrown in jail. "How is Sheila?"

"Still out of commission," I said, feeling a wave of emotion.

Sheila Lowenstein Holmes, the mother of my late husband, George, was out in Palm Springs, California, at a rehab facility, where we hoped that she would dry out. Her drinking had gotten totally out of control. "She'll be happy to come back and be a grandmother again. We're blessed to bring babies into this world, aren't we?"

"And, occasionally, to keep them out of the wrong hands." Bonnie winked, reminding me of Bernice Stottlemeyer, one of her clients who had wanted to adopt for all the wrong reasons. Bernice had been a whack-job of the first order, and she'd very nearly caused a rift between Bonnie and me. But our friendship proved strong enough to overcome the problems that Bernice had caused us.

"Amen to that, sister. Ever hear from our old nemesis?" I asked my friend.

"Bernice and Wesley are getting a divorce."

"Good," I said. "He seemed like a nice man. Her, not so much."

Instead of responding to that, Bonnie smiled. She's very circumspect about her clients, and from her silence, I assumed that she still considered the Stottlemeyers as such.

"This baby might be a C-section. So far, it looks like he's determined to be breech. I'm going to go nuts having to stay home and recover," she said. "Promise you'll come visit me."

"I will," I promised. "I couldn't sit still. I can't imagine you doing it either."

"Getting scrapbookers rounded up and out the door is like forcing parakeets to march in a straight line," Clancy said as she helped me put scraps of paper into plastic bags. "You look exhausted," she said. We'd sort the scraps by color later. It's amazing what you can do with a tiny bit of paper. Absolutely amazing.

"I am tired. Really bushed."

"Sorry I was so rough on you."

"I'm sorry I didn't listen to you and Margit when you tried to talk me out of this...this...frantic schedule."

"Yes, well. We should have backed off as soon as we realized you were already taking heat from Thelma."

4

"How did you know about that?" I rubbed my lower back with both fists.

Clancy shrugged. "We got it straight from the horse's mouth. I use that cliché advisedly because she's been acting like a horse's rear end. Calling here. Demanding to know how many hours you've worked. Practically had poor Margit in tears."

What?" I couldn't have heard her right. "Thelma? Calling here? At the store?"

"I debated over whether to tell you, but you might as well know. She probably calls twice a day, asking if you are here and how long you've been working. I've gotten so I try to screen the calls so Margit doesn't have to deal with her. You know how upset Margit can get over hassles like that."

Yes, I did. What on earth was Thelma up to?

"Look, it's almost over now. You'll have your baby and everything will go back to normal. In the meantime," Clancy took the baggies out of my hand, "why not go and sit down at your desk? Put your feet up. Is Brawny coming to get you?"

"I sure hope so." A tear leaked out and trickled down my face. "Is it so wrong for me to worry about the store? Thelma doesn't seem to understand. And I wasn't nasty to the customers tonight was I? Tell me, please? Do I owe anyone an apology?"

"Let's put it this way. No one nominated you for Miss Congeniality, that's for sure." Clancy took me by the arm, led me to the big black leather chair in the room we still called "Dodie's Office." Until her untimely death from cancer, Dodie Goldfader had been my mentor, my boss, and my friend. If it hadn't been for her, I would have never grown up. She guided me into adulthood after my first husband, George Lowenstein, was murdered. Sitting me down, she'd told me the hard facts of life: "If you don't take care of yourself and your daughter, no one will. You're the adult in the room. Get with the program." That changed everything.

"I miss Dodie. I wish she was here."

"We all do." Clancy slipped her forearm under my calves and helped me lift my legs so that my feet were propped up on top of the desk. "I didn't know her like you did, but there are days when I can feel her presence."

"Are you getting all wooo-wooo on me?"

"No. Okay, maybe. Lately, I feel this sort of happy warmth in here. I figure it has to be Dodie. She'd be thrilled about your baby."

"Yeah, but she'd also be the first to wonder if I can handle it all. Can I keep the store going, be a wife, and raise three kids all at once?"

"Probably. As long as you don't run off the help or the customers."

"I'm not myself." The tap had been turned on. Tears streamed down my face faster than I could mop them up with my sleeve.

"Of course you aren't. You're nine months pregnant. Hello! It's going to be okay. Try to take it easy."

"Yup," I said, but it came out as a mumbled snivel.

I rested my head back against the big leather office chair. Dodie insisted that this seat made her feel like a CEO. I felt like a dwarf. Sleepy. Yeah, that was his name. What were the names of the other six? Dopey? Grouchy? Sleezy? In a Disney-induced fog, I drifted off until Brawny tapped me on the shoulder.

Clancy must have warned the nanny that I was a mess, because Brawny put one arm under my armpits and half-lifted me out of the chair. When I complained that I needed to use the restroom, she walked me inside before leaving me to my business.

By the time I had finished, she was holding open my cape, the one she'd made for me. In a practiced move, she bundled me up, wrapped the scarf around my face and throat, and held open the mittens that Margit had knitted for me.

"Clancy said your feet are too swollen to fit in your boots. I'll pull up the car. The floor mat will be your red carpet tonight, so get ready for your star turn." Brawny wrapped an arm around my expansive waist and guided me to the exit. Clancy joined us there.

"Get some rest," Clancy said, giving me a stiff hug. "I'll take over your All About Me album class tomorrow."

"But you can't—" I started.

"Yes, I can. In case you haven't noticed, I can follow directions. I'm not incompetent, nor am I a moron. Honestly, Kiki, you're the best teacher I've ever had. Don't you think we're prepared for your taking a leave of absence? It's not like you haven't been pregnant for nearly nine months."

She humbled me. I nodded, feeling even more miserable.

"Look. We love this place as much as you do. And we love you, too, even though you're being a dope. Why don't you trust us?"

I opened my mouth and started to complain, "It's not that I don't trust—"

"That's what it feels like," said Clancy. Even though it was ten at night, her makeup was still perfect. However, the big hashtag between her eyes marred how perfect she looked.

"I'm scared," I said, blubbering.

"Of what? Having the baby?" She peered around me, opening the door a crack to see whether Brawny had pulled up yet. A burst of cold air stung my face.

"No. Yes. Some—and scared about business, and how I'll cope, and how Erik will do with a new baby, and how Anya is going to—"

Clancy closed the door between us and the frozen landscape, but the cold had already chilled us to the bones. Her nose was pink from the arctic blast. "Don't forget to worry about Ebola, ISIS, inertia of Congress, tax increases, rat poop in our food supply, global warming, and the chance that spring won't come this year."

"You're making fun of me!" I felt my lower lip quiver.

"No, I am not making fun of you," said Clancy. "I'm helping you get the job done right. If you're going to be a worrywart, no sense leaving any stone unturned. How's that for an ugly mixed metaphor? Come on, Suzy Sunshine. I'm sending you home with the Celtic Warrior Woman. I love you dearly, but I've had enough of you for one night."

5

Saturday

That's how I came to be banned from my own store.

Of course, I didn't know I'd been banned. Not at first. The next morning I got up, ate breakfast, got dressed, kissed the kids and Detweiler goodbye, and reached for my car keys. My keychain was gone.

I called my husband. "Have you seen my keys?"

"Of course I have. They're right here in my pocket." Detweiler looked up from his iPad where he'd been reading the New York Times. My husband was a hunk. Long legged. Lean. Dark blond hair with gold highlights that came naturally. Beautiful slender and long fingers. And a body to die for. Instead of feeling lucky, that last thought made me wonder why he cared.

Yes, he was a hunk and he was married to a whale. Or a tug boat. Or a baby elephant. I couldn't think of a single metaphor that flattered my balloon-shaped self.

"I need them."

"No, you do not. You aren't going anywhere."

"But the store! It's a Saturday!"

"The store will do just fine without you. Margit called Laurel and Rebekkah, the two of them will cover your hours. I suggest you put a kettle of water on the stove and make yourself another cup of tea."

Laurel was a dear friend who looked like a Playboy centerfold and totally disarmed you with her sweet nature. Otherwise, she was so gorgeous that she'd have been insufferable. Customers loved Laurel because of her willingness to help. Rebekkah was the daughter of Dodie Goldfader. Although she was hirsute like her mother, Rebekkah's friendship with Laurel had convinced the young woman to tame her hair and brows. The transformation had been visually amazing. Of course, Rebekkah had grown up in the store, so she was very knowledgeable about products.

Both of my young friends were fully capable of running the store without me. But I wasn't ready to let go. Not yet.

"What?" I was so loud, so indignant, that Gracie came over and rested a big paw on my knee.

"You need to rest, Kiki. You aren't sleeping at night. I feel you trying to get comfortable, and you can't. Not with our baby fighting you for floor space. Why not enjoy the day? Lorraine is coming over to keep you company later this afternoon. She's working on an afghan. You've been saying you wanted to learn to crochet. Now's your chance."

I stomped my foot, which was jammed into my rubber boots so tightly I was sure I'd get blisters if I walked more than fifteen feet. My trusty mukluks were in my messenger bag, the one I'd made by sewing Beggin' Strips bags together. (If you'll excuse the pun, my bag is so doggone cute I could just sit and admire it all day long. Not that I want to sit around all day. Just sayin'.)

"I know how to crochet! I don't want to sit home and crochet!

I have stuff to do at my store! I need to get to work! And I plan to go there the minute Brawny gets back with the Subaru."

He chuckled. "Good luck with that. You planning to arm wrestle her for the keys? Take it from me, you'll lose. She was beating me easily up until the time I got shot. I have a hunch that she'll have your arm pinned in nothing flat."

"You can't do this to me. You should have discussed it with me! It's not fair."

"Babe, what is it that you're always telling the kids? Life ain't fair? I love you. We all love you, and you're being totally unreasonable about staying home so we put our heads together and came up with a solution."

"Oh, we did, did we? We who? I wasn't consulted!"

"You weren't consulted because you've been a little down lately. Brawny thinks it's the hormones getting to you. I even called Dr. Gretski, and he agreed with us. This is for your own good. Think of it as a snow day. You can play with the kids. That'll help them handle the big changes ahead."

He was right, but I was honked off. I felt betrayed by his willingness to go along with my friends in keeping me away from the store. That shop had been my lifeline when my marriage to George was failing. Thanks to Dodie Goldfader, Time in a Bottle had become my home away from home, my happy place.

If I were to be perfectly honest with myself, I needed Time in a Bottle more than the store needed me. Truth to tell, Anya and Erik weren't the only ones facing big changes. Suddenly I felt overwhelmed by the thought of mothering three kids. As a new bride—we'd only been married twelve days—I also felt like I'd missed out on a honeymoon. Not that I needed a fancy trip, but with both marriages, there'd been no chance to run away with my groom. No time to be romantic and alone with my life partner. I'd gotten pregnant after one night with George, and with Detweiler there'd been what he called "equipment failure," so in both cases I'd gone from dating to cohabitation in nothing flat.

I wondered what it would be like to take walks on a beach, cuddle in a big bed with an overhead fan going, and drink tropical concoctions by a tiki bar. Yes, I knew the man I was marrying, but wouldn't it be lovely to get to know each other in a leisurely way? Without someone hollering, "Mom!" in the background? Once in a while, Detweiler would share a glimpse into his past, and I would realize that I didn't know him very well at all. On the other hand, we'd been through so much together that I knew enough to know he had my back—and I had his. But what I really longed for was someone to rub my back. To pay attention to me and only me, just for a while, that's all. In short, I felt cheated, and at war with myself because I knew I was very, very blessed, but I still felt sad. Inside me there was a tug-of-war going on, one side pitted against the other, and I suspect this cognitive dissonance added to my general sense of exhaustion.

Even from my seat at the kitchen table, I could see that the weather outside was truly frightful. Detweiler had studded snow tires on his police cruiser, but I still cringed at the thought of him out there on the roads alone. Much less the thought of him doing his job on the mean streets of our town. Our wedding last month had climaxed not with the taking of our vows, but with a bullet whizzing by. Detweiler's spleen had been nicked, but the doctors hadn't caught his internal bleeding until he lost a lot of blood. Although he was back on his feet, my husband was drawn and moving kind of slow, which is not good when you're a cop. He'd been instructed not to lift anything heavy for six weeks. I couldn't tell if he was adhering to that bit of warning or not, because twice I'd watched him reach for Erik, and he would have lifted the boy, if I hadn't shouted out for him to stop.

Gracie stood at my side, her thick tail whopping me with every wag. She loves Detweiler more than she loves me, even though I rescued her. I don't mind. I think it's cool that they've bonded the way they have. In the summer, when Detweiler picks up his keys and heads out, his leaving is easy on her. In the winter, when he has to get bundled up like this, she whines. All these thoughts raced through my mind, as I watched Detweiler pull on his coat and reach in his pocket for his winter gloves.

He was going to help Leighton put together a bookcase for his lady love, Lorraine Lauber, who was also Erik's aunt. No one had expected Leighton and Lorraine to fall in love, but they had. Whereas Leighton once lived here in "the big house," his family home, he and Lorraine now occupied the small house on the edge of our spacious lot. Having them so close was a blessing. Auntie Lorie could watch Erik grow up, and we were near enough to help out when she had a flare up of her MS.

My lower lip trembled as my husband put one hand on the doorknob.

"Aren't you forgetting something?" I asked, puckering up my lips.

"I could never forget you," he said, sweeping me up into his arms. "You're my whole life."

6

Over the next hour and a half, I was a very busy bee. Scratch that. I was more like a mad wasp protecting its nest. I picked a fight with Brawny and Margit. Added to my tiff with Detweiler, I got into three different scuffles or quarrels, to be precise. Only Erik had avoided the wrath of Kiki.

I overheard Brawny telling Margit not to call me with problems. Evidently, there was a question about an album that I'd set aside for a customer. Since Brawny and Margit already rub each other the wrong way, I bristled when I heard Brawny telling Margit that Clancy could handle the situation when she came in later.

"You could have given me the message, let me solve the problem, and that would have been the end of it. Now I'm going to have an unhappy customer to deal with when I get back to the store."

"The customer will be fine. Clancy will soothe her. She always does."

I decided to let that go, even though it sounded like a criticism of my customer service skills.

We probably would have had words—or at least I would

have had a go at her—except she was scheduled to teach a class at my store. With a smile, she patted my hand and said, "Don't ye dare go into labor while I'm gone."

Less than five minutes later, Detweiler had ticked me off because he kept telling me, "Be careful. Mom says you shouldn't..." and that list was longer than my arm. According to Thelma Detweiler, I shouldn't fret, bend over, pick anything up, stand for longer than five minutes, get too hot or too cold, go without drinking water for more than an hour, and other activities too silly to pay attention to.

I felt trapped in my own home. The image of a Push Me Pull You, the mythical llama-like creature in the Dr. Doolittle books sprang to mind. On one hand, I needed to get outside and soak up whatever meager amounts of sunshine I could. On the other, soft surfaces and mounds of covers beckoned me to burrow down and go into hibernation.

Not surprisingly, I leaped toward my cell phone the second it rang, because I was that eager for a distraction. Thelma Detweiler sounded incredibly cheerful. "How about if we go to St. Louis Bread Co.? I know how you love it."

In St. Louis, we call Panera Bread by its local name, St. Louis Bread Co. and that rhymes with "dough."

"Wonderful," I said. "I'd love to get out of the house."

Since she was driving over from Illinois, I had plenty of time to get ready. Standing in front of the full length mirror, I took note of the extra cleavage I'd grown and how my mighty boobs spilled out from the armholes of my bra. Would I ever be slim? Doubtful.

I'd taken to smoothing my hair with a curling iron. My curls seemed like the only portion of my life I could tame. The styling implement was heating when Anya burst into our bedroom. "Mom? I have to go to the mall. You need to take me. Nicci's there, and she wants me to look at boots with her."

"Anya? I believe you meant to ask me if I could take you to the mall. You surely did not intend to demand a ride, did you?" This was a new tact I'd been taking. Rather than correct her, I acted as if she'd overlooked something important, usually manners.

"Whatever." She pouted. "You know what I mean! Look, I really need to go right now. Nicci doesn't have all day."

Actually, Nicci probably did have all day. Anya's best friend, Nicci Moore, spent countless hours at the mall.

"I'm sorry, but I have a meeting to attend. I need you to stay here with Erik."

"What? Babysitting? I'm not your unpaid slave, you know!"

"That's true. Point of fact, we rarely ask you to watch Erik, because we have Brawny, so it won't hurt you to watch him for an hour or two right now."

I was being (somewhat) unreasonable, and I knew it. Truth to tell, Thelma could have dropped Anya off at the mall and I could bring Erik with me to St. Louis Bread Co. Thelma adored the boy and accepted him as her grandson even though he wasn't related to her by blood. Since I planned on a civilized conversation, Erik was the perfect foil. He would remind both of us, Thelma and me, that we needed to be especially kind to each other.

But Anya's demanding tone struck me wrong. A slave? Could she hear herself talking? If she thought her life was restrictive, she was in denial. Sure, she wanted to be with her friend, but I was going into labor, and then I would be flat out of choices for a long time. It wasn't much to ask for her to stay home with her brother.

Detweiler had encouraged me to find a second-string babysitter for Erik. Laurel and her fiancé Father Joe were always willing, but they were busy planning their wedding. But my husband had foreseen this day, a time when Anya was eager to leave her little brother behind while she did her own thing. To be honest, I'd actively procrastinated on finding a helper. Erik had come so far since moving in with us that it seemed unreasonable to push our luck, especially with a new baby coming. Why upset him by adding a new face to his world?

No, to my mind Anya was acting like a spoiled brat. Her accusation that I was using her as unpaid labor hurt my feelings. Over the summer, I'd hired her to work at my store and paid her more than she could have made babysitting. Since she's only thirteen, she was lucky to find work at all. I couldn't at her age. Now she had a nice nest egg, and it had come directly from my profits—and I'd been generous. I'd expected her to cut me a little slack when I needed her help.

"Look," I said, in an effort to be reasonable, "I'll pay you five bucks an hour to watch your brother. Trust me, Anya, most of us were saddled with watching younger siblings for free."

"Make it ten."

That really got my dander up. "I can't believe this! You're holding me up for money! I'm your mother. He's your brother."

"Not really," she said.

And then I got very, very mad.

7

After grounding my daughter for the rest of her life plus thirty years, I called Thelma and told her I'd meet her at Bread Co. That allowed me to make a clean get away, as I left Anya at home to stew in her own juices.

Thelma was delighted to see the little boy and me. Erik loves Bread Co., so we ordered his favorite lunch, a smoked ham sandwich and creamy tomato soup. I was content with my own bowl of tomato soup and an iced green tea. Thelma paid, and that made me slightly uncomfortable, but I decided to roll with it. We took a booth by the front window. I sipped my tea.

"You shouldn't be drinking that," she said. "It has caffeine."

"I looked it up. Brewed coffee has 95 to 200 milligrams of caffeine, while the same amount of green tea has 45."

She paused while dunking a tea bag in hot water. "Right, but the March of Dimes suggests that women cut back on caffeine consumption during pregnancy. There's some concern that too much can kick you into labor."

"Right now, that sounds heavenly. My skin is so dry I feel like I'm covered in sandpaper. I itch and scratch all the time. I can't sleep. The baby keeps jamming his toes under my ribs. If I push on one side, he strikes at the other. I have heartburn. My thinking is foggy." I stopped. I couldn't believe I was giving Thelma ammunition for why I should stay home.

"I remember being uncomfortable, but all that fades away when they put a healthy child in your arms." There was a slight undertone of disapproval, an attitude totally unlike Thelma Detweiler. "That baby is much, much more important than your stupid store."

The blood drained from my face. I felt light-headed. "Excuse me?"

"Kiki, you've been spending too many hours on your feet. For goodness sake, you're endangering your child! Use a little common sense." Thelma's face must have been as red with anger as mine was white from shock.

"The baby is doing absolutely fine, Thelma. The doctor told me he's active, and healthy, and appropriately sized. There's no reason I can't continue to work up until I go into labor. None."

Her mouth flattened into a straight, thin line. "Things can still go wrong, Kiki. Women lose their babies all the time."

"Mama Kiki, can you lose a baby? Our baby?"

I said, "No," right as Thelma said, "Yes."

That raised my ticked-off meter to boiling hot.

"He doesn't need to hear that," I hissed at Thelma, after I encouraged Erik to go and dump a wadded up paper napkin in the trash.

"It's not right to lie to him." Her tone was odd, and totally unlike the Thelma I knew.

I had had enough of Thelma Detweiler and her sanctimonious judgments on my behavior. "I am not lying to Erik. I'm simply uninterested in scaring the kid half to death. The doctor says my baby is fine, and he is. I'm not a high-risk mother. Sure things can go wrong, but then, we could get hit by a truck on the way home."

A nice clerk had given Erik a bag of potato chips. I didn't notice he was heading back toward our table. He suddenly appeared at my elbow, and the expression on his face told me he'd overheard my casual remark.

"We could get hit by a truck?" Erik dropped his bag of potato chips. As he bent to pick them up, I gently said, "No, honey. Those are dirty. We'll get you a new bag."

His little face scrunched up with worry. "Mama died in a car. An axe-see-dent killed Mama and Van. They died. Are we going to die?"

Then he burst into tears.

I desperately wanted to snap at Thelma, and ask, Couldn't you leave well enough alone? But to my credit, I kept my mouth shut.

8

Monday

"Either somebody gives me a ride to the store or I'm going to call a cab," I said, facing down Detweiler and Brawny as they sat across from each other at the breakfast table. "I've had it with staying home."

Detweiler set his coffee cup down gently. "Kiki, are you—"

"Yes, I'm sure. On Sunday, Lorraine and I crocheted for hours. She was pooped out by the time she left. Could barely sit up in the recliner. For goodness sake! That woman has MS. She's in no condition to be helping me! She's worse off than I am—and I am bored out of my skull."

"Lorraine is fine most of the time," said Brawny. "Lately, she's hit a rough patch."

"So have I, but my rough patch is the direct result of you two treating me like a pet parakeet."

I have no idea where that image came from. The words jumped out of my mouth.

However, they did have the desired effect on Detweiler and Brawny.

“Parakeet? As in a budgie?” she asked.

“A pigeon, maybe. A parakeet, doubtful,” Detweiler said.

“Budgie? What's a budgie? Yes, I mean, no. Okay, maybe. I mean a small colorful bird in a cage!”

Detweiler's sigh was long, low, and loud. “If you think you're up to it, I'll take you. But honestly, Kiki, you've been awfully grumpy lately. Are you sure being at the store is a good thing? For you and your customers? You've gotten mad at my mother, at Brawny, at Anya, and at me. That's not exactly the sort of upbeat attitude that your customers have grown to expect.”

“Since I’m the only person at this table who’s ever been pregnant, I'm a lot more qualified to make judgments on my state of well-being than either of you are.”

“Okay,” said Detweiler, slowly. “You want breakfast?”

“No.”

“I'll make you toast and tea.” Brawny pushed back her chair. I was still plenty ticked off at her so I said, “No thanks. If I wanted toast and tea, I would have made it myself.”

She sank back down.

The drive to the store was quiet. We were half-way there when I realized how much I was craving a McDonald's breakfast burrito. But I would have died rather than ask Detweiler to pull up to a drive-through window. However, my husband knows me pretty well. Five blocks from my store, he took a detour that routed us through a McDonald's. I planned to sit there, stone-faced, but I couldn't. “Sausage burrito, please. Make that two burritos. A hash brown, too. A big bottle of water.”

He handed me the bag.

I couldn't help it. I got the giggles.

“Tough lady,” he said, reaching over to give me a hug. “Hang in there, sweetheart. Three days from now, we'll be holding our baby son in our arms. This will all be over with. I know you haven't been feeling well. Guess what Dr. Gretski told me?"

"What?" I said, cramming a big bite of the burrito into my mouth.

"That you shouldn't have another baby until you grow five inches taller."

"Ha, ha, ha, what a kidder."

"Seriously. He explained to me that because you're so short, the baby has nowhere to go. That's one of the reasons you're so uncomfortable. No room at the inn, so to speak."

"Great. Instead of an ob/gyn, I got a comedian. Ha, ha, ha."

"He said that you're irritable because you're uncomfortable and tired."

"Right." I swallowed hard rather than say, I'm irritable because your mother keeps sticking her nose into our business.

"You sure you're okay?" he asked.

"I'm peachy-keen."

I didn't tell Detweiler how worried I was. How could I possibly be a good mother to three children? Erik needed me desperately. When he first came to live with us, he'd been stand-offish toward me. That was fine. I knew I couldn't replace Gina, his mother. But over the last few weeks particularly, he'd become a little love bug. He would sidle over to me and rest his head on my shoulder. He'd slip up behind me and take my hand. I'd feel his tiny fingers reaching for me at odd times when we were all sitting together on the sofa. At night, he hugged me until I pulled his arms free from my neck.

After having lost one mother, he was naturally worried about losing another. So his kindergartener mind decided that keeping an eye on me, holding on to me physically, was his best option for keeping me safe, because to him, close by and safe were the same thing.

I wondered how he would manage when I went into the hospital. I could imagine him being frightened at my absence.

Halfway through my breakfast burrito, I quit eating. The meal that once seemed so appealing no longer interested me.

9

Monday dragged on and on. We give out coupons with our classes, as a way to encourage our students to come back quickly and make another purchase. That's in addition to a hefty coupon for a discount if they sign up for our mailing list. It's all part of our strategy for staying in touch. We also want to help them feel successful right off the bat, so our first email to them reminds our new friends we're here to help. Often they'll get home and then discover they have a question. Typically, we see or hear from our new scrapbookers within a week after they take their first class.

Case in point: Jana Higgins. She hadn't let any grass grow under her feet, metaphorically. She came in, clutching her coupon in her gloved hands. Her head swivel in a wide arc as she took in all the marvelous options we offer for saving memories.

Rather than ask how I could help, I decided to be more direct. "How's the pregnancy going?"

"Fine, how's yours?"

"I am tired of being pregnant," I said. "I'm ready to have this baby and get on with my life."

Her smile blinked off and on. “Me, too.”

“Where are you having yours?” I asked.

“Uh, I haven't decided. How about you?”

That took me a minute to process. “You haven't decided? Where does your doctor want you to go?”

She quit smiling and shoved the coupon in her pocket.

“You aren't thinking of having it at home, are you?”

“Um, maybe.”

“Wow, that's courageous. I guess if you're healthy and everything goes well, it could save you a lot of money.”

She nodded vigorously. Then she asked, “You have other children, don't you?”

“One girl and one boy. How about you?”

“This will be my first.”

I opened my mouth to say more, but the door minder rang. Lee Alderton stepped inside, shaking off snowflakes from her hair as she tugged at a pair of earmuffs. What a contrast she made with Jana. Both wore quilted coats, but Lee’s was a sleek black Burberry with cuffs that turned back to show the famous plaid, except in blue and black. Jana’s reminded me of a gray sleeping bag because it was so puffy. Both women favored mittens, but Jana’s looked to be of a clumsy acrylic when Lee’s were a rich merino wool.

“Lordy,” Lee said, giving Jana a tiny wave of greeting. “Makes me wish I was back at our house in Palm Beach.”

“Sounds like a plan to me,” I said. “How’re the plans for your daughter’s wedding coming?”

While Lee and I pondered how best to memorialize Taylor and Ryan’s upcoming nuptials, Jana wandered around, collecting page kits we’d already made up. I noticed she was primarily interested in ways to scrapbook her baby, and I had decided to go over and remind her about our upcoming class when Lee asked, "What do you think of these embellishments? They seem sort of ordinary to me."

"Yes, I agree. Nice, but common place.Too bad they aren't having it in that vineyard in France," I said with a sigh. "We have so many cute embellishments with grapes and grape leaves."

But Lee only laughed. "Right, but Jeff is a wine connoisseur, so I bet we can use the grape images somewhere, don't you think?"

I nodded, thinking of how her husband had introduced Detweiler and me to a wonderful pair of wines called Romeo and Juliet. "Do you have the labels from the wines Jeff plans to serve?"

"Why?"

"Well, why not incorporate the labels into your design?"

"That's clever!" Lee nodded her approval. She brought her supplies over to my worktable and spread them out.

Jana wandered over and watched us consider various combinations for Lee's daughter's wedding album.

"Kiki? You really know a lot about scrapbooking," Jana said. "How did you learn all this?"

"Taking classes. Reading books. Asking questions. I also learn from all of you. Lee has taken classes in interior decorating. Her daughter is in fashion merchandising. They both have a terrific sense of style." I didn't want to sound pushy, but having Jana stand over us felt uncomfortable. I wanted to get her going so Lee and I could enjoy our time together. "Do you need me to ring you out? Have you signed up for the 'A Star Is Born' class?"

Jana hesitated, but only for a second. "Yes. You'll send me a reminder, right? An email? Good. I really should get back to work, anyway."

10

Tuesday, January 14 and Wednesday, January 15
Kiki's due date

Tuesday dragged on and on. I worked six hours because I was too proud to back down and say I was exhausted. I gave a weak protest when Detweiler came to pick me up at the store. Secretly I was happy for an excuse to go home and put my feet up. I awakened Wednesday to the sensation of a tiny elbow pushing against my ribs.

"Show time?" asked Detweiler, in a hopeful tone.

"I'm not sure."

An hour later, nothing had changed, except the position of the tiny elbow. With my sleep shirt pulled up to expose my baby bump, we could watch my passenger's progress as he moved under my skin.

"Amazing, awe inspiring, and slightly creepy," said my husband. Leaning over to kiss my navel.

"You can say that again."

"You aren't going in to work, are you? Today's the day. As soon as you go into labor, I'll take the next three days off. Hadcho will cover for me. I hope Dr. Gretski is good at math."

Detective Stan Hadcho was Detweiler's partner and best friend.

"It's not just math. One theory is that there's a tipping point where my body can't support both of us, and labor is nature's way of saying the show's over. I've also read that when a baby's lungs are mature, a hormone is released that starts the mother's body into labor. So, from what I gather, it's more a matter of the baby deciding that he's ready, than a simple mathematical formula."

"Like I said, I hope Dr. Gretski knows his stuff."

"Dr. Gretski's never been pregnant. Everything he knows is hearsay. You wouldn't depend on it in court, would you?"

"No, but he doesn't need to go through labor to be an expert observer, does he?"

I decided to humor my husband and let him retain his confidence in my doctor. Frankly, I thought Gretski a bit of a bonehead, but the obstetrician who'd delivered Anya was retired, and Gretski took over for him. Rather than search for a new doc, I'd stayed with the practice.

I pulled on the only pair of maternity pants that fit, threw a top over my head, and tried to make myself comfortable on the couch. I was sitting in the same place when Detweiler and the kids came home.

Detweiler kissed me. "Any progress?"

"No. I might as well be watching paint dry. Not even a twinge of a contraction."

He laughed. "I'm going to help Brawny in the kitchen. You stay comfortable."

"How's the weather outside?"

"Looks like we're in for another ice storm. It's sleeting right now."

"You have to be kidding me!" I shivered from my spot on the sofa.

"Not to worry, with those studs on my tires I can go through anything."

That was mildly reassuring, but my teeth began to chatter anyway.

"I'll throw another log on the fire," he said. "Do you want me to run up and get you a heavier sweater?"

"Nah." It was always a little cool-ish in the living room. By keeping the curtains closed and putting pillows around my body, I'd been able to pretend I was in a warm cocoon. I'd also been able to avoid the drafts that swept through the room. The house badly needed weatherizing. Detweiler assured me we'd get to it next year. As if reading my mind about the drafts, he grabbed an afghan from a chair, threw it over my feet and legs and tucked it in carefully.

"Thanks," I said. I sat and stared at the logs burning in our fireplace. The sweet smell of wood smoke brought a smile to my face. I had been reading Bad Girl Creek, a book by Jo-Ann Mapson, when I dozed off, only to be awakened by a very angry little boy.

"Where is our baby?" Erik stamped his foot on the floor. Those warm chocolate eyes of his were blazing with anger. "Isn't he coming yet? That baby is supposed to be here. You said he was coming today. I've been looking and looking for him."

I gathered the little boy into my arms. Although my belly was too big for him to sit on my lap, Erik could prop himself up against me by leaving one foot on the floor and sprawling the other over my leg. "You've been looking?"

He nodded solemnly. "Anya told me he'd be driving up in a

big car. A shiny one. So I was look-et-ing out the windows for a long time. My fingers is cold. See?"

When he pressed his tiny digits into mine, they were like ice.

"Anya?" I called out to my daughter. She was lying on the rug on the floor in front of a crackling fire, pretending not to be listening in on our conversation. So I tried again. "Anya? What did you tell Erik? Hmmm?"

With great reluctance, she set down her pen, pushing aside her notebook, and turned to blink at me. My daughter, sweetness and light, feigning innocence. Slowly she opened her mouth and said, "What? I didn't hear you."

"Then we need to take you to an audiologist and get your hearing checked, young lady. What did you tell your brother? Did you mislead him? Cause him to stand and stare out the window?"

"She's a poopy face." Erik pointed an accusing finger at his sister.

"No name-calling," I said.

"Anya? I think you owe Erik an apology."

I tried to keep my voice neutral, because the family therapist had warned us this would be coming. The honeymoon between the siblings was officially over. When Erik first came to live with us, Anya had treated him like an honored guest. Over the past two months, reality had set in. The boy was adorable, but he was also a pesky younger brother. As such, he often bugged his older sister.

In many ways, this was good news, because it signaled the start of a normal relationship. If Anya had continued to hover over him, Erik wouldn't have learned to fight his own battles. Her willingness to tease him signified a deeper acceptance of the boy as a member of our family.

Instead of acting like two strangers, they were building a stronger bond. It would be messy, but once they had gone through the initial stages of digging in the dirt to lay the foundation, it would be indestructible.

"I told him that because he was getting into my things!" she said, raising the emotional water level in the room. "I asked him twice not to draw in my journal, but he did it anyway!"

"Erik? You have to leave Anya's things alone. You have your own—"

I gasped as a cramp hit me hard. I was seated in a side saddle position with both legs up on the sofa and to the side. Suddenly I felt a release, as though someone had pulled a plug and warm water ran over the top of my right thigh.

"Did you wet your pants?" Anya stood over me, staring at the wet splotch on our sofa.

"No. My water broke. Remember? I told you this would happen. Please go get Detweiler."

Instead of moving, she stood where she was and screamed at the top of her lungs, "Detweiler! The baby is coming! The baby is coming!"

11

Detweiler stumbled on his way down the stairs. I knew this because the rhythm of his feet stopped, there was a slamming noise, and a few mumbled curse words. He came limping around the corner, his face a study in pain and shock. With one foot tucked up behind him, looking more like a stork than a human, he hopped into the living room.

"Baby?"

We'd had our practice run three weeks ago when I'd been doubled-over with Braxton Hicks, false contractions. My hospital bag had been packed for a month. When last I looked it was sitting by the door to the garage. Its ominous presence a daily reminder that this day was coming.

Brawny heard the hue and cry. She came skidding around the corner, her feet sliding on the tile. To my surprise, she looked panicked, too. Since she's been trained by the military and a graduate of nanny school, I'd expected her to stay unruffled. But the look on her face was priceless. You'd have thought Anya would have called out, "Incoming torpedoes! Duck and cover!"

"Our baby is coming!" Anya shrieked. With that, Gracie

made her move. The doggie gate in the kitchen came clattering down as the big dog barreled into the room. She hopped up on the sofa next to me, put one paw on each shoulder, and covered me in doggy kisses,

"No, Gracie, no!" Detweiler lunged for the dog. As he did, he stepped on a stack of magazines I'd been reading. Like tectonic plates, they shifted. But he didn't let go of Gracie's collar, and she wasn't ready to leave my side. He yanked, and she yanked back. His feet went flying, slipping on the slick paper of the magazines. In slow motion his legs moved upwards in an arc. His arms spiraled in the air. And he came down hard.

"Great day in the morning!" That was as close to a curse as Brawny would allow herself. She squatted over my prone husband.

Meanwhile, Anya and Erik had joined hands to dance around in a circle, chanting, "We're going to have a bay-bee, we're going to have a bay-bee."

"Detweiler? Detweiler?" I reached down and shook my husband's shoulder.

"Baby?" He turned shocked eyes on me.

"Yes. It's time."

"Baby." He struggled to his feet, clutching his side. "Suitcase."

"Are your stitches okay?" I barely got out the words when another cramp gathered power in my abdomen. It was as if every muscle fiber south of my waistband contracted at once. What had begun as a pinch turned into a painful chokehold, leaving me breathless.

"Suitcase." Detweiler stared down at me.

"Upstairs. Our bedroom."

"Baby!" My husband stood there, frozen.

"Brawny? These are powerful. They're coming fast, one right after another, and my water's broken."

Gracie nuzzled me and sniffed at my thighs. “Get down, girl,” I told her sternly, and she obeyed, but she stayed two feet away, wagging her tail and watching me carefully.

“Come on, girl.” Detweiler grabbed her by the collar and pulled. Gracie fought him every inch of the way. Her high-pitched whining built to a full-blown howl.

“Let me help you to your feet, Kiki. We need to get you to the car.” Brawny reached down for me with strong arms. I grasped her hands, but I didn't get far. The pressure returned, and with it came the urge to push. This was nothing like what labor had been with Anya. I'd eased into that journey, going from annoying cramps to gradually building waves of intensity. No, this was accelerating faster.

Gasping, I let go of her and fell back onto the sofa. “I don’t think we're going to have time for a car ride.”

The logs in the fireplace crackled, one popped, and a tiny puff of wood smoke wafted into the living room.

The color drained from Brawny's face. Behind her, the children stood, a study in shock. Erik clutched at Anya’s waist. She hugged him tightly.

“Anya?” I managed. “Please take charge of Erik. My phone’s in my purse. Grab it so he can play Angry Birds.”

That normally was a real treat for the little guy, but he didn’t smile. His lower lip quivered. “Is Mama Kiki dying?”

“No, sweetie. I’m fine. Our baby is—” A contraction cut off my wind.

“I’m getting towels,” Brawny said.

“I’ll go heat up the car.” Detweiler hobbled up behind the kids. One hand clutched at his side. I knew what that meant: He’d hurt himself. Now I had three onlookers, all stunned into inaction. But that was okay, because my body was busy doing its own thing. Any control I once had vanished as I gave myself over to the cramping waves sweeping through me.

"Aren't you going to the hospital?" Anya's jaw was slack.

"Maybe not," I said between clenched teeth, as I rode the roller coaster of a contraction up, up, up to the point that time stood still, and then down again. "Detweiler, don't go. Stay here. This baby is in a hurry."

"Okay." He froze in place.

Brawny raced over with an armful of towels. Detweiler came to his senses enough to help her slide them under me. She also tossed a sheet over my legs. It wasn't much, but the covering blocked the view of my private bits so the kids didn't see everything.

"Your water is broken," Detweiler said, in a strangely robotic voice as he pinned one towel between the sofa cushions. He pointed to the wet puddle growing beneath me.

"Help me pull down my pants," I said, gasping with exertion. As I hoisted my hips, Brawny put cold hands on my britches and gave them a tug. The material released its grip on my belly as it came to rest on my thighs. "Brawny, I'm not joking around here. I think this baby—"

"Is coming right now," she finished for me.

12

"I'm calling 911," Anya said.

"Mama!" Erik wailed.

"I'm fine!" I yelled to the boy. "Come here, sweetie, and hold my hand." He laced those fingers through mine. I was panting, but I managed to say, "It's okay. The baby is coming, sweetie, and he's in a hurry. That's all. I'm…fine."

Since Erik stood by my head and the sheet was draped over my nether regions it afforded me a bit of privacy while Brawny peeped at my progress. "Fully dilated. Progressing well."

Anya had handed the cell phone to Detweiler. He stumbled over our address. At the end of the call, he shouted, "And hurry!"

I've seen my husband in all sorts of emergency situations, and he's usually Mr. Calm, Cool, and Collected. Not this time. I giggled, but stopped abruptly when another contraction hit me hard.

Brawny's fingers gently brushed the inside of my thighs. Her face was hidden by the odd angle, but when she finished her exam, she gave me a nod of approval. "On his way, he is. Detweiler, get behind Kiki. We need to prop her up so the baby has room. He's crowning."

My husband dithered over where to put the cell phone and finally decided to tuck it inside his waistband. His strong arms wrapped around my body and pulled me upright. I heard Gracie whining. Detweiler must have put up the dog gate in the kitchen.

"A crown? Our baby has a crown?" Erik was totally confused.

"That means his head is nearly out." Anya had read *What to Expect When You're Expecting* from cover to cover. "That's good news. Our baby will be here very, very soon. Right, Mom?"

"Right." My body had taken over, doing what it needed to do instinctively. Resistance was futile. I went along for the metaphorical ride, huffing and puffing, trying to catch my breath.

"He's crowning," said Brawny, her voice filled with excitement and awe.

Warm liquid ran down my legs. The sofa would never be the same.

Neither would I. This kid was barreling into the world faster than I could blink and sputter.

Brawny yelled, "Push hard!"

"Don't you think I should try to wait?"

"Not now. He's too far along. He's in the birth canal and almost here. You have to keep pushing because he might have the cord wrapped around his neck," she said. The look she gave me was bleak. Suddenly we both realized the gravity of the situation. Sure, it had been mildly amusing before, but now it was flat out terrifying.

The energy gathered, bunched up my muscles, and I gritted my teeth. I saw Anya's face reappear over Brawny's shoulder. Erik huddled beside her. The metallic scent of blood was in the air, along with a smell more primitive and raw.

"Push, Kiki, push," said Brawny.

"I am pushing hard!" I wanted to slap her up the side of her head, and I would have, too, except I'd taken to grasping Detweiler's forearms, a reaction to all the pain.

"He's halfway out," she said. "Another good push should do it."

I ground my teeth together and huffed and puffed and gave it my all.

Brawny yelled, "Anya? Get ready with a towel. Erik, hold the end of the towel, my wee man. You two are going to get to be the first persons to hold your brother. Are you ready?"

"Uh-huh." Anya's voice sounded far away. Along with it came a clicking sound. Familiar, and yet, I couldn't figure out what it was.

"Push, push, push," said Brawny. In the distance, an ambulance wailed. The sound was coming closer and closer as I took a deep breath and bore down with all my might. I pushed and pushed and pushed until I felt another sensation of release. A sliding wetness. A zing as my organs ricocheted back to their original spots. My muscles went slack. Brawny was fussing about, but I couldn't see exactly what she was doing because the afghan over my knees blocked my sight. Anya's head ducked down.

"Woohooo!" yelled Detweiler.

"Hurrah!" said Erik.

When Anya straightened up, her face was full of wonder—and she beamed with joy as she presented my son to me.

13

~Detweiler~

Ever since I can remember, I've wanted to be a father. In fact, I can't remember a time when I didn't want kids. Yeah, I know that most men don't feel this way. I've had friends on the force who've proudly avoided procreating. Others who've denied their involvement in pregnancies.

But to me, there's nothing more important that a man can do than being a good dad. Maybe I get that from my father, because he's always been there for me. He's the man I admire most in the world, so I guess it's natural I'd want to follow in his footsteps.

After I married Gina, who had been my high school sweetheart, I would lie awake at night and imagine us having a child. When I broached the subject, she was quick to shut me down. "Are you nuts? We can hardly make ends meet as it is."

She was right, but I figured we'd find a way. If we wanted to. But she didn't want to, and she made that clear. There was that day she dropped her purse. Out spilled a diaphragm case. The sight felt like a swift kick in the gut. Without any explanation, she calmly took the equipment from me.

We didn't discuss it. What was there to say? She'd made it clear she hated our life. I didn't make enough money. She was bored. Just how bored I didn't realize until the day she left me. The news that she'd gotten pregnant, and that the father was an African-American police officer, came as a shock even five years after she'd gone. Of course I would give her son, Erik, a home. Especially when he looked so much like his mother.

Brenda? She was a mistake. An error of ego. I thought I could save her from herself. Instead, she nearly drowned me, the way a person does when flailing in deep water. Have kids with her? No way. Brenda was on drugs from the beginning. Inside I knew it, but I would have been hard pressed to admit as much. After all, she was my sister Patty's good friend. I had practically grown up with her. Each time I looked at her, I saw the gawky teenager she'd once been.

But Kiki was always different. Even from the start. Sure, I had to consider her a murder suspect. It's always the spouse, isn't it? Just doing my job. That said, she couldn't have done it. That woman has this honesty about her, a clarity in her eyes that lets you see right through to her soul. Watching her with Anya, I recognized a kindred spirit. Kiki loved her daughter the way I always expected to love a child.

At the very least, I wanted her as a friend. When times got tough, she was the type of person you could depend on.

The worst time in my life were the weeks and months when she refused to speak to me. Not when I was accused of murder. I could live behind bars if necessary, as long as I had Kiki in my corner.

Over the time we've spent together, I've seen that woman

grow. After George died, she was this butterfly struggling to unfurl its wings. Once that cocoon broke away, she used every bit of her strength to expand to her best self. Taking on challenges with the store. Standing up to Sheila. Becoming the head of a household. Encouraging me to bring Erik home. Agreeing to become my wife. When she first told me she was pregnant, I felt like I'd hit a home run. My mother warned me that being pregnant and having a healthy baby were not the same thing. She worried about Kiki, especially when she realized Kiki wasn't going to sit home and wait for the baby to come.

But we can put that behind us now.

Watching her cuddle our son, I thought my heart would burst in my chest. Erik dropped to his knees so he could stroke his baby brother's head. Anya took over the armrest of the sofa so she could be close to her mother. The four of them. They're my whole life. My brain took a picture just as Brawny snapped one on her phone. I plan to keep that photo in my wallet the rest of my life. I'm going to tell everybody that I'm a dad!

"Can you believe it?" Anya proudly pointed at my son. "I'm grabbing my phone to take the pictures! Can you believe him? Huh? He's so wrinkled!"

"A baby! A baby!" Erik moved away from the sofa and was doing a hip-hop, his version of skipping. His tiny hands clapped in a rhythmic pulse.

"You better call your parents." Kiki smiled at me. She looked marvelous.

"I can start making the calls." Brawny slapped me lightly on the shoulder. "Savor this moment." I sank down next to Kiki on the sofa. But for the longest time I couldn't see, couldn't make heads or tails of the bundle in Kiki's arms because my eyes were brimming with tears.

And then, wonder of wonders, Brawny helped me lap one

arm over the other, making an oval, a protective circle. Slowly, with great tenderness, Kiki placed a bundle in that cradle. A small shape, warm, red, wrinkled and squirming. Too light to be real. Too new to be understood. And yet when I looked into his eyes, I felt a shock of recognition. This was my son!

14

Three days later

~ Kiki ~

Anya was taking her sweet time about naming the baby, but she'd promised us that she'd come up with a name by Sunday, which was two days away.

"When the pediatrician asks me what to call this little guy, what do you expect me to say?" I rocked the baby in my arms while Detweiler was outside heating the car. Today was our baby's first visit to the pediatrician, Dr. Yee. After the baby had been born, we'd gone to the hospital via ambulance. There the attending physician had checked me over, delivered the placenta, and given the baby a once-over before pronouncing him "fit as a fiddle." I figured that Dr. Yee would say the same, but this well visit would go a long way toward putting my mind at ease. After all, we certainly hadn't planned for a home birth.

"I'm not telling you his name because I want everybody to

find out at once," she said. "The whole family will be here on Sunday when Father Joe and Laurel come for the blessing ceremony. Mimi and Pop, Ginny and Jeff and Emily, and Patty and Paul, and Amanda and Catherine, and even Grandma Collins."

Fortunately, my daughter is far too smart to call my mother "Grandmother Collins" to her face. My mother would come unglued. As far as she's concerned, she's far too young to be a grandmother. Under any other circumstances, the lack of a label for a grandparent would be problematic. But my mother is barely involved in my kids' lives. In fact, she is barely involved in anything or anyone but herself, so references to her are blessedly meager.

"You're sure you won't drop a hint to us about what you plan to name the baby?" I asked Anya. Admittedly, I was concerned. What if Anya came up with some weird, wacky name? Something like Moonwalker or Pedro or Manfred? I'd offered her the privilege as a sop, a way of helping her come to grips with her new role as big sister. Also, I'd hoped that by naming the new baby, she'd feel less alienated. When she first heard that a baby was on the way, she'd worried about being the only Lowenstein left, because Sheila was now married to Police Chief Robbie Holmes. Over the past three months, Anya had seemed to be at peace with our blended family. I only hoped that the peace was genuine and long-lasting.

"No," she said. Her smile was one of supreme happiness. "I'm not telling anyone. It's my secret. I've even got Robbie and Gran planning to join us by Skype."

"That certainly was smart of you." I tried to tamp down my fears.

"You ready to go?" Detweiler walked into the kitchen. He was wearing his winter coat, a sheepskin that made him look faintly like a rancher from Montana.

"Ready," I said, as I picked up the diaper bag from the back of a kitchen chair.

Detweiler was puffed out like a peacock. You'd think he'd done all the pushing, although to be fair he also told anyone who would listen, "Kiki was so brave and strong. It must have hurt like crazy, but she was a total trooper. If guys had to give birth, our species would disappear from this earth. Trust me."

Erik seemed to be more curious than jealous.

Anya? She was playing her role to the hilt. That mysterious clicking sound I'd heard had been my daughter documenting the birth of her brother. When she announced what she'd been doing, I nearly fell on the floor and foamed at the mouth.

"You are not, under any circumstances, allowed to take that camera or those pictures to school," I had told her.

"Why not?" she'd said. "Childbirth is a natural biological function."

"Yes, and that was my natural biological function. I deserve a modicum of privacy."

"Modicum?"

"That means, a 'little bit' of something. I deserve a little bit of privacy."

"But, Mom!" she had wailed. "You're always talking about how important it is to learn new things. Just think how much my friends will learn when I show them the pictures. Who would have ever guessed it would be so...messy?"

"They can learn from another source. I'm warning you, Anya. You show those pictures to anyone—*anyone*—and I will ground you for the rest of your life."

"Gee whiz," she had said, stomping around in a circle. "One minute you're all about education and learning and the next you're withholding information. You need to make up your mind!"

"And you need to get out of my bedroom. You're upsetting me and your little brother."

I hadn't meant to snap at her, but she'd pushed me over the edge. Her ploy, the suggestion that the photos were educational, was only half-way successful. In truth, I knew that she wanted to show off the pictures because she was probably the only kid in her class who'd actually witnessed a birth up close and personal.

Was I being a hypocrite because I'm such a big believer in documenting our lives—and here I was telling my daughter to hide the documentation?

I scooted down in the bed and pulled the covers over my head. I didn't care if I was being hypocritical or not. Most of the CALA parents thought I was a little weird anyway. There was no good reason to give them more ammunition. Besides, my daughter had learned a lot about photography from me. We weren't talking about blurry photos taken at a distance. We were talking sharply focused shots of my Southern Hemisphere, complete with the Parting of the Seas, and the Birth of a Nation.

That was definitely not something I felt like sharing.

15

All our family members and friends dropped by to meet our newest addition. The parade seemed endless. Prize-winning cattle are viewed with less interest than my son and I were. My sisters were both giddy with joy. The crew from the store came bearing gifts and goodwill. My mother stayed away, claiming a cold. Detweiler's sisters and his niece brought a huge selection of stuffed toys. When his parents arrived, my antenna went up, because Louis is generally the most happy of men. His hug felt strained. His eyes barely focused on me. But then, I was nursing and that makes some men uncomfortable. As for Thelma, she seemed stand-offish. There was a pain behind her smile. Her fingers reached for the baby almost like she was grasping for a last straw. Normally effusive, she said little.

Even Anya asked me later, "What's with Mimi?"

"I honestly don't know."

"She was fighting with Detweiler. I heard them. They were in the laundry room with the door closed."

"Anya, you shouldn't eavesdrop."

"I consider it research, Mom."

That made me laugh.

Over the next few days, Detweiler seemed remote. Pre-occupied. Distant. I overheard him querying Brawny, asking questions about my labor. Although the post-partum visit to the hospital had resulted in me being pronounced, "Fine," I didn't feel like myself. My dreams troubled me and I woke up emotionally spent. I went through the motions of caring for my son, but there was an emptiness I couldn't shake.

Finally, I decided I needed to talk to someone about what I was feeling. A voice inside told me it wasn't normal. Dr. Yee, our pediatrician, had always been a good listener. He was a pro-mother doc, a man who put great store by the instincts of mothers. "If Mama say baby getting ear infection, but I no see problem, I listen to Mama. Mama knows," he'd explained to me. "Mama and baby are connected. I am only observer."

I wasn't surprised when Detweiler announced he was coming with me to our son's first appointment. But I wasn't thrilled about it either.

"Looks like you've got a keeper here," said Dr. Yee, his almond-shaped eyes crinkling with good cheer. "Everything is where it should be, and he's hale and hearty. How are you doing, Mama? How are your spirits? Any signs of depression?"

I opened my mouth to say that I'd been a little down, actually, but Detweiler beat me to it.

"Kiki's wonderful. Terrific. A fabulous mom. Came through everything like a trooper."

"And your other children?"

"Anya took pictures," Detweiler continued, handing the camera over to the doctor. "Now I can always revisit what it was like to see my son being born."

Dr. Yee took the camera from Detweiler's hands. I'd forgotten that I'd put it into my purse as a way of safeguarding my privacy. Detweiler must have seen it when he helped me into the car. I had ordered the camera in bright red, as a way of making sure I didn't lose track of it. Sitting as it was on the top of all the other junk in my handbag, the gizmo would have been easy to recognize.

While Dr. Yee scrolled through the pictures, I looked at Detweiler. He was in charge. I opened my mouth again to tell the doctor that I wasn't feeling very perky or happy, but Detweiler interrupted.

"Of course, we'd planned for the baby to be born in the hospital. In fact, I was stunned that Kiki went ahead and pushed rather than waiting. They specifically told us in the Lamaze classes what to do. Thank goodness the baby is okay."

What on earth had gotten into him? My heart took an elevator ride to the soles of my shoes. My whole body flushed with anger, making me so hot I had to fan myself. "Dr. Yee, would you please explain to my husband that once labor began in earnest, I didn't have a choice? It wasn't like I gave birth at home on purpose?"

"I never said that!" Detweiler whipped his head around.

"I know you didn't, but that's what you're wondering." The baby squirmed in my arms. He could tell I was upset, and that bothered him.

Dr. Yee didn't look up at us. He kept staring into the camera. While Detweiler and I glared at each other, the pediatrician grabbed a magnifying glass from a pencil holder on his desk. Holding the camera under the lens, he gazed down at the picture for a long, long, while.

Leaning against his desk, the doctor kept the camera in one hand. "Once labor has started and the contractions are five minutes apart, there was no way that Kiki could have stopped herself from pushing. It was a biological imperative. Totally instinctive. It would have been like stopping a sneeze or a cough, only ten times harder."

I could see Detweiler's shoulders relax somewhat. But he still had an irritated expression on his face. I watched a muscle tense in his jaw as he said, "My mother told me we were lucky, really lucky, that our baby wasn't hurt...or worse. She says Kiki should have fought the urge or paid more attention to her body and asked to go to the hospital earlier."

I was speechless with rage. Thelma had gone behind my back and used her own nightmarish experiences to poison her son's joy. If that didn't beat all!

"I never argue with mothers," Dr. Yee continued. "They're more often right than wrong. Your mother is right. All three of you were lucky. But the credit for your healthy baby goes to your wife. It's a good thing that Kiki followed her instincts and pushed hard despite the fact she wasn't in an ideal situation. Look right here."

He held up the photo and centered the magnifying glass over a picture of our son's head coming out of the birth canal. "See that white thickness at his neck? That's the umbilical cord. That's the reason we prefer hospital births to home births. If Kiki hadn't pushed, if she hadn't delivered your son right then and there, there's a good chance that he would have strangled because of that cord being wrapped around his neck."

16

"I'm so sorry," said Detweiler, after we strapped the baby into the car seat. While the rear-facing seats are safer, they're also awkward to use because you have to lift the baby over the seat itself. But Detweiler did it with ease. I'd have to get used to making the climb.

Right now, all I wanted was to go home and lick my wounds. My husband's revelation that his mother thought I'd made a mistake hurt worse than my sore girly bits. How could Thelma have done such a thing? The fact that Detweiler had listened to her hurt me deeply. I tried to keep a smile on my face, but as he pulled out of the parking lot, I had to avert my eyes and stare out the window. I couldn't stand to look at him. I felt the warm trail of a tear running down my cheek.

"I've been a real jerk. You deserve better."

"I'm disappointed by your mother's actions. It's not like her to interfere."

"I should have been more trusting. I tried to keep my feelings under control. Honest, I did. But when she told me this last night, I thought I'd go crazy. The idea of losing our child drove me out of my mind."

"I could tell you were upset."

"Right."

The drive back to the house was uncomfortable to say the least. More so when we pulled up and discovered a truck parked beside our garage. That could only mean that Detweiler's parents were visiting. Had Thelma decided to show up and lecture me? Was this her way of driving home a point? I badly wanted to ask if Detweiler had expected this visit, but I was so upset that I knew better than to voice my concerns.

Instead, we quietly got out of the car. I let him take the baby, while I followed like an obedient servant. An angry, seething servant at that.

My mood darkened to black when we pushed through the side door and heard strident voices. Brawny was saying, "Respectfully, you are wrong."

Detweiler and I came to a complete, dead stop in the hallway. All I could see was his broad back. The baby had fallen asleep on the drive home. Our entrance had been soundless. I could see him tense up, and I knew he was hesitating. He loves his parents, truly he does, but he's enough of a grownup to realize when they have crossed a line.

At least, I hoped he was.

"But you didn't even go to the childbirth classes!" Thelma said. Her voice was pitched unnaturally high.

"Aye, I didn't."

"You didn't know what you were doing! The baby could have died. All because Kiki is so involved in that store that she wouldn't take time off and listen to her body."

"I dinna take the childbirth classes because I'm a trained midwife. That was part of the education I got even before I went to nanny school."

"Midwife?" Thelma scoffed. "You have to be kidding me. No

midwife is qualified to deliver a baby. A class? That's all? You endangered my grandbaby."

I literally saw red. If Detweiler hadn't been blocking the hall, I would have attacked Thelma. As it was, his presence prevented her imminent demise.

Fortunately, Brawny took this accusation in stride. Our unflappable nanny said, "With all due respect, Madame. You're wrong. I have personally assisted more than thirty births in dicey situations. I'm a trained medic, from my time serving the Queen. If I'd thought Kiki or the babe to be in distress, I could have kept them both alive long enough for us to make it to hospital. Second babies always come fast. Again, I want to be respectful, Madame, but you need to have a re-think about this."

Louis Detweiler's soft tones intervened. "Sweetheart, I think you're being unfair. I know how scared you get—"

"Don't you patronize me, Louis Detweiler!" It split the air as a shriek.

And that's when our infant son began to cry.

17

To call the next two days "rocky" would be the understatement of the decade. Detweiler promised me he'd get his mother to calm down. "Dad will help. He knows she's being overwrought."

Holding my tongue took every particle of energy I had left. Rather than greet his parents the day we walked in on Thelma's tirade, I took the backstairs to our room. There I slipped into our adjoining bathroom, turned on the shower as a covering noise, and had a loud, sloppy crying jag.

After that, I crawled into bed and fell asleep until the baby needed to nurse. Holding him, I reminded myself that Thelma had been wrong. We'd get over this as a family.

But a mean voice inside me said, Really? She sure seems reluctant to let this drop.

I tried to turn my attention to Sunday, the day that Anya would name our child and we'd "officially" present him to the family. I was doing a pretty good job until the day of, when my mother arrived.

"Too many cats," she said, standing on my threshold and sniffing the air. "Smells like cat litter in this house, doesn't it?"

As a matter of fact, it didn't. Anya had changed the litter half an hour ago. We've been using a new product by Arm and Hammer that really keeps down the smell. Besides all that, the litter pan was in the basement, and the two cats accessed it via a cat door that led them downstairs. We make it a habit to douse the air with a good squirt of Febreze at least once a day. So I was absolutely, totally positive that the house didn't smell like cats.

Besides all that, my mom has lost her sense of smell. I know that because my sister found a rotting pumpkin in the back of her closet. Mom didn't remember putting it there, but the stink alerted everyone in the house that something was amiss.

Now Mom stood in the middle of our foyer, complaining loudly about the smell of cat pee. My sisters, Amanda and Catherine, rolled their eyes in concert. Pretty soon we'd need to have a sit-down discussion about "what to do about Mom." She was getting too weird for my siblings to handle. Okay, beyond weird, she had become downright dangerous. On a whim, she'd lit a half dozen candles in her bedroom. The smoke alarm saved the house from going up in flames.

"Mom?" Amanda took her by the elbow. "Let's go into the living room. There's a lovely fire there."

"Smoke," she said. "I'll smell like smoke."

Actually she always reeks like a certain brand of hairspray, which shall be nameless. I think she must have confused it with perfume, the way she sprays it on. This is incredibly unfortunate for me because I'm allergic to the fragrance in that particular hairspray. Each time I get close to Mom, I start to sneeze. Amanda has removed the hairspray from Mom's bathroom several times now, but new cans seem to appear regularly. In fact, I could tell that she'd managed to secure yet another stash because as she walked past me, my nose started to run. I sneezed repeatedly.

"Sorry," mouthed my sister.

Catherine, my other sister, shook her head. "I have no idea where Mom gets that stuff. I'm thinking she must buy it from other old ladies at the Senior Center, because Amanda tosses a can out of her bathroom on a regular basis. But she must have a supplier somewhere."

I couldn't answer for sneezing.

Luckily I wasn't holding the baby. If I had been, I'd have dropped him. It's amazing to me that a sneeze can totally overpower you. Repetitive sneezes were so crippling that I had to lean against the wall to keep from toppling over.

"Can I get you anything?" Catherine asked.

"Benadryl. Master bathroom. Medicine cabinet," I gasped.

She trotted up the stairs, while I concentrated on not wetting my pants. The sneezes had me so much in their thrall. Meanwhile, my eyes had started to water, and tears ran down my face.

Mom had taken her place in the large recliner. As I sneezed, I could see her staring at me. I wondered, "Does she realize how sick she's making me?" The answer was, "Probably." The next question was, "Does she care?" And the answer to that was, "Only because it's fun for her. You're sick and she's amused."I would never, ever understand that woman.

While I was staggering around in the kitchen, using paper towels to mop up my running nose, the Detweiler clan had arrived. I re-entered the family room to find Thelma holding my son. Since that day we'd walked in on her complaining about me, I'd been overly polite to her, the best way I knew of for disguising my anger. I said hello to the older Detweilers and to Emily, Ginny and Jeff Volker's daughter.

Lorraine and Leighton had also arrived. The two lovebirds had made an assortment of appetizers. They helped Brawny put finger food on the coffee table.

"I want something to drink," said my mother. "Leighton? Would you get something for me?"

She batted her eyelashes at my neighbor. He was too much of a gentleman to tell her to take a hike, even though she was perfectly capable of hoisting herself out of the chair and walking into my kitchen. "What would you like?" he bent his head close to hers to take her order.

Father Joe and Laurel came through the back. They're like members of the family. Anya worships Laurel. Erik adores Joe. At some point in the future, Detweiler and I plan to ask them to serve as our kids' legal guardians in case anything happens to us. We know from sad experience that you can't plan to live forever. Regina Detweiler Lauber's death being a case in point.

"Aunt Kiki?" Emily tugged on my hand. "Mom and Dad said to tell you they're sorry they couldn't come. Dad's parents are visiting from Iowa. Grandpop is too grumpy to expose to neighbors. That's what Dad says, and I think he's right. Mom said she wants to come over next week. Aunt Patty and Uncle Paul couldn't make it because they can't get out of their driveway. Aunt Patty's really mad at Uncle Paul because he didn't get out there with the snow-blower right when the snow started coming down. But I think they didn't come because they had a fight about having a baby of their own."

This amused me. Emily had all the down and dirty details on the family. She delivered all this scuttlebutt with a lack of drama, but we both knew she was ratting out her Aunt Patty. I wiped my nose and reached out to give her a hug. "Emily, I'm sorry they aren't here, but I'm pleased as punch that you are."

"Anya told me she got to see the baby come. She said she has pictures. I can't wait to see them. He's pretty cute, isn't he? The baby, I mean. Except that his face is kind of squishy, isn't it? Anya showed me the spot on this head where you can watch his heartbeat. Seriously weird. Ugh."

I laughed. My sister Catherine handed me a box of tissues and the Benadryl. "I'll go grab you a glass of water."

I sneezed my thanks.

Emily was staring at me. Time to shift into "teachable moment mode." "Yes, that soft spot is weird isn't it? You can see why you have to be so careful with babies, can't you?"

"Right, and he's so little. I can't believe he was squished up inside of you."

"It's hard for me to believe, too. I'm glad he's out. Things were getting crowded."

Emily leaned close and whispered, "My mother would like another baby, but my dad keeps saying no. I don't understand that. Everybody loves baby. That's all Aunt Patty ever talks about."

I struggled to keep the smile on my face. This was the sort of casual bombshell tidbit that felt like a hot potato in your hands. You didn't dare drop it. You couldn't lob it to someone else. You had to juggle it until you could find the right place to put it.

"Uh, that happens a lot. Even when two people love each other, they might not always agree."

"They fight over it. All the time. They think I'm not listening, but I still hear them," she said, in a confidential manner. Her eyes were wide as she waited for my response. Not knowing exactly what to do, I hugged her close and whispered, "Does that worry you?"

"Y-y-yes. My friend Daisy's parents got divorced because they were fighting all the time," she whispered to my shoulder.

"It can be scary, but I don't think you have anything to worry about. Honest. Sometimes folks argue because they love each other, and they're trying to communicate, but their emotions are bigger than their words. I know they love you, sweetie, and I think they love each other."

I let her go and planted a kiss on her forehead. "Why don't you go and ask Mimi if you can hold the baby?"

Catherine handed me a glass of water, and then nimbly walked through the gathered crowd to hand a similar glass and a spoon to Detweiler that he used for tapping on the side of a water glass. "Everybody? Hello? Everyone? Thank you all for coming. Especially for braving the elements. Everyone made it but Cara Mia Delgatto. Her flight had a connection in Charlotte, and that airport is closed down, so her plane was canceled."

I did my best to keep smiling. The others might not notice or care about Cara's absence, but I felt a sharp edged pain, an emptiness. I knew she would have been here if possible, but it still hurt that she wasn't.

Brawny circulated, offering cocktail napkins.

The voices died down and came to a stop as everyone but my mother gave my husband the attention he deserved. She kept chattering on to Lorraine, who'd taken the chair next to Mom's. Even though Lorraine put a finger to her lips, Mom didn't shut up. Joe reached over and took Laurel's hand. His dog collar lent him an air of authority, but the soft expression in his eyes was total mush. He and Laurel were meant for each other.

Would Detweiler and I be able to get back on track?

I worried and I didn't worry at the same time. I just felt...blah.

Detweiler waited patiently for my mother to shut up. Amanda went over behind Mom and told her to shush. She turned to my sister with the sort of angry look that would peel the skin off an onion, but she was prevented from lashing out because Leighton handed her a glass of champagne.

"For you, pretty lady," he said, giving Mom the glass while winking at Lorraine. With a tray balanced on one hand, he wound his way through the assembled gathering as he dispersed glasses of apple cider to the kids and bubbly to the adults.

"Please raise your glasses in a toast to our newest family

member," said Detweiler, "and to my wonderful, beautiful wife for fulfilling all my dreams."

"Here! Here!" Louis cheered. Thelma smiled but it didn't reach her eyes. The children all clapped.

"We tried to get Sheila and Robbie by Skype, but it didn't happen." Detweiler explained. "Maybe they couldn't figure out how to make it work. Robbie's a bit of a Luddite."

"Anya? We've been waiting, sweetheart," I said, by way of encouraging my daughter. "What have you decided to name the baby?"

Anya was sitting next to Emily, who was snuggled deep on the sofa with the baby on her lap. Emily was regarding the infant with a mixture of awe and interest. Anya carefully lifted her brother from her cousin's grasp. With the accomplished motion of a practiced hand, she turned the baby to face all of us, while supporting his tiny head in the crook of her arm. I couldn't help the tears that started. My daughter looked so grown up. I could imagine her as a young mother with a babe of her own. Catherine came over to stand next to me, and slipped an arm around my shoulders. I couldn't bring myself to look at Detweiler. This should have been a happy moment, but he and his meddling mother had done their best to ruin it for me.

"I've been thinking a lot about this. Names are very important. They're almost sacred. Our new little brother is extra special. Partially because we got to see him arrive."

Thelma winced.

Erik had been seated at Anya's feet, stroking Gracie's head, but now he gave his older sister his full attention. His dark chocolate eyes solemn in his dear little face.

"Erik and I talked about this little guy, and I told Erik how much I miss my real dad, and he told me how much he misses his father, too. But we both love Detweiler, our new dad. So we decided to name the baby Tyler George Lowenstein Detweiler, because Tyler was Van Lauber's real first name, and George Lowenstein was the name of my daddy. Of course, you all know that this baby is a Detweiler. Erik and Mom are now Detweilers. I'm hoping that I can become a Detweiler, too."

PART II

18

January 31

Thelma kept her distance from me, which in itself signaled a problem between us. Typically she's very affectionate and interested in all I'm doing. Not today!

I didn't trust myself to figure out anyone's mood because mine seemed seriously out-of-control, but the way my mother-in-law held herself, the stiff posture and the turned down lips, told me Thelma wasn't happy about something. By contrast, Louis had been over-the-moon with joy that Anya wanted to become a Detweiler. But Thelma acted like she didn't hear Anya or care. That in itself was unusual. Typically, she encouraged Anya to feel like part of the Detweiler clan.

When the urge to tinkle hit me, I decided not to go upstairs. On a whim, I went quietly down the hallway past the kitchen. On my way back to the living room, I overheard Thelma complaining. Pausing, I pressed my ear to the wall so I could listen better.

"It's a pity that Anya didn't name your son after his father," Thelma said.

"That's fine, Mom. The baby is a Detweiler. That's enough for me," Detweiler answered. "Come on. Ease up a little."

"How can I? Your wife doesn't seem to care about what's best for your baby."

"What? Mom, that's not true or fair and you know it. In fact, you ought to be thanking your lucky stars that Kiki didn't spend more time in the hospital."

"What do you mean?"

"I mean it's my job to read the police reports. Another attempt was made to steal a newborn."

"You have to be kidding me!"

"I wish. That makes two in less than two weeks. We're stretched thin on manpower, as usual, so Prescott Gallaway in his infinite wisdom has decided not to warn the public. But he's got a meeting scheduled with hospital administrators to go over their security protocols."

"Nobody steals dead babies. That's what has me worried. That Kiki isn't concerned enough about keeping your baby alive."

"That's ridiculous," Detweiler said.

At that point, I'd heard enough. I tiptoed back to the bathroom, slammed the door behind me and spent five long minutes growling in fury at my reflection. How dare she accuse me of being careless! I had no idea what bug crawled up Thelma's backside, but if she didn't watch her step I was going to...

To what?

There was nothing I could do. I wasn't about to ruin my marriage over a nasty mother-in-law. I'd been through that rigamarole once before. You can't come between a mother and a child, nor should you try. You'll only splinter your family if you persist. I'd learned that lesson the hard way with Sheila, my late husband George's mother.

Sheila! If only she'd get out of rehab and come home, I could blow off steam to her. But Robbie had phoned to say that they'd had a "setback." I needed to know more. Each time I tried to get him on his cell phone, the call rolled over to his mailbox.

Did they even know I'd had my baby? We'd sent photos via our cell phones. But Sheila was missing out! Ty was already growing and gaining weight. He ate like a champ. He slept like a tired athlete. He cried only when he needed food or changing.

Then why was I so out of sorts?

I had every reason to be happy. What was wrong with me?

19

"You're sure the alarm system was triggered?" I asked my husband as he helped me out of his car. "Margit is usually very good about making sure this place is locked up tight."

We stood near the back door of my store. Detweiler had gone ahead, clearing the place so he knew it was safe for me to enter. The call had come at eight p.m. on a Saturday. Both the older kids were having an overnight at Laurel and Joe's apartment. I'd been stretched out on the sofa. The stain from childbirth had been easily removed by a drycleaner. Getting up and out of my comfortable position was a chore, but it couldn't be helped. Margit didn't answer her phone. If we didn't check on the alarm, I could be liable for any losses incurred.

Detweiler held my arm and guided me over the threshold. He'd used his flashlight to do his walk-through. "I think something tripped a circuit," he said.

"The breaker box is in a panel up front."

"I'll lead you there."

I picked my way through the place that had always been a second home to me.

"Surprise!" A loud chorus of voices almost sent me reeling. The overhead lights flicked on. A store full of faces smiled at me.

"What on earth?" I felt my jaw drop.

People started laughing and clapping. Friends crowded around me, waving miniature flags made out of baby blue paper and taped onto soda straws.

I turned and shook a finger at Detweiler. "You sneak!"

He laughed and pulled me close. Ever since I'd overheard him talking to Thelma, there'd been a strain between us. Sure, he'd taken my side, but I wished he'd been more forceful with his mother.

"Are you surprised, Mom?" Anya came over, joining Clancy, Laurel, Margit, and Rebekkah as they gathered me into a group hug.

"Yuppers," I said, laughing at the flashes going off. My friends were largely my customers, too, and since we're all scrapbookers, no one could resist the chance to take candid photos.

"You need to get off your feet," said Clancy, as she escorted me to the big black leather office chair. Usually it's behind my desk, but for tonight, they'd rolled it into the center of our sales floor. They'd also pushed back the display shelves of merchandise. Thanks to the casters on the bottom of the units, we could re-arrange the space and open up room in the center of the store.

"Here," said Margit, propping up my legs with an ottoman.

"Where did that come from?" I asked, staring down at the cube covered in fake leopard fur. Not only was it the right height, but the fun fur totally upped its cuteness quotient. That's a barometer that I rely on heavily. I constantly ask myself, "On a scale of 'yuck' to 'awesome,' how cute is this?" The answer guides a lot of my day-to-day decision making, especially when it comes to my store, Time in a Bottle, Missouri's premier scrapbooking and crafting outlet.

"We made it just for you," said Laurel. "Margit contributed a Styrofoam cooler that her mother's insulin is shipped in, Clancy donated an old jacket made of that fake leopard-skin, and I used my trusty E-6000 to whip it all together. Isn't it cute? Don't you love the fake leather trim? You can even pop the top off—"

She broke the footstool into two pieces. Looking down inside, I could tell how she'd repurposed a small, but thick Styrofoam cooler. Inside there was a well, a secret compartment about six by six inches square. A cold Diet Dr Pepper waited there for me.

"You get two pieces, with storage," Laurel continued. "How nifty is that?"

"I absolutely love it!" I giggled. "You three have been Skyping with Cara Mia Delgatto again, haven't you?"

"Guilty as charged," said Clancy. "Actually the footstool was Cara Mia's idea. She's introducing them at her shop because Styrofoam is so hazardous to the ecology of the beachfront."

"She calls it the gift that keeps on giving," said Laurel with a twinkle in her eye. "Only she substitutes another word for 'gift' and it rhymes."

I really laughed at that.

Now that I was comfortably seated with my feet propped up, I took the opportunity to look around at all the decorating my friends had done. Blue and white crepe paper hung from the ceiling. Three big white Chinese lanterns dangled over my worktable, which had been covered with a white vinyl tablecloth. Tiny blue storks were glued to small stakes stuck in jars filled with blue and white jelly beans for centerpieces. The whole scene was so uber-cute that I said to Detweiler, "I need my camera!"

That got everybody laughing. Lee Alderton said, "We've got you covered, girlfriend," and she snapped a photo with her iPhone.

"Wait!" hollered Clancy. She dug into a big black plastic garbage bag and pulled up a red velvet robe. With a flourish, she unfurled the robe and positioned it over my shoulders.

"Your crown, ma'am," said Rebekkah Goldfader, as she sank into a deep curtsey. As she bobbed down, I caught a fleeting image of her mother, Dodie, standing there and smiling at me. That's been happening a lot lately. Although Dodie died several months ago, her spirit is still alive and well. She's found all sorts of charming ways to let us know she's still keeping an eye on her scrapbook store, and on us.

"Arise, princess," I said, tapping Rebekkah on the shoulders with a yard stick that Laurel had painted gold. The hilt had been fashioned from foam core board and wrapped with gold glittered duct tape.

Rebekkah gently positioned the crown on my head. "We pay our fealty to thee and thy offspring," she said in a formal, distant voice.

"I swannee," I said with a giggle, "y'all have been watching way too much of that Outlander series on Starz."

"Guilty!" came the response from several voices. My customers have convinced me to have an Outlander night once a month, replaying an episode of Diana Gabaldon's popular series. That's spawned a whole new income stream for me, as we've been happily producing Outlander-themed scrapbooks and paper craft items. A few of the women have even tried their hands at making food from that era. Of course, Brawny, my Scot nanny, is a big part of the draw. In her tartan skirt, brogues, and sporran, she's the living embodiment of a different culture. Brawny's been giving lectures about the strife between the Brits and the Scots, a conflict that still has overtones in today's world.

"Did you think we'd forget the gifts?" Lee said. "You know how I love wrapping things and making them extra-pretty. It's the presentation that counts, right? Let's get this party started!"

Since I love presents, and I adore tearing the wrapping paper off boxes, I dug right in. Lee handed me an elaborately wrapped box. “This is from all of us,” she said.

Under the blue and white paper was a robin’s egg blue box. I knew immediately it was from Tiffany’s, but I didn’t squeal with joy. My friends are thrifty. The box could well be a leftover from another gift—and really, where it came from shouldn’t matter.

But it did.

I opened the lid on the blue box and parted the white tissue paper. Inside was a silver spoon.

“We chipped in to buy that for you,” said Bonnie. Her eyes were moist with tears. “You might not have been born with a silver spoon in your mouth, but any kid lucky enough to have you as a mother has found a real treasure, indeed. We wanted to make sure your son never forgets that he’s rich beyond all others, having a wonderful woman like you for a mother.”

At that, I dissolved into tears.

20

~ Cara Mia Delgatto~

As we approached West Palm Beach International Airport, Poppy surprised me by taking the divide marked "Short Term Parking" instead of heading toward the DEPARTURES lane.

"No need to park. You can just let me off at the terminal. I'll be fine."

"Nope. I wanna see you on that there plane myself. You never can tell about flights. There's cancellations, delays—"

"Poppy, they won't let you past security because you don't have a ticket."

"Then I'll walk you inside the terminal and up to where they got it cordoned off."

I swallowed down a sigh. My stubbornness could be traced directly back to my grandfather. Once he made up his mind that was all she wrote. Instead of complaining, I stared out the window at the swaying palm trees. A short line of cars had pulled to the right rather than wait in the cell phone lot. I wondered how long they'd get to stay there before getting ticketed.

"You check the weather?" Poppy craned his neck to find an empty space for his old Toyota truck that he'd painted a bright John Deere green.

"Every day. Sometimes twice a day. The wind chill is thirty below. Ice storm moving in." I fingered the handle on my backpack. Tucked inside were beautiful gifts for Tyler George Lowenstein Detweiler. My friends and co-workers felt like they knew Kiki, because I'd talked so much about her. Upon hearing that Dodie Goldfader had nicknamed her "Sunshine," EveLynn McAfee sewed a baby quilt in a starburst pattern of cheerful yellows. Her mother Honora hand-quilted the blocks.

Being an expert in all things vintage, MJ Austin searched for and found a stuffed baby alligator. One touch of the leathered and withered exterior confirmed it was real. "I know it's weird, but boys like stuff that's bizarre. He'll appreciate this when he gets older. Besides, it's a vanishing part of Old Florida culture."

When I pointed out the alligator might make a grand chew toy for Kiki's dog, MJ produced an alternative gift, a hand-painted child's mug, bowl, and plate set. In the foreground, a brightly colored orange hung from a leafy branch, while the logo FLORIDA was done in a very mid-century modern font.

"Much better," our pal Skye Blue said. She showed off her present, a small mirror framed by tiny seashells, set in a sunburst pattern. I knew collecting, sorting and mounting them had taken her weeks of work.

"Hope you don't freeze your butt off," Poppy grumbled. He didn't like me leaving. Although he knew it was going to be a short visit, he had become very dependent on me lately. That proved miracles still happen. When I'd first contemplated a road trip from St. Louis to Miami, Florida, I'd had every intention of driving right past Stuart, Florida. My relationship with my grandfather had soured after he didn't show up for my father's funeral. But we'd since made amends and grown closer than ever to each other. Poppy wouldn't come out and say he didn't like me going away for a while, but he'd complained enough to make his opinion clear.

"I hope I don't either." I leaned over and gave him a peck on the cheek.

The walk from the car park to the terminal gave me the chance to tell him once more how to care for my pets. When the pneumatic sliding doors wooshed open, he dropped back. Airports were unfamiliar territory to him these days. I pointed to the American Airlines check-in desk. We were early, so there wasn't anybody in line. Or so I thought.

Fifteen minutes later, we were walking back to the green truck. Poppy held his tongue rather than remind me that he'd pestered me to keep checking the weather. I could fly as far as Charlotte, North Carolina, but after that...no go. An ice storm was blanketing the mid-Atlantic.

Fighting tears I text-messaged Clancy: *All flights from Charlotte canceled indefinitely. Won't make it to the baby shower. Give Kiki my love — CM*

21

~ Kiki~

Detweiler stayed long enough to watch me open a few of our gifts. Then he gave me a kiss and announced, "Ladies? I've got paperwork to catch up on."

To me, he said, "Clancy has promised to drive you home. Don't let this rowdy bunch tire you out too much. Clancy? She needs to get home before ten."

"Aye, aye, captain," said my friend.

The baby shower went on for nearly three hours. Detweiler had been right to worry about my stamina. If I hadn't been seated so comfortably, I would have never made it through the entire event. The stream of presents seemed endless. I was shocked and humbled by the haul. (I was also daunted by the thought of the number of thank-you notes I'd be writing.)

It's a well known fact that I hate—loathe—baby and wedding shower games. But in this instance, I was willing to play along because Laurel and Rebekkah had organized them. Tasting baby food and guessing what flavor it was about caused me to turn green. Watching ice cubes with plastic babies in them melt wasn't so bad. (The person whose cube melted first screamed out, "My water broke!" and won a prize.) Watching my crafters write messages on plastic diapers was silly, but fun. ("When you're changing these in the middle of the night, you'll get a giggle," suggested Lee.)

Clancy whispered in my ear, "You don't know how lucky you are. Someone suggested a game where people have to eat artificial baby poop. You make the poop by melting candy bars."

"You have to be kidding me."

"Cross my heart and hope to cry," said Clancy.

"Thank you for sparing me."

"You are welcome." She patted my knee and got up to distribute yet another game, one she called "Baby Literature, or as it's affectionately known, 'Chick Lit.'"

I shook my head. "Nope. Chick lit is a genre known for protagonists who love shoes, make snappy retorts, and have endless problems with their weight and men. Bridget Jones' Diary is an example."

"Huh," said Clancy. "A baby bird is a chick. 'Lit' is short for literature. Put them together and you get 'chick lit.'"

This was an argument I couldn't win, so I threw in the spit-up towel and guessed the titles of a lot of kid lit. Probably because I read a book to Erik every night. After accepting my prize (a Baby Ruth bar), I watched as my friends took turns decorating baby onesies with trim, iron on patches, and fabric ink.

"Has everybody signed the guest register?" Laurel waved a light blue autograph album over her head. "Everyone? Because I'm going to draw names from it. I have to have your name to give you a door prize."

Listing the proper names of baby animals was cute and harmless. Clancy won that, hands down. I knew that a baby kangaroo was a joey, but who knew that a baby sharks are called pups? And what on earth was an echidna? Clancy even knew that its baby was called a puggle!

Guessing the number of M&M's in a baby bottle was more my speed, since I've never met an M&M that I don't like. The color does not matter one bit to me; however, Clancy had found a place that sold her blue and white candies, just for this event.

"No fair! "We all know that Kiki knows her candies!" shouted Lee Alderton from the back, when Clancy announced that I'd won the M&M's guessing game.

That brought a lot of laughter and a hearty hug from Lee. Laurel announced, "Time to dig into the refreshments. Ladies? Help yourselves."

My mouth had been watering for some time, as the wonderful smell of baby bacon and cheese quiches filled the air. Margit brought me a plate with two of those, two blueberry and chèvre cheese quesadillas, and two pigs in a blanket. "More to come," she said. "I made strudel. One for you to take home. I know how the detective likes it."

I think she has a secret crush on my husband. She's always sending home food for him.

"He'll love it," I said. "Thanks so much."

She gave me a big hug. "I am so happy. This baby, you will bring him to the store, ja? I want to hold him. I couldn't come to the blessing ceremony because I was watching the store."

"I meant to thank you for doing that," I told her. "Of course, I'll be bringing Ty to the store. As soon as the wind chill isn't so brutal."

"Ach," she said. "I wish Dodie was here."

"So do I."

I hadn't expected a hug because Margit isn't physically

demonstrative. But the embrace she gave me was surprisingly full of emotion.

"Uh-oh." Over Margit's shoulder, I saw Bonnie Gossage grab her belly with both hands.

"I think my water just broke," the attorney said.

22

Bonnie's labor kicked our party into high gear. Literally. Rather than have a repeat of my home birth drama, Clancy loaded Bonnie into her new white, four-wheel drive Range Rover, the car she'd bought so she'd never have to fear our Midwest weather again. I hesitated on joining them, because I didn't want to seem rude. However, the other attendees shooed me out the door.

"Who knows when and if Bonnie's husband will make it in time?" Laurel handed me my scarf and gloves. "He's picking up his parents at the airport. She needs somebody, and you're it. None of us knows her as well as you do. Besides, you have the most recent, first-hand experience."

That was true enough. Things definitely had changed since I'd had Anya thirteen years ago. Besides all that, Bonnie had chosen to have her child at Southeast, the same hospital I'd visited after Ty was born. Given all those stellar reasons, I quit arguing and grabbed my purse.

Clancy proved her usual unflappable self, getting us to the ER in record time. I held Bonnie's hand and helped her time her contractions.

"Hard to believe I've been through this twice before," Bonnie said between grimaces. "Both times, Jeremy was by my side."

"My ex-husband was the last person I would have wanted with me when I gave birth," Clancy said. "He is so squeamish."

"I'm sorry that Jeremy isn't here, Bonnie, and that you have to put up with me," I said.

"Huh." Bonnie sniffed. "I'm glad you're here. You, too, Clancy. Jeremy also fainted both times. So far, you two are doing a much better job. He can't come with me into the operating room if I still need to have that Caesarian. They don't have time to scrape him off the floor and take care of me. Some things never change. He's a wonderful guy, but he goes limp at the sight of blood. How did Detweiler do?"

I thought it would be disloyal to complain about the problems created by my mother-in-law, so I kept the conversation very neutral. "Fine. None of us expected a home birth, but Brawny knew what she was doing. Obviously, it felt different—and I'm glad the kids got to participate. I think that's helped them bond with their new brother. I'm glad Ty's here and healthy, but I'm tired all the time and I can't find the energy to do much."

Bonnie smiled although her teeth were clenched. "Maybe you need to give yourself time to recover. Of course, that might be the only upside to working for other people. It's the law office's responsibility to cover for me."

Clancy let us out at the ER entrance. I walked Bonnie into the ER and got her paperwork started. An orderly found a wheelchair for her, while I pulled up a chair by her side. We weren't there five minutes until Clancy joined us. "Lots of parking. I guess most people don't want to be out in this weather. There's another ice storm coming. Or that's what they've predicted. Poor Cara Mia. She was so upset about not joining us."

"I can't wait to see her." I stepped away from the window where they were taking Bonnie's personal information. "I've missed her so much."

A hospital worker came over and strapped an identifying band around Bonnie's wrist. "We need to move you," she said to our friend as another wave of contractions hit her. By my calculations, they were fifteen minutes apart. Maybe even longer because I'm so bad at telling time it's a joke. Anya has suggested I take remedial classes. Detweiler wants me to ask Siri, the voice on my iPhone. I prefer to continue on my merry way being chronically misinformed because my inability is so well-known by now that no one expects me to be accurate.

Clancy and I took two steps to follow Bonnie in her wheeled chariot, but an armed security guard intercepted us. "Sorry, ladies. No one but hospital workers and personnel are permitted beyond this point. Unless, of course, one of you is actually that lady's husband in drag."

He thought he was being hilarious. Clancy and I looked at each other and rolled our eyes.

"Kiki? Clancy?" Bonnie called out to us. "Grab a couple of magazines for me from the gift shop will you? I might be here a while. I'll go nuts without reading materials."

"Sure. Want us to grab a couple from the waiting room, too?" I asked.

"Yuck! No way," Clancy said. "That's one of the secret places germs hang out. Magazines on airplanes and in waiting rooms. We'll go grab a few for you, Bonnie."

"I did not know that about magazines in waiting rooms," I said.

"Also doorknobs, phones, pens handed to you to sign things, handrails, handles of utensils at salad bars, salad bars, salt and pepper shakers, the list is endless."

With one gloved hand, I smothered a smile. Clancy is

borderline OCD. If anyone would be able to recite such common bacterial hideaways, she'd be the one.

"Steering wheels on cars, the bottoms of purses because most women set them on the floor in restrooms—" Her list went on and on.

The gift shop beckoned, so I kept walking while she warned me of lethal infestations lying in wait. The magazine rack offered a pleasing selection of reads. We both picked two.

To the right of the cash register was a wall of fame, saluting Star Employees.

"I'll get these," Clancy offered.

"No, I'll use the store charge card. It's a promotional item, I think. A gift for a customer, right?" As I pulled my wallet from my purse, I did a double-take. One of the photos on the wall caught my eye. I squinted. The face seemed familiar. I leaned across the counter.

"Excuse me!" A volunteer in a pink smock stuck her head up from where she'd been unpacking new merchandise. She peered up angrily, a strangely incongruous sight because she was planted on a footstool. "What do you think you are doing? Leaning on that glass. Well, I never."

"Sorry," I mumbled.

With a sour set to her mouth, she rang up our purchase and shoved the bag our way.

"Ah, well, let's go back to the store," Clancy said after we'd delivered the bag to a grateful Bonnie. "There's lots of food there."

"And M&Ms. I can get excited about them."

"Do you know what Bonnie's baby will be?"

"Yup. Remember? She asked for blue. Another boy. I think she and her husband were a tiny bit disappointed. Three boys. They would have loved to have added a girl to their household."

Clancy laughed. "She told me she always wanted to have a

big family. What do you want to bet this won't be her last trip to the birthing suites?"

"If at first you don't succeed," I said, "try, try again."

PART III

23

February

~ Kiki~

As predicted, Bonnie had another boy. Despite the fact we'd raced to the ER, Bonnie wasn't ready to go into hard labor. In fact, she didn't give birth for another 24 hours. But unlike me, Bonnie managed to make it to the hospital.

Since I'd given birth at home, Dr. Gretski wanted to see me sooner rather than later to see how I was doing. The appointment came as a surprise to Detweiler. He'd been prepared for a six-week post-natal visit, but not one so soon.

"Don't worry," I said. "I can handle this without you."

When he grunted an "okay," I turned so he couldn't see my expression. Secretly, I'd hoped he'd find a way to come with me. Yeah, I could sound all brave and self-sufficient, but inside I felt crumbly. Like the spine I'd finally built at great cost and intense effort was suddenly riddled full of holes. This porous scaffolding could give way at any minute.

But I didn't share that with Detweiler.

He had his own worries.

His boss, Prescott Gallaway, didn't get much done, because he spent all his time calling do-nothing meetings and following up on them with press conferences. "Makes me sick," Detweiler had complained over his morning coffee. "He's doing everything possible to position himself to take over Robbie Holmes's job. He keeps telling the media all these shortcomings he's supposedly found and fixed. Or fixing, because this obviously is going to take him a while. But all that's a joke. It's make-work. Everybody knows what he's doing. The mayor is on board, because he's never liked Robbie. He can't bend Robbie to his will."

I inserted, "Uh-huh," and other comments designed to prove I was paying attention. But my mind had skipped ahead to the doctor's visit. I planned to tell Dr. Gretski that I wasn't myself. Every morning I spent part of my time in the shower sitting on the floor and sobbing. At night, I stared at the ceiling and wondered what it would be like to be dead. Would it hurt?

I held Ty and felt nothing. No joy. No attachment. Only intense responsibility. And I knew, deep down inside, that I was not myself. That I'd fallen into a deep pit of depression. But I told myself, repeatedly, that if I kept going through the motions eventually I could climb back out. Except...how could I scale those impossibly high walls if I only had enough energy to keep putting one foot in front of another?

Several times while Gretski examined me, I opened my mouth. I intended to say, "I need help," but the words weren't there. It was like they were library books and another patron had checked them out, leaving only an empty spot on the shelves.

Instead of speaking up, I stared at the shiny bald spot on

Gretski's head and tried to avoid eye contact. He had this funny, peering look about him. You could imagine him as a Peeping Tom. Of course, maybe he was. Only he'd been smart enough to get paid for having a look-see.

"Any questions," he said, after plopping down behind his computer and entering notes on my exam. He seemed equally happy not to lock eyes with me. Perhaps he thought that my having the baby at home was a personal failure. Or maybe just a costly mistake, since he couldn't charge me for delivering my baby.

"Um. I'm not happy like I should be. I'm just blah. That's the best way I can describe it. I don't think it's normal," I complained to Dr. Wade Gretski, my ob/gyn. Anya thought it hysterical that my doctor's name that sounded so much like that of the great hockey player. She even suggested that I was having a "hat trick," the slang for scoring three goals, because I now had three kids, and that Dr. G would show up for the delivery wearing a hockey mask.

"In cases like this, it's best to review your lifestyle. Ease up. Get more rest."

"But I have a nanny! Brawny lives with us. She's really a terrific helper and—"

He interrupted me. "How many hours a week are you working?"

I added it up in my head. "I've only been to the store once, for a party."

"Are you getting enough rest? Going to bed at a reasonable hour? How is your husband sleeping? He's recovering from a gunshot wound, right?"

"Not well—"

"How many times a night do you get up to urinate or nurse the baby?"

"At least three. Sometimes four."

"What's a typical day like for you?" His fingers danced over the keyboard. Gretski might share a name with a hockey player, but he had the typing skills of a darn good secretary.

"Get up around six. Feed the animals, two cats and a dog. Shower, get dressed. I nurse Ty and then I get the kids ready for school. Brawny takes them, but I've been trying to give them extra attention. So I drive the kids to school and drop them off. Of course, I take Gracie along with. She's our Great Dane. She's no trouble at all, except that she misses going for walks. There are thank-you notes to write and—"

With a kick of his feet, he wheeled away from his computer. "I don't think we need to continue. Here's the point: Like most of my patients, you are pulled in a dozen different directions. Of course you're tired. Nanny or no nanny. You're probably exhausted. Anyone would be, but especially a thirty-three-year-old mother! Staying at home with the baby should be like a vacation."

I burst into tears. "But it's not! I don't feel like myself. I'm sad."

"Kiki, I'm not chastising you. I'm simply pointing out that you have every reason to be tired. Be kind to yourself. Try to sneak in a nap or two. Put your feet up when you can."

"But will I be okay?"

"Of course. You're healthy and hormonal. You'll get over this. What's on tap for you the rest of the day?"

"I've got a book to read, thank-you notes to write, an afghan to finish, and a phone call to make."

Dr. Gretski shook a finger at me. "I'm ordering you to go home, put up your feet, and get some rest."

"Okay. Got it. Thanks for your help. I'll get right on that." As I glanced over Dr. Gretski's shoulder, I saw his nurse shaking with laughter. A telepathic moment passed between us. I could read her thoughts: This man is nuts.

24

I did go home. I did curl up on the sofa. But I didn't get any rest. For days now, I'd been worried about the "setback" that Robbie had reported to us regarding Sheila's rehab for alcohol abuse. Each time I called, his phone went to voice mail. From my spot on the sofa, with Gracie on the floor and both cats curled up behind my knees, I tried again.

"How's Sheila doing?" I asked the minute Robbie answered.

"Up and down," he said. "Last week someone grabbed her 400-count sheets out of the dryer by mistake, and she had to sleep on regular linens. That caused a real problem. Not so much because the sheets were rough. More because it reminded her she wasn't in her own home, and that she didn't have control of her life anymore."

"Could you describe 'setback' for me? In detail? I'd like a sense of what you're dealing with."

"She bribed a member of the cleaning crew to bring her vodka. The dope put it in a Pine-Sol bottle to hide it. Unfortunately, he hadn't rinsed the bottle out properly, so Sheila started puking almost immediately. Then that idiot of a housekeeper started laughing, because her vomit was so sudsy. He suggested that she move it to the hallway, because that way he could wipe it up and clean the tile at the same time."

I groaned. Sheila had obviously sunk to a new low. Thank goodness Anya couldn't talk to her, at least not yet. I did not want my daughter to know all these gory details. Maybe someday, but not right now.

"The next day," continued Robbie, "she was upset, so Sheila sprayed Aqua Net into her mouth."

"Come again? Aqua Net?"

"Turns out, hairspray is 77% alcohol. Someone had smuggled in a can. Sheila traded her diamond earrings for a three-dollar can."

"Oh, no!" Sheila's first husband Harry had given her those earrings, and I'd hoped that one day they'd go to Anya, because her grandfather had been so thrilled to learn she was on her way. Sadly, Harry had died before she was born, but even on his deathbed, he'd thanked me repeatedly for carrying his grandchild.

Once I recovered from the shock of her giving away jewelry so sentimental, the impact of her desperation hit me. Hard. I couldn't imagine squirting hairspray into my mouth. What sort of compulsion was this? I wondered, and a voice in my head answered, Mental illness. That's the point: If you knew you had it, you would be mentally healthy. But you don't know what's happening, and you can't exert willpower over what you can't recognize.

"Kiki? You still there?" Robbie prodded me.

"Yes."

"Sad, isn't it?"

"Uh-huh," I said, as I wiped tears from my eyes. "Doesn't she know how much we love her? Can't she feel it?"

"No. Not right now. All she can do is fight the cravings. It's like driving along a highway on a foggy night. She can't see more than a couple feet ahead, and at the end of the headlights, there's a nice warm hotel room, the comfort she's missing. In a bottle. That's the siren song, calling her name."

"I miss her," I said. "I miss the old Sheila, the one before this woman who is acting so weird."

"I do, too."

25

~ Cara Mia Delgatto~

After living in Florida for nine months, my blood had thinned considerably. I'd actually forgotten what it felt like to be cold. That's the only way I can explain why I'd walked out of my house in my sandals when MJ came by to take me to the airport. As she stood there beside her pink Cadillac, I wondered why she didn't climb behind the steering wheel. Maybe she was taking a long last look at my beautiful Spin the Bottle hibiscus blooms. They were especially glorious that morning, with their deep magenta centers and yellow tips.

A woman of few words, MJ looked me up and down. Her frown of disapproval struck me as a fashion commentary.

"FitFlops sandals? Hello? Have you checked the weather in St. Louis? You might as well be flying into Siberia. I refuse to take you to the airport if you don't go inside and change immediately. Frostbite is ugly."

Needless-to-say, I did as she suggested, although I felt silly wearing knee-high black boots in the West Palm Beach Airport. But MJ assured me that it was smarter to wear them than to try and jam them into my suitcase. "Once you give Kiki all those gifts, you'll have room in your bag again, but not now."

The flight proved blessedly uneventful. As my father always said, "Any time they can reuse the plane, it was a good flight."

Inside the jet way leading to the terminal at St. Louis International, a wave of cold air smacked me silly. Literally, it took my breath away. I'd forgotten how frigid temps could deal your body such an unexpected assault. Not to mention how it could make your bladder holler, Howdy! I raced into the bathroom after exiting the arrivals area. After time well spent in a stall, I caught a look at myself in the mirror as I washed my hands. My dark curls were a wild mess, thanks to the humidity I'd just left. Probably not my best look. But the glow of my skin balanced out the unruly mop on my head. There was a natural blush to my cheeks and a sparkle in my eyes. In a word, I looked happy. Time in Florida had been good for me.

As I stuck my hands under a dryer that didn't work, and searched for one that did, I reflected on the fact that I owed my newfound well-being to another mechanical failure, the ominous coughing my Camry had made, a warning wound that forced me to take the exit to Stuart, Florida, where my grandfather had owned a small gas station.

One thing led to another. My character flaws dragged me from one challenge after another. Call me a slow learner. My temper has always gotten the best of me.

In the end, it was just that—a temper tantrum—that led me to impulsively buy The Treasure Chest, a small shop specializing in upcycled, recycled, and repurposed goods with coastal living theme. Yes, it had been unplanned, but my new life turned out to be a perfect fit for me. Sure, I still missed my old friends and St. Louis. But deep down, I realized that I'd bumbled my way home, the real place where I was always meant to be.

Yet, here I was, returning to my old life—sort of—by coming back to St. Louis. This place felt familiar in a comfortable way, a sensation that quickly proved deceptive. Instead of asking for directions to the rental car lot, I relied on my memory. That proved to be a stupid decision. In short order, I found myself on a shuttle bus headed for the outlying long-term parking lots. Being jostled around in a poorly heated bus proved to be a tortuous wake-up call. My automatic pilot had failed me. Things had changed here at Lambert Field since I'd been a local. Without my permission, or my knowledge, life had done what it does best: It had moved on. I needed to prepare myself for the reality that Kiki might have changed, too, in ways beyond my reckoning.

After my unplanned tour of long and short term parking at Lambert Field, I hopped off the bus and asked for help at an information booth. My second attempt proved more successful. And so, only an hour after my plane had landed (ha!), I climbed into a freezing rental car. The smell and feel of the upholstery reminded me of two things I had left behind: toasted ravioli and ice storms.

I'd planned to go directly to Time in a Bottle, Kiki's store, but my fingers turned numb from the cold of the steering wheel. Seemed that a quick trip to Target was in order. There I treated myself to a whirlwind shopping tour, buying a pair of Thinsulate lined leather gloves in black, a fuzzy knit cap in purple, and a matching scarf in purple, black, and white. In a rounder at the back of the women's section, I discovered a black jacket with faux leather trim. When I pointed out a rip in the seam under the arms, the clerk called over a manager who discounted the item.

Now I was ready to take on "the Lou."

My face hurt from smiling by the time I pulled into the parking lot at Time in a Bottle. Rather than chance waiting outside the back door, I went through the front, the same as any customer might do.

"Hello? Guess who just flew in from Florida?" I yelled.

"Oh, Cara, it's so good to see you." Kiki hurried over to greet me. Her hug was extra strong, as if she were holding on to me to keep herself upright. A few curious scrapbookers glanced up from their work, but not for long.

"Nothing could keep me away. Except ice storms in Charlotte," I said, relaxing into the warmth of Kiki's embrace. "I'm sorry I missed the naming ceremony, but I'm here now. When do I get to hold my godson?"

"Welcome back, Cara," said a deeply masculine voice. Chad Detweiler stepped forward to show off the new addition to the Lowenstein-Detweiler family. The tall detective cautiously tilted the bundle so I could meet Tyler George Lowenstein Detweiler, live and in person. What a thrill! Two bright blue eyes blinked up at me from a red and wrinkled face. Ty's rosebud lips puckered and quivered. The sweet scent of baby powder wafted up from the tiny package.

"Hello, little lamb," I said, taking the newborn gently from his daddy.

Ty responded by puckering and pursing his lips. A tiny mewling sound escaped. That little mouth started working overtime. I recognized the signs. "Kiki? Somebody's hungry. I'm a poor substitute for your mommy, aren't I?"

"One milkshake coming up. How about if we go into the office?"

"What about your customers?"

"They'll be fine without me. Lee Alderton is here."

"She is?" I craned my neck and sure enough, Lee came out from the back room. After giving me a heartfelt hug, she agreed to help the other crafters while Kiki and I got caught up.

But Lee wasn't the only surprise waiting for me. Detweiler had been hanging out in the back room, too. After greeting me, he put a hand on Kiki's arm. "Babe, I'm heading in to work. Brawny's giving me a lift."

Kiki's nanny was only two steps behind Detweiler. Here in St. Louis, she cuts quite the figure. I'd never seen a woman wearing a tartan skirt, brogues, and sporran until I met her. At first, the outfit seems weird. Comical, even. But once I got to know her, it was absolutely "spot on," which is Brit-speak for "perfect." Not only is she a character, but Brawny's a Scot, through and through. Proud of it, too. With her deep voice and that unmistakable accent, she's definitely one of a kind.

"I'll run the detective to the police department," she said. "I needed to get back to the house and do laundry anyway. We're having stew for dinner. I hope that's all right with ye."

"Brawny is a spectacular cook," Kiki said. "I've never eaten so well. Brawny? Cara Mia's family owned that restaurant I'm always raving about. The two of you should compare recipes."

"I'd like that," I said.

"And I as well," Brawny said, just before she and Detweiler headed for the back room.

"What? We've been married just a month and you don't kiss your wife?" Kiki called after him.

Properly chastised, Detweiler hurried back to give her an enthusiastic smooch. "Hadcho will give me a ride home later."

"Lee is willing to help out with the scrapbookers, but I need to let Margit know you're here and we're busy. That way she can listen for customers." Kiki nodded her head toward the needle arts room. There I found Margit bent over a tiny sweater that could only be destined for Ty.

"Margit, how are you?" I asked.

"Cara Mia!" The older woman toddled over to give me a stiff hug.

"We're going into the back," said Kiki. "Ty is hungry."

The tiny senior citizen waved. "Ja, ja. You go. I am fine."

"How's everyone doing?" I asked, as we walked away from the sales floor. "Detweiler, Anya, and Erik? Get me up to speed."

Instead of answering, she nodded toward the counter. "Help yourself to coffee, tea, or hot chocolate. You're probably freezing."

I did as she suggested while she rocked from side to side and answered my question.

"Erik has his moments. He's taken to calling me Mama Kiki, which is fine. I would never push him to accept me as his mother. Once in a while, something will remind him of his parents or of California, and then he's weepy. Mostly, he's been enchanted by snow and ice. You know that his Aunt Lorie moved here, right? She moved in with Leighton. That's been helpful. Lorraine and Leighton are like surrogate grandparents for the kids."

"Anya?"

"She's a handful. Helpful one minute and a pain in the backside the next. I guess that's typical."

"And Detweiler?" I added almond milk to my coffee, two Stevia packets, and then I stirred it to perfection.

"He's recovering pretty well from that bullet that nicked his spleen," she said with a shrug, "but he doesn't like to admit when he's tired, like now. He still exercises every morning with Brawny, but they've worked out what he can and can't do. I think the exercise is helping him keep up his spirits. For a while, he felt helpless and that was hard for him, you know? Hadcho took a bullet, too. Fortunately, his was a through-and-through in the shoulder. Bicep, actually. His is healing rather nicely."

She paused to brush a tear from her eyes, and then she

continued, "It's a lot, you know? So much happening at once. Sheila's still out in the rehab facility in California. Erik has been wetting the bed, off and on. He's talking in baby talk, like he's only two. I've been told that's a common response to a new baby. Anya has been sassy. I know everything will be all right, but I'm exhausted. Mentally and physically."

"Oh, Kiki," I said, and I threw my arms around her, being careful not to squeeze Ty in the embrace. "Doesn't Detweiler see that you're exhausted?"

"Not really. He's tired, too, but he and Hadcho have been relying on each other more since the shooting. Neither will admit he's hurting. A macho man type of thing, I guess." Backing into the big black leather office chair, Kiki sat down with Ty in her arms. She attempted a smile. "Detweiler still gets a bit lightheaded. I can always tell because he hands Ty to me and says the baby is hungry. But he's not. Detweiler can't fool me. I think he went back to work too soon."

Quickly unbuttoning her blouse, Kiki guided Ty to her breast. A kissing sound told me he didn't need any encouragement. Once he was settled, she put her feet up on a fake fur leopard footstool. I recognized it as being an upcycled item that her friends had made especially for her after my friends suggested the design.

"That footstool turned out so stinking cute. We've been making them like crazy. Can't keep up with the demand. Everyone loves the fact we're reusing Styrofoam containers that would have hurt the environment."

"It's so handy. Hey, could you grab a spit up cloth out of my diaper bag?" Kiki pointed to the cute black bag with white polka dots. It hung from a hook behind me. Just as she finished draping the cloth over Ty's head, we heard the back door fly open.

Detweiler raced into his wife's office with his cell phone

pressed to one ear. The office door banged against the wall behind him, but he didn't seem to notice. His full attention was on his phone. "Uh-huh, right, got it. Will do."

He ended the call and blurted out: "Someone just kidnapped Bonnie Gossage's baby."

26

Kiki sat bolt upright in the chair, yanking Ty away from his dinner. His whole person quivered with indignation. How dare she take the food right out of his mouth!

"Waaaaaaahhhhh!" Ty's scream hit a crescendo before breaking into a wail.

"Sh." Kiki moved closer so he could reattach. Instantly, Ty's stiff little body relaxed.

"Someone stole Bonnie Gossage's baby?" I sputtered. "You're kidding, right? Is this a sick joke?"

"Afraid not." Detweiler ran a shaky hand through his hair. "I was worried about something like this."

Brawny was still wearing her gloves, scarf, and hat when she walked into the office. Her face was an angry mask of concern. She must have turned around and brought the detective immediately back to the store.

"What do you mean? You're saying you thought this might happen?" I asked the detective.

"I hoped it wouldn't, but Hadcho and I both saw it coming. See," and Detweiler pulled up the empty chair and sank down, "there's been a rash of attempted kidnappings of newborns.

Three separate occasions. Three separate hospitals. We brought it up to Prescott Gallaway, and he paid no attention."

Brawny glowered at the mention of Gallaway's name. I waited for Kiki to weigh in, but she didn't. Instead she fixed her gaze on the spot above my head. There used to be a photo there that Dodie had taken of a turtle. Where had it gone?

I sifted through what little I'd heard about Prescott Gallaway. I remember that he was the acting Chief of Police, while Robbie Holmes took a leave of absence to be with Sheila while she was in rehab out in California. In fact, my family restaurant had catered Robbie and Sheila's wedding, so I had seen firsthand how Prescott had lusted after Robbie's job. Whenever possible, Prescott stepped into the limelight. And when that glow of public attention wasn't available to him, he manufactured situations to make Robbie look bad while making himself look good.

"Prescott's attitude all along has been, Why worry about a problem that hasn't happened?" Detweiler continued. "No matter how much we pushed him to take a closer look at all three scenarios, he refused. Several of us told him we needed to alert all the hospitals. We could have checked out their security procedures. But no, Prescott was too busy making himself look like a hero. His big thing is to point to what he calls 'Robbie's lapses in judgment' and criticize his brother-in-law. That way Prescott doesn't need to move forward or make any decisions that can come back on him. Now we've got a crisis on our hands. The person who did this has a head start. The weather forecast calls for more freezing rain. That'll tie up our resources as we respond to fender-benders..."

He didn't need to finish.

"Is Bonnie okay?" I asked.

"She is and she isn't," said the cop. "According to the first responders she's hysterical. She's claiming she must have been drugged. This whole thing went down less than five minutes ago. I mean, no one noticed the child was missing, and they've yet to construct a timeframe."

Ty had finished nursing. Kiki tidied up her clothes with one hand. A milk bubble formed and rested on the baby's lips like a butterfly kisses a flower. His eyes fluttered closed, opened, and sagged closed again.

"Where did this happen? When?" I asked.

"The abduction was discovered less than ten minutes ago. Bonnie's at Southeast Hospital. The floor supervisor went to check on her and discovered the baby was missing. Bonnie was out like a broken light bulb. Rather than sound the alarm, the supervisor quite appropriately checked with all other hospital personnel. She figured another nurse had the baby for some reason or another. That's how she realized Bonnie's little boy had been abducted."

Brawny had slipped back into the office. She was still wearing her boiled wool jacket and a scarf around her neck. She frowned and said, "None of this makes any sense. Infant abductions are extremely rare. Over the past ten years there's been increased security in hospitals. Most babies are fitted with a RFID device right after birth. The bracelet or ankle monitor is securely locked on right after the baby's footprint is recorded. It's highly unusual for a baby to be stolen from a hospital in this day and age."

"But somebody did do it," Kiki said, more to herself than to us.

"And they pulled this stunt while mother and child were still in the hospital," Detweiler agreed. His face was stormy with anger. "So the first thing we need to do is figure out how it happened. That might help us narrow down who did it, and where the baby is."

When his phone rang, he got up and walked out of the office.

27

Kiki let her head loll back against the black leather chair. She looked as if she was ready to follow Baby Ty in taking a nap. But then her lips moved and I heard her say, "I can't believe this is happening. Especially to poor Bonnie."

"Poor wee mite and his mother." Brawny shook her head. "Acting Chief Gallaway doesn't think beyond how he's looking on the telly. It's a shame Robbie Holmes isn't here. That's a man who uses his brain. But Prescott? Detweiler's been telling me tales when we go for our morning runs."

"You're still running?" I probably looked as surprised as I sounded. Sure, I walked the beach every day since moving to Jupiter Island off the coast of Florida, but running? In this weather?

"'Tis more of a fast walk than a run, but the detective wants to keep up our routine. Don't worry yourself. I keep a good eye on him. He's not healing as fast as he'd like. No, I'm worried that if the kidnapper gets spooked by Prescott Gallaway's shenanigans, the baby might be put at risk. What if he or she decides to abandon the child? In these low temps, that could mean..."

"I need your help." Detweiler rejoined us.

"Huh," Kiki scoffed. "I can't help you with this. I'm the mother of three kids. A housewife. There's nothing I can contribute. I think the world of Bonnie, you know I do, but there's no way I can help. I should be home darning your socks."

The edge to her voice shocked me. The unspoken message was clear: She was angry with her husband.

"Yes, you can help us," he said, evenly. "In fact, you might be the only person who can be of assistance. Bonnie is so distraught that her doctor recommends sedating her. If he does that, she's no good to us. She won't be able to report what happened. At least, she won't be able to talk to us in a cogent way. You're one of her best friends. If I can get you over to Southeast Hospital, you might be able to calm her down. I could interview her. We could get this investigation rolling."

That made sense—and the way he put it, Kiki couldn't say no, and yet she hesitated, frowning down at her son's cherubic face. I waited, fighting a sense of shock. Since when did Kiki refuse to help a friend? Especially one whose child was in danger? This was soooo not Kiki.

"Sorry, but you're on your own." Kiki sat forward and tugged on her blouse, settling it over her hips.

"Let me get this straight," Detweiler said. "The woman who's stuck her nose into countless crimes won't help me recover a stolen newborn, the child of her good friend, Bonnie Gossage, who got her out of jail a couple of years ago. Do I have that right? Furthermore, you're refusing to help us find a baby that's less than 24-hours old, even though it's bitterly cold outside, and that child could freeze to death if the kidnappers get spooked and decide to off-load their prize."

As I watched, Kiki's face lost its hard-edged look. In particular, her eyes softened and moistened. Her lower lip trembled. We waited and then she said, "What could I do that would possibly help Bonnie? I'm a mother and a housewife, remember?"

"You know a lot of the women Bonnie socializes with. What her habits are. Since your friend—our friend, Bonnie—is an attorney, it's remotely possible that someone has taken her baby in revenge. Hadcho can cover that angle. But right now I'm more worried that Bonnie Gossage is too hysterical to talk with us. Our best and only witness is incoherent. We need to know what she can remember—and we need to know it fast."

"What about her husband?" Kiki's face, usually so open and welcoming, had shut down like a window blind being pulled closed. "Why is Bonnie so important? I'm sure her husband can be as helpful as I can. Probably more so. And just where was he when this happened? Why wasn't he by her side? Protecting her? Taking up for her? What kind of guy allows other people to harm his wife?"

The words carried a message to Detweiler, one beyond their simple meanings. As I watched, he flinched before answering, "Jeremy Gossage has two other little ones to worry about, in the care of his elderly parents, so he's somewhat distracted to say the least. He'd gone home to see how his older kids were doing when the baby was stolen. Needless-to-say, Jeremy would give his own life for his family."

Wow. There was definitely a nip in the air, and it had nothing to do with the weather outside the building. I felt like I'd fallen down a rabbit hole into an alternate universe. What was going on?

"That leaves you asking me for help? I endanger babies or hadn't you heard?" Kiki glared at Detweiler.

The urge for a close examination of my boots proved overwhelming, so that was exactly what I did. I paid total attention to how the bits of snow had melted to form patterns on the leather. Where the stitches started and ended. Important stuff like that.

I'd never heard Kiki talk this way to Detweiler. In fact, I'd never heard her talk this way to anybody, anytime, anywhere. An undercurrent of anger swirled around us. All three of us were staring at Kiki, our faces must have been a study in surprise.

"Here's the deal. As you are well aware, my husband, I can't be of any help," Kiki said. "I'm not capable of it. In fact, I'm barely able to make good decisions about the welfare of my own family."

I swallowed a gasp.

Detweiler leaned his hands on the desk so he was practically in Kiki's face. "Please listen to yourself. I know you're hurting, but this isn't like you. Not at all. You are blurring the lines here. Are you seriously telling me that you can't help Bonnie Gossage, or that you won't? Kiki, can you live with that? Because I can't. Do I want to involve you? Of course not. No way! But Prescott won't allocate the resources we need. That was Hadcho on the phone, telling me that Prescott has decided to give it twenty-four hours and see if the baby shows up before he allocates resources to the case. He's convinced himself the child was simply mislaid. Mislaid! Can you hear how feeble that is? And twenty-four hours? That's one whale of a head start. By the time we get our butts in gear, the child might be dead."

28

Of course, Kiki caved.

Instead of having Brawny take Detweiler to the police station, it was agreed that the nanny would pick up the older kids from school.

That left Margit as chief babysitter. She was thrilled to have the chance to spend time with baby Ty. Since Lee Alderton was in the next room, she offered to help out. Her face practically glowed with happiness as she took the infant from Kiki's arms.

"Hello, little one," said Lee. "You remind me of my son, Bradley, when he was tiny. Don't worry about us, Kiki. I could hold this sweet child all day."

"*Ja*," Margit said. "We are good here. Take as long as you need."

"I'll drive us to the hospital," I said. "I rented a Kia Sorento because they're good in snow and bad weather. After we stop by the hospital, I can swing back here to pick up Ty if you have a car seat."

"Speaking of which, hand me your keys and I'll go warm it up for us now," Detweiler said, and I complied.

"No fair teaching him how to decorate a home while I'm

gone," said Kiki with a wink at Lee. "Cara? Wait until you see the photos of Lee's new home down in Palm Beach. She and her friend Peter had this brilliant idea to turn a garage into a kitchen. The place looks outstanding."

Lee laughed. "I didn't realize you live so close to us in Florida. We'll have to get together down there, Cara. As for the baby? He might be a bit young to go antique shopping with me. But I'll work on teaching him the names of furniture styles while you're out. By the time you get back, Kiki, he'll be an expert. Trust me."

"I do," Kiki said, "with my life."

Margit's smile grew even broader. "Ja, and I will teach him my mother tongue. He will learn fast, this one will. I know it. German will be a second language to him."

After Kiki planted a kiss on the baby's forehead, I helped her put on a cape that buckled in the front. "Is this the one that Brawny made for you?" I asked.

"One and the same." Kiki wound a long knitted scarf around her neck, jammed a hat over her unruly curls, and pulled on gloves.

I did the same with my new purchases from Target. Boy, was I glad I'd taken the time to complete my winter wardrobe. "Out into the frozen wasteland, we go," I said, trying to keep our spirits up.

As we trudged through the dirty old snow toward my rental car, I shivered. "I'd forgotten how cold it gets up here."

Detweiler had offered to warm up the Sorento for us. When we got closer, he hopped out of the driver's seat and let me take his place. I knew that ceding control must have been hard for him, but the damage from his gunshot wound made turning the steering wheel painful. After making sure Kiki was safely ensconced behind the passenger's seat, he attempted to play navigator while I drove. "Head back to Highway 40, going east."

"She lived here for thirty-some years," Kiki reminded him in a crisp voice. Whatever was happening, she wasn't about to let her husband off the crochet hook where he was firmly skewered.

"Okay. Kiki, do you have any ideas who could have stolen Bonnie's baby?" Detweiler asked his wife. "Off the top of your head? Anyone that Bonnie has mentioned as stalking her or being predatory?"

"As a matter of fact, I do. There's at least one person I know of who would dare steal Bonnie's baby. Who has long held a grudge against Bonnie...and me."

"Really?" The detective's head swiveled around to stare at my friend who was sitting in the back seat. "Who?"

"Her name is Bernice Stottlemeyer. Remember her?"

He shook his head, no.

"Bernice and her husband Wesley wanted to adopt, and they knew one of the mucky-mucks at Bonnie's law firm. So this senior partner assigned the case to Bonnie, because after all, Bonnie is a mom. He made a huge issue about how Bonnie was uniquely qualified to help the Stottlemeyers approach a birth mother about giving up her baby. The idea was that once they appropriately convinced a birth mother that the Stottlemeyers would be excellent parents, Bernice and Wesley would use Bonnie's firm to help them with the legalities involved in adoption."

Although I was listening, I still paid attention to the roads. Drivers in St. Louis are unpredictable in the best of times. It's an old joke that when four residents come to a four-way stop, at least one of them will run the stop sign, expecting the others to put on their brakes. That's a bad enough habit on dry pavement, but when the weather is miserable like this, it's deadly.

"But how did you get involved?" Detweiler wondered.

"Birth mothers today can afford to be choosy about the adoptive parents. These young women want a sense of the families who'll be raising their babies. One way to provide that is by showing them a family album. These albums are usually quite elaborate. Bernice couldn't possibly get up to speed in time to make one, so Bonnie told Bernice that I was the best person for the job."

"Why do I sense this project didn't turn out so good," Detweiler grumbled.

"Bernice was turned down by the birth mother. She got it in her head that I'd sabotaged her album, so she decided to trash the place. Did a pretty good job of it, too, until Aunt Penny nailed Bernice's purse to the floor and we duct-taped the woman to a stool."

"You are kidding!" I nearly slammed on the brakes. "You did what?"

"You have to understand," said Kiki in a soft voice, "Bernice had gone bonkers. Using her purse as a weapon, she'd knocked over displays. She broke bottles. Later we learned she'd slashed all the tires on my BMW. Good thing I didn't confront her while she was wielding that knife. Aunt Penny put a scare into her with the nail gun, but we needed a way to keep her from walking off, and the duct tape was handy."

"Bernice Stottlemeyer was not exactly Mother of the Year material." Detweiler chuckled.

"Nope. Of course, it goes without saying that I did not sabotage her album. In fact, I worked really hard to make her and her husband look good, but I couldn't manufacture a happy home where none exists. I've never met anyone less suited for parenthood than Bernice. That woman is just plain nasty."

"You're thinking she took Bonnie's baby?" Detweiler pressed the subject.

"Yup."

"Isn't that a little obvious?" I asked Kiki. "I mean, wouldn't the trail lead right back to this Bernice woman? You'd have to be nuts to try something like this."

"You're assuming that the person who took the baby is rational. Bernice had a mental breakdown. I know about it because we were going to press charges for the damages she did to my store. Hadcho was the first responder. He called in the locals to take her away." Kiki paused.

"I remember that," Detweiler said. "He laughed about it for days."

"When I went to give my report at the station, they took it but they warned me that Bernice's husband was trying to have her committed to the psych ward at one of the local hospitals. But the laws are complicated and Missouri only has half the beds we need for psychiatric patients. A few days later, Wesley Stottlemeyer himself called me. He asked me if I'd be willing to drop charges if he paid for all the damages. He explained that Bernice was undergoing a psychiatric evaluation. According to him, she had longstanding psychological problems, exacerbated by the hormone therapy she'd undergone while trying to have a child naturally. The birth mother's rejection of the Stottlemeyers set Bernice off. In her mind, they were perfect parenting material. Wealthy. Well-educated. Church-going. Bernice had looked up all the qualities and she was convinced they fit the bill. The only problem was that she had no compassion. Perfection, yes, in a clinical way, but love? That wasn't part of the equation."

"What did you tell Wesley when he asked you to drop the charges?" I asked, as we bumped our way down residential streets. I'd decided to take the back way to the hospital rather than the highway.

Kiki stared out the passenger side window for a long time. Finally, she said, "Bonnie has done me a million favors. After Bernice went bonkers, I called Bonnie and asked if we could get together and talk. Strictly off the record, which means I'm breaking a vow by sharing this with you. But her baby's life is at risk, so... whatever. After Bonnie assured me that Wesley was doing his best to get Bernice into treatment, I decided that I wouldn't press charges. He paid for the damage to the shop. I figured there wasn't any reason to pursue the situation further."

"You're convinced that she's the one who took Bonnie Gossage's baby?" Detweiler asked.

"I'm sure of it. Bernice blamed me, of course, for being rejected by the birth mother. But she also blamed Bonnie. Beyond all that, she was livid that I was pregnant. She said as much while she was slinging her purse around. That suggests to me that she would have gotten equally upset with Bonnie for being pregnant."

"But someone tried to take other babies at other hospitals," Detweiler said. "Which would mean that Bonnie wasn't the original target."

"That's one way of looking at things." Kiki fingered a button on her blouse. A thoughtful expression clouded her eyes. "Or it could mean that Bernice Stottlemeyer practiced on the other babies. Once she perfected her technique, she waltzed right in and kidnapped Bonnie's little boy."

29

Of course, I have known Bonnie Gossage for years. She and Jeremy were regulars at my family restaurant. However, we didn't really become friends until we took classes together at Kiki's store. She always cracked me up with her funny observations about life. Although once or twice she showed up in a business-like jacket, blouse, and skirt, typically she wore mom jeans, a tired University of Missouri sweatshirt, and sneakers. You'd never know she was an attorney, except when she opened her mouth and commented thoughtfully. That's when you realized she was whip-smart. Her observations generally shed a thoughtful light on any subject. Her eyes would narrow as she'd explain an aspect that had eluded the rest of us. Make no mistake about it, Bonnie Gossage was a mental powerhouse.

Or had been. I wasn't prepared for the shell of a woman whom we encountered at the hospital.

We had a sense of the disorganization the minute the elevator doors opened on the maternity floor. Two security guards roamed the hallway aimlessly. The tense postures of the nursing staff suggested they felt the entire weight of what they probably saw as failure. I couldn't blame them. I'd feel the same.

Detweiler introduced himself at the nurses' station. He had called the situation correctly. Prescott Gallaway had not sent even one uniformed city officer to the rescue.

“Thank goodness, I'm only working part-time,” Detweiler muttered. “Otherwise, Prescott could complain about me being here.”

Kiki and I waited while Detweiler handed both guards his business card and ordered them, “Don't leave. I'll want to talk to you after I speak with Mrs. Gossage.”

After a polite rap on the door, Kiki led the way inside her friend's room. There, a broken Bonnie Gossage sagged in a hospital bed, while sobbing and gibbering in an unintelligible speech. A bleak-looking man sat on the far side of the bed, his eyes vacant and listless.

“Bonnie, Bonnie, it's me,” said Kiki, hoisting herself onto the bed next to the attorney.

Following Detweiler's lead, I went over and said hello to Jeremy Gossage. “We've met,” as I explained that he'd seen me at my family's restaurant and at the scrapbooking store. Jeremy nodded, but obviously, he wasn't in the mood to talk about fine dining or scrapbooking, I pressed my body against the far wall, trying to be as unobtrusive as possible. Detweiler pulled his phone from his pocket and retreated to a far corner of the room. Once there, he kept his back to us and he spoke in low tones.

“How does this even happen?” Jeremy slapped his palms against his thighs. “Explain it to me. They put a bracelet on our son's foot. They gave us this song and dance about how tight security is. But someone comes right in and walks off with our son? This has to be a bad dream. My parents are at home with the other two. I told Dad to lock all the doors and get my Sig out of the gun safe.”

That caused the hairs on the back of my neck to stand at attention. "Um, is that really necessary? You have two small kids, right? Couldn't they get hurt?"

"Sure they could get hurt, but our baby has been abducted, so I have to do something, don't I?"

I swallowed hard. "Right, but your parents are probably upset, too? I'm not sure how easy it'll be for them to keep careful eye on your boys, under the circumstances. And little kids are fast. Especially little boys. I raised one. We used to call him Tommy 'Quicksilver.'"

Jeremy studied my face for a long, long time. Then, very slowly, he pulled his cell phone from his pocket. "Ma? It's me. No news. Oh? You did? Right. Good thinking. Thanks, Ma."

He hung up and said, "My mother wouldn't let Dad go and get out the gun."

With relief surging through me, I concentrated on what Kiki was saying to Bonnie as she rocked the other woman in her arms. "Tell me everything you remember, Bonnie, okay? It's going to be all right. We're here to help."

Detweiler put his phone away and stood respectfully at Bonnie's bedside.

Bonnie's gasping sobs devolved into noisy, but infrequent hiccups. It had taken a while, but our friend was calming down. Kiki patted her back repeatedly, treating the attorney like an emotional child.

"She came," Bonnie said. "I forget her name. She said she was in a room down the hall when she heard I was still here. So she came by."

"You can't remember her name?" Detweiler prodded.

"No."

"What was she wearing? Do you remember? Can you describe her?" Detweiler asked.

"A gown. Like this." Bonnie plucked at her own faded cotton smock.

"She was only wearing a gown?" Kiki repeated for clarification.

Bonnie paused. She tilted her head to one side. "Boots."

Kiki frowned. "Boots? Here? In the hospital?"

"Yes. I remember because they were like those UGGs that Anya has. Loose. Sloppy. They didn't click on the floor when she walked. They were wet. The nurse came by and had to mop up the mess. That's the last thing I remember, except that I was holding Riccardo. In my arms."

Detweiler took a notebook from his back pocket and scribbled on a page. He'd caught the discrepancy, as had I. A patient wouldn't be wandering around in wet boots. The tile floor would become slippery. Bonnie's description didn't make sense. Or did it?

"Was Jeremy here at the time?" Kiki asked.

"I ran home to check on the other boys and my parents. They're not accustomed to dealing with two rambunctious guys in diapers," he sounded a tad defensive, as if to suggest that it wasn't his fault the abduction had occurred. Of course, he'd blame himself. If the baby wasn't found, their marriage might suffer. How could it not? They would always wonder, What if?

"That woman brought me a Vanilla Coke." Bonnie gasped and pointed to her trash can. "Where is it? The can was here. Then I drink a little of it and fell asleep, but I hadn't finished it. Next thing I knew, Jeremy was waking me up and asking where the baby was."

Detweiler slipped out of the room. Straining to listen, I heard him tell the security guards to search all the trash and recycling containers for an empty Vanilla Coke can. He also told the head nurse that he wanted a comprehensive list of all the patients in the other rooms on the maternity floor and a list of anyone coming and going, staff and visitors.

"No, no, no," moaned Bonnie.

"Bonnie, this isn't the time to go to pieces. Your son needs you. You have to put him first. You can cry all you want later, but right now, you need to focus," Kiki said.

To my relief—and to the obvious relief of everyone in the room—Bonnie nodded her head. "You're right. I know you are," she mumbled.

"Can you get a police artist here?" Kiki asked her husband. "Or someone trained in using an Indenti-Kit? It sounds like you need to help Bonnie with a description."

"I know who gave me the cola," Bonnie interrupted.

"You do?" I couldn't help myself.

"It was that woman who was in our baby album class with me. Jana something or other."

30

"I can't believe it," said Detweiler, shoving his hands into his pocket. "The security guards and first responder couldn't get anything useful from Mrs. Gossage, and then Kiki asks the right question and *pow.* Now we're getting somewhere."

"Bonnie needed to calm down," I said. "Kiki had the right effect on her. I sure hope Margit can find that woman's registration information."

"This is the information our customer gave us," said Kiki after she got off her phone from calling Time in a Bottle. "There's her street address, phone number, and email address. But odds are, she lied. If she was planning this from the start, it would make sense to lie, wouldn't it?"

Detweiler showed the paper to the head of hospital security, Anthony Zenino, who left us with a promise he'd distribute the information through their IT system. "I'll know in minutes if anyone with these details checked in as a patient."

"I'll beg a favor from Lucy Edelman," Detweiler said. "She's the woman who's in charge of our composite images. Today's her day off, but she's a mom with five kids. I know she'll respond to my request. That way if this Jana Higgins lied about her identity, at least we've got a picture."

As Detweiler predicted, Lucy was willing to help. She arrived within an hour. That gave the head of security time to double-check the hospital's system for our abductor. No joy.

Meanwhile, the nursing supervisor put her head together with everyone else working on the floor. They created a list of visitors, at least of those who had signed in. The supervisor admitted to Detweiler, "It might not match the official list, so I might be wasting our time, but there's always the possibility this woman slipped past someone at a desk."

One of the nurses found an empty can of Vanilla Coke in a trash container in the family waiting room. Bagging it in plastic, she was able to hand it to Detweiler. He called in yet another favor, and Stan Hadcho showed up shortly thereafter.

"My shift is over. I'll take this to the crime lab and get it analyzed." Hadcho tucked the can into his pocket. "The real reason I stopped by is to warn you that Prescott is on the warpath. The hospital administrator heard what you're doing and phoned Prescott to thank him. He thought Prescott changed his mind about waiting twenty-four hours. After accepting the man's gratitude, Prescott blew a gasket, yelling like a banshee about your insubordination."

Detweiler clapped Hadcho on the shoulder. "Good old Prescott. Always comes down on the right side of serving and protecting, huh?"

"That customer of mine might not have ever been a patient on this floor," Kiki said as she studied the list the nursing staff had cobbled together. "Jana Higgins' name certainly isn't here. I wonder if she might have slipped in another way."

"What do you mean?" I asked.

"Well, Cara," Kiki said, "I'm thinking that she could have been a visitor just like us but used an assumed name. Once she got inside the hospital, she could have grabbed a gown and changed in a bathroom."

"That's certainly a possibility," Detweiler said. "We need to widen our search to the other floors and any security cameras. We need to view the footage, see if we can get a glimpse of this woman coming in or going out. I'll tell them to get ready for an image they can distribute." He turned his back on us and phoned the head of hospital security.

A rap at the door told us that Lucy Edelman, the police artist, had arrived. Detweiler gave her a nod of greeting and introduced Lucy around. After removing a hot pink silk scarf from around her neck and black leather gloves, she pulled up a chair next to Bonnie. Lucy's demeanor instantly calmed all of us down. Although her personal style was dramatic, with a sharply cut bob of silver hair and leopard print glasses, her manner was as soothing as a prayer.

For the next twenty minutes or so, Bonnie responded to questions while Lucy hit keys on a small computer. When they were finished, Kiki confirmed that the picture they'd developed adequately represented a woman known to us as Jana Higgins.

Detweiler thanked Lucy before she left. "No problem. We'll all be happy when Robbie Holmes gets back."

"What else can you tell us about this Higgins girl?" Hadcho asked Bonnie. She had settled down considerably. Her posture had relaxed and her eyes seemed more focused.

"Jana told us she was going to have a baby. Her due date was the same as mine. While Kiki was busy helping another scrapper, Jana whispered to me that she was engaged to be married, but they wanted to wait until after the baby came so they could include the baby in the ceremony." Bonnie's voice was flat and lifeless.

"Any idea where she lives? Any mention of where she'd driven in from?" Kiki asked. "Remember, some of the city streets hadn't been cleared yet. Could she have talked about having difficulty getting to the store? That might help us figure out who she is."

"No. She didn't mention the driving conditions."

"What did she say when she came in here? When she greeted you?" Detweiler asked.

Bonnie's face puckered as she struggled to think clearly. "She said, 'Hello. Oh, what a cute baby.' Things like that. My head hurts. Could someone get me an aspirin?" With that she started to cry again, softly.

"What if Jana Higgins, or whatever her name is, came through the ER?" I said. "Every time I've gone to the ER, they've made me change into a gown. Put a band on my wrist, too. Isn't it possible that she did that under an assumed name? Have you looked at the log down there? Could you take that sketch downstairs and show it around?"

"Won't do any good," said the nursing supervisor, who'd been standing by the door. "The shifts have changed. Anyone who saw the abductor won't be on duty now. You'll have to wait until tomorrow."

Hadcho cursed under his breath.

"No one by the name of Jana Higgins is in the drivers' license database for the State of Missouri," Detweiler said after checking a text message.

"A fictitious name and address from a woman taking a scrapbooking class?" Hadcho rubbed his hand through his hair. "Now I've heard everything. Here I always thought that scrapbookers were such wonderful people."

"They are," said Kiki. "Jana Higgins couldn't scrapbook her way out of a paper bag album."

"She planned this from the start," I said.

"Let me ask Margit how she paid for the class." Kiki opened her cell phone.

A few minutes on the phone and Kiki confirmed that Jana Higgins had paid in cash for the class. "With a one-hundred-dollar bill no less. Which is weird in itself because she didn't look like she had two cents to rub together."

"We keep hitting dead ends," Jeremy said.

"Yes, and we're eliminating a lot of blind alleys," Detweiler said. "That's important. We're already discovered this was well-planned and cunningly executed. That tells me someone wanted to keep your baby alive—and that gives me hope."

31

Detweiler's summary of the Gossages' plight was mildly encouraging.

Hadcho picked up the thread and continued, "We need to construct a timeline. Kiki? Bonnie? You two first saw this Jana Higgins when?"

"January 10 at our crop," Kiki said.

"Any sightings after that?"

"Yes. She came to the store a couple of days ago to redeem her coupon. I waited on her."

"What next?" Hadcho asked. "Mrs. Gossage, walk me through what happened, minute by minute. Your baby was born, when?"

"Last night around eleven."

"That leads me to wonder how this woman knew you'd given birth," Detweiler said. "Hospitals no longer post photos of new arrivals until after mother and child have gone home. It's a security risk."

"Only Jeremy knew. Okay, and then he was supposed to call Kiki and my law firm this morning."

"But I never got the chance," Jeremy interrupted his wife.

"Because I went home to tell the kids about their new brother and to give my parents a break. When I came back this morning, well, you know what happened."

"I fed our son a bottle. We decided that we'd use formula this time because when I'm in court, it's a real hassle otherwise. I put him down for a nap in that crib," and Bonnie pointed to the crib next to her bed.

"The nurse on duty came by and checked on Mrs. Gossage and her baby," said the floor supervisor. "No one was here who shouldn't have been."

Bonnie nodded. "The baby was sleeping after he'd eaten, and I was watching television. Then there was a knock at the door. It was Jana. Or whatever her name is."

"What was she wearing?" Hadcho asked. "Get me caught up."

I knew this was a successful interview technique. Asking for the same information over and over encouraged the interviewee to elaborate. To think of new details.

And it worked.

"A hospital gown, boots." Bonnie paused to think. "Like Uggs but gray. Wet. On her wrist was a bracelet like mine."

Holding up her wrist, Bonnie showed us the regulation plastic bracelet that most hospitals use to tag patients. So now we had a new piece of the puzzle to work with.

"Could you tell if the bracelet came from this hospital?" Detweiler probed gently.

"I'm sure it did. It looked exactly like mine."

"If she didn't have her coat on," Kiki said, "she must have gotten dressed in that thin cotton gown after getting inside the hospital, right? It's twenty below outside."

"That means she must have gone through the intake procedure and been given a gown. She simply used a fake ID. I'm on it," Hadcho hustled his way out of the room.

Bonnie rested her head on Kiki's shoulder and cried softly. Kiki kept murmuring words of comfort.

"So where did she go with our son?" Jeremy wondered.

"The head of hospital security is checking the video feeds. There are all sorts of security cameras on this campus," Detweiler said.

"It's so cold outside," said Bonnie.

"Bonnie and Jeremy, remember this: She wants the baby to raise for her own," Kiki said. "She's not going to let anything happen to your little boy. If Jana didn't want to be a good mommy, she wouldn't have shown up for a scrapbooking class."

"That's right," Detweiler echoed.

"I'm sure she wants to keep your baby safe," Kiki repeated as she raised her eyebrows at me. I kept my mouth shut. I figured Kiki and I were thinking the same thing: Accidents do happen. Look at the kidnapping of the Lindbergh baby. The abductors dropped him as they were climbing out of the bedroom window. The baby was never ransomed because he didn't live through his abduction.

32

Excusing myself, I walked out to the nurses' station. "Could you tell me where your vending machines are?"

A woman in pink scrubs with gray kittens on it looked up from a computer screen. "In this building or on the hospital campus?"

"This building," I said. I couldn't imagine Jana braving this freezing weather to try and find a Vanilla Coke.

"Sure. Here's a brochure for this building. On the second page, you'll see all the vending machines are listed."

"Thanks." I took it and walked back to the room.

Kiki was talking quietly to Bonnie. Detweiler was talking to the intake desk. After Jeremy left to update his parents, I said, "I'll be right back." I had a mission in mind. In the hall, I discovered we'd been joined by a uniformed officer, who was keeping an eye on the door to Bonnie's room. "Are you going to stay here? To safeguard Mrs. Gossage? Did Prescott Gallaway send you?"

"I'm actually off-duty, but I'll stay long as I can, because Hadcho asked me if I'd help out," he said. "If Chief Holmes was in town, he'd assign a detail, but with Prescott Gallaway in charge, it's anybody's guess. Gallaway likes to brag about being fiscally conservative. Penny wise and pound foolish if you ask me. Since he's never been in charge for long, the impact of his poor decision-making has escaped notice."

I was shocked that the officer would be so candid, and I guess my face betrayed my surprise.

"If you're a friend to Mrs. Lowenstein, I mean Mrs. Detweiler, then I know I can be honest with you," he explained.

"Thanks for anything you can do to help Bonnie. This is purely awful, isn't it? I get the impression we're dealing with a whack job here."

"Aren't they all?" said the cop, with a crooked grin.

According to the brochure, there were vending machines in every lounge on every floor, and two sets on the ground floor. One set by the entrance and one back in the family waiting area. The cafeteria was also on the ground floor, so I started there.

Twenty minutes later, I had my answer, and I returned to Bonnie's room.

"She's cried herself to sleep," said Kiki. She rested one hand on the shoulder of our friend, who was snoring lightly.

"I made a tour of the vending machines. Nothing but Pepsi products. That means there are no Vanilla Cokes to be had."

"Huh?" Kiki moved off the bed where Bonnie was sleeping. She tiptoed over by me. "What's this about Vanilla Coke, and why does it matter?"

Detweiler looked up from the text message he'd been composing.

"The Vanilla Coke matters because Jana, or whoever she is, brought the cola with her when she came to the hospital. Maybe I'm making broad assumptions here, but that tells me she came here specifically expecting to see Bonnie. If that's the case then—"

"That further confirms that someone here at the hospital

was watching specifically for Bonnie to have her baby," Kiki said. "That person must have contacted Jana and told her Bonnie had been admitted."

"Right," I said, feeling rather pleased with myself.

"Good thinking," said Detweiler, "that means our abductor probably had an accomplice. It's easier to catch two people who're in on a plot than one person, acting alone. Someone here, who's part of the hospital staff, or who has regular access is involved. The hospital administration is going to go nuts."

"I've been thinking and thinking about Jana," Kiki said softly so she didn't wake up Bonnie. "We usually take out the recycling on Wednesdays, but we had that ice storm last Wednesday."

"So?" Detweiler arched an eyebrow.

"I wonder if Jana left behind any trash after the crop. She brought a package of photos with her. As I recall, they'd been developed at Walmart. I wonder which store and what name she used. I'll give Margit a call and tell her to hold onto the recycling," Kiki said. "I'll also ask her how Ty is doing."

By the time Hadcho came back, we had a lot to tell him.

33

Bonnie roused briefly, until the duty nurse gave her a sedative. The baby had been a C-section, so our friend needed all the rest she could get. Hysteria would not speed her recovery. I had a hunch that crying used more muscles than lying there happily in her hospital bed, but I didn't bother to ask for clarification.

Hadcho had gotten a list of everyone who'd checked into the emergency room over the past 24 hours. None of the names looked familiar to Kiki. None of the "guests" (that was the hospital's terminology) presented as being in labor.

"We're back to where we started," said Detweiler, rubbing his jaw. "Let's hope your recycling provides us with a few answers."

Kiki looked worn out. She'd perked up while we related our theory about an insider, but in the aftermath, she'd grown increasingly quiet. Sitting in the big recliner, she reminded me of a limp dishrag. Definitely not the image that usually came to mind when I thought, "Kiki Lowenstein."

"How about if I take you to the store and then drop you off at your house?" I wanted to dig into that trash and see if we could come up with anything.

"Sounds good."

Detweiler and Hadcho decided to stay at the hospital and conduct more interviews. "I'm hoping the CCTV will show a good picture of the woman who took Bonnie's baby. The Indenti-Kit image is never as reliable as a photo."

Hadcho agreed. "It might also indicate where she came from and where she went. Maybe the baby is still on the premises. That would explain why the RIFD alarm didn't go off."

Kiki gave Detweiler a half-hearted hug. I followed her out the door as she led the way to the elevator bank.

"Where are you staying?" she asked.

"Probably at one of the Drury Inn hotels. Free breakfast and dinner, plus a glass of wine in the evening. What's not to love?"

"You're welcome to stay at our house."

"That's very kind, but I don't think you need another person underfoot."

She didn't argue about that. Back in the rental car, Kiki was uncharacteristically quiet.

"Okay, what's eating you?" I asked as I keyed the ignition.

She didn't respond.

"Kiki, I've bared my soul to you more than once. Don't you think it would help you to talk about whatever it is that's bugging you? You aren't yourself, you know."

"Have you ever felt totally and wholly inadequate? That's how I feel. I look at Erik and Anya and Ty, and I think, 'What if I'm a worse parent than my mother? What if Erik notices that he doesn't match his siblings, and he never fits in? What if I rely too much on Anya?'"

"You're over-thinking this."

"Maybe. Erik has started wetting the bed. He didn't do that when he first came to live with us. He's been waking up and crying at night. That's new, too. The timing of all this is wrong. If I hadn't gotten pregnant—"

"Then you and Detweiler wouldn't have moved up the ceremony. That would have left Erik in a precarious position. No mother. Just a working dad who's got an around-the-clock type of job."

"But he would have had the chance to acclimate. Instead, he's been asked to adjust to a lot of changes all at once."

"He has the same caregiver that he's had all of his life. Brawny provides him with tremendous stability. How about Lorraine? His Auntie Lori? She's right next door. Short of importing palm trees and a coastline, you've done everything possible to make Webster Groves his home."

"But he's regressing!"

I was temporarily stunned into silence. Kiki's usually not like this. She's usually the one who acts like a rock for the rest of us. This turn of events had loosened her moorings. Like the mythical island that tears loose from its foundation, she was floating, tossed by currents, and getting ready to sink.

Okay, it was my turn to be her anchor. I could do that for her.

"Regressing is a very normal response to a new sibling. Erik is acting like a normal five-year-old who's just had a new addition to the family. Did you hear the word I repeated? Normal and normal. Cut the kid some slack, and cut some for yourself while you're at it."

We'd reached the parking lot of Time in a Bottle. I eased my rental car up over the slight bump in the concrete and pulled into an empty space.

"What if I can't take care of him? And Anya? And Ty? What if I'm not up to this? Three kids and a full-time job?" Kiki's voice was strained and her eyes were filled with tears.

"Of course you're up to this," I said, in the calmest voice I could muster. I wanted to grab her and shake her, but instead, I gripped the car keys extra hard. "You've been through worse. After all, your children are safe."

But she didn't respond.

34

When we walked back into the store, Lee Alderton was sitting in the office chair and holding Ty in her arms. "He's such a good baby," she said. "I can't wait to be a grandmother. Thanks so much for letting me hold him. Margit is up front helping a customer."

Kiki thanked the sweet woman, hugged her, and watched as Lee tossed on her coat and waved goodbye. Margit joined us, explaining, "It's quiet now. No customers, but I listen for the dinger, *ja?*"

Of course, we had to tell her and Clancy what we'd learned.

"Bonnie and Jeremy must be frantic. Going through the recycling bin is a great idea. You're right, Kiki. We haven't dumped it out lately." Clancy's hand shook as she handed me a cup of Earl Grey tea. This easy camaraderie reminded me of my store down in Florida. In that parallel universe, we also served hot drinks to each other in times of stress. The back room at The Treasure Chest had become a gathering spot for food, friends, and fun. It was there that we had cemented our relationships by sharing tidbits about our lives.

"Kiki puts the scrap into scrapbooking." Clancy pointed to a recycling bin that was actually two large trashcans duct-taped side by side. They were filled to the brim with paper pieces.

"Oh, boy," I said. "Those are honking big bins. How about if we use plastic trash bags so we can sort through this mess one piece at a time? I'm assuming all this is...recent?"

"Yes," Kiki said. "I keep anything that's at least an inch by an inch or bigger. Then the scraps get divided by color into these smaller plastic bins. You wouldn't believe how handy these pieces are."

"You're right. I wouldn't believe it. Looks like garbage to me."

Ty whimpered and nuzzled Kiki's neck. He was hungry. She was tired. I volunteered to take her home and come back and sort through the confetti.

"Not yet," she said. "I'll stay here while you look. I might be the only person who can recognize leftovers from Jana Higgins' baby album. I can go and nurse Ty in the office. Call me if you see anything that might be a piece that Jana threw away. Do you remember what any of her photos looked like, Clancy?"

"Yes, I do. You're looking for a photo of a man and two little girls. Jana made an offhand comment about her fiancé having daughters from another relationship. I'll go get fresh trash bags for us to use while sorting." Clancy turned and headed for the kitchen.

Margit and I watched as Kiki carried Ty into Dodie's office.

Even though it's been months since Dodie Goldfader died, I can't help but think of that room as "Dodie's Office." It's as if Dodie's spirit lingers there. Once Kiki closed the door, Margit removed her glasses, pulled a gray square from a pocket, and wiped the lenses. After replacing them, Margit shook her head. "Kiki is not herself."

"You're right. What do you think it is?"

Margit shook her head. "So much all at once. You know about Sheila, right?"

"No. How about if you tell me what's up with her while I go through the paper?"

"I can help, too," said Margit, but she didn't look steady on her feet. The woman has to be in her late seventies, if she's a day. Without asking, I pulled up a chair and gestured for her to sit. Clancy returned with the trash bags. After opening one, Clancy would pull out a wodge of paper from the recycling bin, hand half of it to me, and we'd untangle the pieces.

"Give me something to do," Margit demanded. Since she was seated, she didn't have the range of motion that Clancy and I did. I loaded a small empty plastic bin with papers that she could sort.

"Sheila is in rehab in California," explained Margit.

This I knew, but I didn't say anything. I wanted to let Margit and Clancy lead the conversation.

"Robbie took her there himself," Clancy said. "He planned to handcuff her to the car if she didn't agree to go. That poor man even drove her there himself because he figured she'd make a fuss on the plane. Anything to get out of going for help."

Margit picked through papers, examining each one carefully. "Last week Sheila had a set-back. She drank hairspray."

The papers in my hands fell to the floor. "She did what?"

"Actually, not that uncommon," said Clancy. "I looked it up. Usually people drink cologne. She must have been really hankering for a fix."

"What is this 'hankering'?" asked Margit.

"That means she was really aching or longing for alcohol," I explained. "Wow. I didn't realize she was such a mess."

Clancy pulled out two pieces of paper and set them aside. "I can't tell if these are anything. There's a man in them. I'm not sure what we're looking for."

"Best to ask Kiki," I said. "If they are from this Jana Higgins character, Detweiler and Hadcho might be able to track the fiancé down, and that might lead us to the kidnapper. Was Sheila really that bad? I never saw her drunk. A little lubricated, but still..."

Clancy examined more chopped up pieces of photos. "Robbie was covering for her. As were people at the country club. Linnea, her maid, covered up some of her misdeeds. Even Kiki, although Kiki didn't totally realize what was happening. Anya, too, I guess you could say. Turns out, that Anya was talking her grandmother out of driving places on a regular basis. That poor kid had to make snap judgments as to whether her grandmother was too drunk to get behind the wheel."

I rocked back on my heels. I'd dropped to a squat to retrieve the papers that had fallen to the floor. "You have to be kidding me! Sheila was driving around drunk and with the kids in the car?"

"We think so." Clancy frowned. "After Brawny started working here at the store, Sheila volunteered to pick them up from school two days a week."

"Brawny teaches knitting classes here," explained Margit.

"At least twice that I know of, Sheila was a bit tipsy when she got to the carpool line. On one occasion, she took Erik and Anya straight to her house under the guise of having forgotten her cell phone. Instead of running in and grabbing the phone, she parked the car, took the kids inside, and poured herself a gin and tonic. Fortunately, Anya refused to get back into the Mercedes with her or to let Erik go either."

"That's awful!" I blurted out.

"Kiki blames herself," Clancy said, "because she grew up with a father who was a drunk. Although she knows better, Kiki feels like this drinking business has something to do with her. Goodness only knows what!"

"*Ja,* and it makes no sense, but when does the human heart understand logic? Where there is emotion, logic hops on his horse and rides away. Now Sheila can be no help to Kiki, and Detweiler is struggling."

"You mean with his wounds? He does look tired."

"*Ja*, the good detective is still healing, but there is more to their problems. It's his mother, you see," Margit said with a disapproving click of her tongue.

Clancy shot Margit a dark look. "I think you shouldn't have shared that."

"Cara is an old friend. She needs to know," Margit protested.

"Thelma has a problem? Something physical?" I got to my feet so I could stretch out my back. After sitting on the plane, it had stiffened up.

"Nothing that a good, swift slap across the face couldn't cure." Clancy kicked one of the plastic recycling bins. "Or a kick in the butt."

"Huh? From all I've heard, Thelma Detweiler is the perfect mother-in-law. That's changed?"

The co-workers became co-conspirators. Margit and Clancy bent their heads close to mine so they couldn't be overheard. Clancy explained, "Thelma made no secret of her disappointment that Kiki didn't stop coming to work sooner. She phoned here often to keep tabs on Kiki. We never told her what Thelma was doing, because we didn't want to upset her. Then when the baby came so fast, and because Kiki had him at home, Thelma really got her tail feathers in a twist. She practically went bonkers."

"*Ja,* she told Detweiler that Kiki could have had the baby at the hospital. She said Kiki should have waited. It would have been safer for the boy. Thelma is a good woman, but *ach, Man muss die Dinge nehmen, wie sie kommen.*"

"Translation, please," I said.

"You must take things as they come," explained Margit. "Kiki did not want to have the baby at home. What else could she have done?"

"Thelma keeps telling her son that she's worried that the baby is not safe. That Kiki is not being a good mother," Clancy said.

My mouth dropped open. It took me a minute to gather my thoughts. "You have to be kidding me. What does Detweiler do about this? Surely he's ignoring Thelma. Or telling her to stay out of their business?"

Again, the co-workers exchanged glances that signified there was more to the story. Slowly, Clancy said, "Thelma has managed to make Detweiler nervous. See, this is coming at a time when he doesn't feel capable any way. So she's dealt him a low blow. Worst of all, Thelma is throwing Kiki off-balance, you know? She's always counted on Thelma being supportive and helpful. Now suddenly, she's causing this riff between Detweiler and Kiki. Kiki's already got so much to handle—but Thelma keeps adding to the pressure. It doesn't make any sense. Neither of us can figure out what her problem is!"

"Oh, my goodness." I processed all of this. "No wonder Kiki looks so beaten down. Besides all that, it's cold and dark outside. She's never done well with winter, has she?"

"No," said Clancy.

"Not ever," said Margit.

35

On that somber note, we continued our separate tasks. Margit, Clancy, and I kept combing through the scrap paper pile until we'd reached the bottom of the bins. As a result, we had a nice little mound of scraps to show Kiki.

"Could you go through these, please?" I asked, as she came out of her office. "See if any of them look like what Jana Higgins had. I think we might have found something, but you're the only one who can really confirm what we have."

"Sure," Kiki said, handing Ty to me. His tiny head bobbled in the transfer.

I inhaled deeply, filling my soul with the fragrance of innocence while simultaneously stirring my own desires to have another child. Brushing my chin against the top of his head, I was transported to my son's early days. Babies are crowned with velvet, and the sensation of that gentle new sprung hair is intoxicating.

Kiki had just dumped the bits of paper on a lap desk when Hadcho walked in, stamping bits of ice off his shoes. With a deft hand, he brushed snowflakes off his shoulders. More flakes dotted his jet black hair. "Detweiler sent me to see what you'd found. You okay holding the baby, Cara? That's my godson, you know. I can take him any time you want." After taking off his coat, Hadcho extended his arms, but I didn't hand over the baby.

"He's my godson, too, buddy. I love holding him," I said, cradling Ty to my chest. "I adore babies. Absolutely adore them."

"Yeah," he said. "Someone else does, too. Enough to steal one of them."

"Kiki? You want a Diet Dr Pepper?" Margit paused behind the refrigerator door. When Kiki said she did, I took it as a good sign. Her interest in her favorite soft drink seemed like a step in the right direction.

After laboriously piecing one image back together, Kiki said, "That's Lois Kimmel's son and daughter-in-law. Not what we're looking for."

Pulling a magnifying glass from a nearby top desk drawer, she worked patiently to assemble yet another shredded photo.

A buzzing signaled that Hadcho had a new message. He checked his phone and stepped into Kiki's office leaving me to rock Ty while Kiki worked with miniscule pieces of a photo.

Because of where I was seated, I could hear the detective talking on his cell phone. He seemed to be talking to another law enforcement officer, giving commands to interview all the hospital personnel. Last but not least, he talked to someone about reviewing camera footage from the hospital exits. That must not have gone well, because he cursed and snarled.

When Hadcho opened the office door, a chill swept through the back room. It reminded me of the subzero temperatures outside—and that gave me a thought.

"There had to have been two people. Either that or the abductor used a cab service or Uber."

"How do you figure?" His dark brown eyes glittered with interest.

"You wouldn't walk outside with a newborn in this cold weather and get into a cold car. You'd want the car to be warmed up, wouldn't you?"

"That's assuming this person is thinking straight. We don't know that."

"But Cara's right," Kiki said. "We know that the abductor is a plotter and a planner. We have every reason to believe she wants to take good care of this infant. Why jeopardize his health by loading it into a cold car? If the vehicle was warmed up and sitting outside for her, maybe someone at the hospital saw Jana get inside. Maybe a security guard took notice of a woman fitting her description carrying a baby? Or even any woman carrying a baby out of the hospital earlier today."

Hadcho called that in.

When he finished, Kiki handed him a photo. "This man? He's the guy that Jana identified as her fiancé. I remember it now, because Jana said he had two kids from a previous marriage. Daughters. That's one reason she must have wanted to steal a boy. She said something about men wanting sons."

Hadcho leaned close to look at the snapshot. Unfortunately, there was a stray bit of paper that was stuck to the man's face in the picture, obscuring his features.

"That piece of paper can be removed," said Kiki. "It's glued down. But it would probably be best to have a lab tech do it. I mean, we scrapbookers have our ways, but that would be tampering with evidence. Let me go through the scrap paper recycling again, okay? I seem to recall that Jana did a little journaling. Let me run to the bathroom and then I'll see if I can dig that out."

"I hate this," Hadcho said, after she left. He carefully tucked the photo into an evidence bag.

"What do you mean?"

"I hate knowing that seconds and minutes are ticking past. Gimme," said Hadcho.

I passed the baby to him. He held Ty very naturally, rocking ever so gently in his chair. Ty's eyes fluttered closed. Hadcho's face creased into a smile totally at odds with what I knew of him. The scene caused me to wonder if we really know anyone. Unless we've seen that person in every situation imaginable, our perspective is sorely limited.

"Let's work this through, okay?" I said. "This Jana person takes a class at Kiki's store. A baby album class. Why would a person do that if she wasn't pregnant? Or if she didn't have a close friend or family member who was expecting?"

"That's the point." Hadcho scooted down into the chair so he could relax while holding Ty. In an almost sleepy voice, he said, "Here's what I learned from the National Center: There's a very narrow, very typical, and very specific profile of an infant abductor. In nearly all the cases, the abductor is a woman who desperately needs to produce a baby because she's been pretending to be pregnant. Usually, there's a man involved. Usually, she has told that man that she's having his child. Often she's tried to have a baby and failed. As the months go on, she needs to come up with a kid, right? So the abductor will actually seek out and target a woman about to give birth. Typically she does this by lying and saying that she's pregnant, too."

I felt slightly ill. "You mean to tell me that this person might have been watching Bonnie for months?"

He opened one eye and stared at me. "Bonnie and Kiki and maybe even another mother-to-be. But the good news is that our abductor wants desperately to prove she can be a good mother. That she can take care of a baby. She's highly invested in playing the part of a loving parent."

"That means Jeremy and Bonnie's baby should be safe."

"At least for now." Hadcho opened one eye and shifted his weight. "The problems could occur when—and if—our abductor is challenged about giving birth. And there's one more possible hiccup. What if it's beyond the abductor's abilities to take care of the infant? Then what does she do?"

36

Kiki bent over the recycling bin. After a few minutes of digging around, she held up a crumpled sheet of paper with handwriting on it. Previously, we'd overlooked this scribbling, because we hadn't known what we were searching for. But Kiki had recognized Jana Higgins' handwriting. The journaling said: Derrick and the girls, last summer at the annual picnic. He's going to love my new baby more than he loves these two, I just know it. He told me he'd love to have a boy.

Hadcho passed the baby to me and took the paper out of Kiki's hands.

"Now we need to find some poor sap named Derrick who has two daughters." He slipped the paper inside a second evidence bag.

"Wait a minute," I said. "How do you know she didn't lie about the man's name? If she isn't Jana, maybe he isn't Derrick. Maybe they're in this together."

He shook his head. "Highly unlikely. In most cases like this, the husband or man involved has no idea that the woman is perpetuating a lie. In fact, he is usually convinced that his partner is pregnant. But when she disappears and mysteriously pops up with a baby in her arms, he starts to wonder. Bit by bit, it dawns on him that the woman's shape hasn't changed, and that for someone who's just given birth, she seems particularly spry."

"Spry?" Such a quaint sounding word. I couldn't help but get hung up on it.

"Right. In this case, spry means active, unchanged, not tired, the whole nine yards. If this poor dude hasn't been in a relationship before, it might take him a while to put two and two together. But if this information is correct," and Hadcho waved the evidence bag, "we're looking at a guy who already is a dad. He's been through this before. He'll realize Jana Higgins, or whoever she is, is lying to him. I'm thinking that if we publicize this abduction, this dude is likely to stop by a police station and casually ask a few questions. Might even turn his partner in."

Kiki nodded. "I'm going to ask Margit to go through all our transactions for the date of that class. Even though Jana paid cash, there's a chance she signed up for our newsletter or even for another tutorial. Maybe she left behind her real name or contact information."

"I sure hope so," said Hadcho, getting to his feet. "I've got plenty to do. Detweiler messaged me from the station. He's waiting for the results of tests on the liquid left inside the Vanilla Coke can, and he needs a ride home. It's already five o'clock."

"Let me see how Margit is doing, closing up for the night, and if she can look over the transactions this evening from home," Kiki said.

"No wonder I'm so tired," I told Ty as he fluttered his long lashes at me. "I've been up since four a.m. I'm ready to hit the sack. How about you, little boy?"

"Okay, Margit's taking home the paperwork so she can look it over. She's offered to give me a ride, even though we're the opposite way." Kiki walked to the lights panel and started switching things to a night time mode.

"Don't do that. Let me give you and Ty a ride home. There's a Drury Inn not far from you," I continued to rock Ty in my arms while she grabbed her things.

"Cara, would you reconsider staying at our house? We've got plenty of room. The guest bedroom is all ready for a visitor. I know Anya would love to spend some time with you. I think it would reassure her. She needs to see that some parts of our lives haven't changed very much at all."

"I don't want to be a bother, and I had planned to stay at a Drury Inn." I handed over her sweet little bundle, grabbed my outerwear, and picked up my purse.

"I can understand you wanting your privacy," my friend said.

That made me laugh. "Kiki, I live on a scarcely populated island all by myself! Down in Florida, I have scads of privacy. I'm hesitant to take you up on your invitation because I don't want to create more work for you or to put you out."

"I get it. It's not a bother. Really it's not. Brawny is a great labor-saving device." She blinked back tears.

"Hey, are you okay?"

"No, no, I'm not. I'm not myself. I can't explain it. I feel disconnected. Numb."

"Maybe you're just tired?"

"Maybe."

"Here's the deal, I'll agree to come and be your guest as long as I'm not an inconvenience. If it seems that I'm in the way, I'll get a room. How's that?"

"Perfect." She text-messaged Brawny, explaining that I'd drive us home.

"What about a car seat?"

"I keep one here. Since we're always switching kids around, we bought an extra for the store," she explained while transferring the baby to me. "What's more, this one turns into a stroller. When Ty gets fussy, I can load him up and walk him around the shelf units until he falls asleep. Tell you what. Let's put him in it now, and go see if Margit has any news for us."

Reaching to the side of her bookcase, she pulled out a folded contraption. With a quick motion of her wrist, the stroller clicked into its upright position. I gently set Ty down so he could finish his nap, and then we left the office and headed for the front counter.

A clipboard next to the cash register announced: Upcoming Classes. Margit was busily waiting on a customer, so she shook her head at us, a signal that she hadn't had the chance to look over the signup sheet. I grabbed it and skimmed through the names listed while Kiki moved the stroller back and forth.

"Remind me the date of the class."

"January 10."

I flipped back to that signup sheet and read off the folks who'd requested being added to the newsletter.

"I know most of those women," said Kiki. "Jana, or whoever she is, isn't in that batch."

She slumped down on the stool beside the counter. "Want to know what's totally weird about this?"

"What?"

"I would have sworn on a stack of Bibles that the person who took Bonnie's baby was Bernice Stottlemeyer."

I put the clipboard away. "Yeah, I can see why you'd think that."

The Stottlemeyers often patronized our family business, a restaurant my parents had named after me. Bernice was such a pill that our servers would fight over who had to wait on her. If her husband,Wesley, came in alone, they fought over waiting on him, because he was such a nice guy and a good tipper. But Bernice was nasty, mean, and hateful. She constantly found fault. Nothing was up to her standards. She reveled in humiliating our wait staff, once telling a young woman, "Do you really think all those holes in your face are attractive? I have news for you, they aren't. You look stupid."

"Given all the threats she made and how determined she was to have a child at any costs, I would have bet money she was behind this."

"I can see why you want to believe that Bernice was involved. But do you have any real proof? Anything to suggest she was anywhere near Bonnie earlier today?" I asked.

"None. I know I'm being silly. It's just that she's such a horrible person, and you weren't here to see the evil look she gave my belly. I'm sure she was every bit as envious of Bonnie's pregnancy. Cara, I swear, that woman was purely evil. It's too convenient that Bonnie gives birth and, right away, her baby goes missing."

"How would Bernice have known? Who would have told her that Bonnie had given birth? And she couldn't have known which hospital, right?"

"Right. At least, I guess you're right. Maybe I just want it to be Bernice because she was so hateful.

37

The guest bedroom at the Detweiler house reflected the taste of Leighton Haversham's mother, because she had always hoped to have a daughter. Consequently, she'd appointed the room in grand style with a white French provincial four-poster bed, matching dresser, and make-up table. She'd chosen pink and green and white as the colors. The unabashedly feminine decorating scheme took me back to my teenage years.

After escorting me to my room, Kiki did a slow circle, taking in the room's ambience, as if this was all new to her. "I rarely come in here. Brawny keeps all this clean and ready for guests. But this? This decorating scheme definitely has to go. Sorry about how juvenile it looks. All you need is a stack of Barbara Cartland romance novels and you're all set."

"I actually love Barbara Cartland novels." I ran my hand over the curved footboard. "I wish my friend Skye Blue was here with us. She'd have this transformed in nothing flat."

"By hauling it to Goodwill?"

"No." I sat on the mattress and pulled away a pillow so I could get a better look at the headboard. "She would saw off these posts. That would give you a more modern silhouette. Then she would stretch thick foam over the headboard and staple it down on the wrong side. With a glue gun, she'd cover the foam. Finally, she'd attach nail head trim or a thick braided ribbon."

Kiki sat down next to me. "You sound pretty confident. I remember a Cara Mia Delgatto who didn't consider herself a crafter."

"Amazing what you can do when your back is up against the wall. At first, I left all the crafting to Skye. But that didn't work, because she's full-time at the deli across the street. I needed to get up to speed fast because I hadn't lined up vendors—and I needed to fill my store with merchandise. Out of necessity, I picked up a paint brush and started stenciling furniture. I've never looked back."

"What colors would you use?" Kiki cocked her head and studied the fussy pink room with its rosebud wallpaper. The place was cloyingly sweet.

"Eggplant, tan, and aqua."

"You're kidding."

"Nope. The pink and green are nice, I guess, but I'd make this wall behind the bed a dark eggplant. I'd paint tan and cream stripes on the other three walls. For an accent, I'd use aqua pillows, an aqua comforter, and I'd spray paint the base of this lamp aqua, too. Then I'd recover that stuffed chair in tan and cream. I'd also replace this ugly light fixture with a small chandelier. Since that's bound to leave a big hole in the ceiling, I'd hide it by gluing fake flowers in a circle, trimming the circle with a thick flat braid, and then spray painting all that cream to match the ceiling. No, wait. I'd cut the flowers out of thick cardstock. I'd cover them with Elmer's Wood Putty to make them 3-D, and then I'd glue them to a cardstock oval. Trim that out. Spray it cream and glue it to the ceiling."

She didn't say a word.

I waited, even though I was pretty pumped up. I could imagine installing mirrored tiles to the closet doors. That would reflect the headboard, the new color scheme, and act as a floor to ceiling mirror, while adding more space and light.

"You've really blossomed," she said at last. "I'd love for you to makeover this room."

"Since it's freezing outside, I'll take a pass for right now," I said, as I laughed, "but I'll come back in the spring or summer, and we'll do it together. How's that sound?"

"Just grand," she said, and then she smiled. For the first time since my visit, she looked like my old friend, Kiki Lowenstein.

38

Shortly after midnight, I roused enough to grab my cell phone. Footsteps on the stairs suggested the detective was home. For a guy who needed to heal up after taking a bullet, Detweiler was working a lot. Maybe even too much. He and Kiki were both looking drained, and I had a hunch it wasn't just because of Ty.

Like all classic over-achievers, Detweiler and Kiki found it nearly impossible to slow down. Through the soft fog of sleep, I recalled a stress test that had floated around years ago. It assigned point values to moving, taking on a big mortgage, getting married, having a child, changing jobs, and so on. Although I couldn't recall the numbers, I knew that Detweiler and Kiki were poster children for high achievers on that test.

And that was the sort of test were a high score was not a good outcome at all.

I was nearly asleep when I heard one word: What?

Followed by: You are kidding me!

Whatever Detweiler had shared with his wife, it must have been a doozy. Otherwise, why would she have been so shocked? Kiki had practically yelped in surprise.

Ty must have thought so, too, because a mewling cry rose out of the night, like a bat flies through the darkness. I pulled the covers up tightly around my neck. Kiki or Brawny had thoughtfully made the bed with a multiple of layers, including a wool blanket between softer sheets. In the chill of the night, with unfamiliar sounds coming from the bedroom down the hall, I snuggled back into the cocoon of warmth and quickly fell back to sleep.

The next morning the wonderful smell of bacon and coffee nudged me awake, so I dressed hurriedly, pulling on jeans, a tee, and an old gray cashmere sweater that had once belonged to my father. He'd gifted it to me after I accidently washed it in hot water. Even though I'd washed it since then, I could still smell Dad's aftershave, the spice and the moss of it. Or at least, I thought I could, and it warmed my heart even as I shivered my way down the stairs to the Detweilers' kitchen.

What a wuss I'd become. This normal Missouri weather felt like torture to my joints. I gave myself a good mental slap: Okay, the ocean would still be there when I got back to Florida. Meanwhile, I would be "in the moment," and enjoy my time here with friends. The scent of fresh coffee wafted up the stairs, promising warmth and a hazelnut treat.

Detweiler stood over the frying pan, turning crispy bacon with a long-handled fork. Anya leapt up to give me a huge hug. "How's Florida?"

"I love it," I said as I smiled first at her and then at the solemn boy sitting next to her. Noting his beautiful brown eyes and caramel-colored skin, I offered my hand for a shake. "Hello, my name is Cara. You're Erik, right?"

At first he ducked his head shyly, but encouragement from Anya worked its magic as he extended his small, plump hand for a shake. We studied each other. His curly red hair surrounded his face in a cherubic cap. His bright eyes indicated an alert mind. This boy was an old soul, as my father would say, because behind that intelligence was a sadness, a sense of loss.

"I have a boy at home, too," I said. "Except he's at college most of the time. His name is Tommy. He loves animals. Do you?"

"We haff a donkey named Monroe," said Erik. "Want to see?

"Yes, I would love to see Monroe. Can it wait until after breakfast? I'd like to eat first. Is that toast good?"

He nodded vigorously. "We gots bacon, too."

"I think she might have already noticed the bacon." Anya gave him a smug smile.

Gracie wandered over and regarded me lovingly, her brown eyes searching mine as she leaned against my leg. "Hi, sweet girl." I rubbed her head.

"Did we wake you up last night?" Detweiler gave me a concerned grin. His hair stuck out in five different directions. He was sensibly attired in brightly plaid flannel sleep pants and a sweatshirt.

"Not really. I heard you, but that's because I'm accustomed to living alone. It roused me, but I didn't really wake up, if you know what I mean." I helped myself to a cup of coffee from the coffee maker.

"Yummy." I took a seat between Erik and Anya. Detweiler slid a plate of food in front of me. As enticing as it was, first I am fueled by coffee in the mornings and I'd already finished half of what I'd poured, so I got up and refreshed the cup for myself. Just as I scooted back into my chair, the back door flew open and Hadcho came stomping into the kitchen. His entrance admitted a blast of air so cold it took the wind out of me. Gracie jumped to her feet, recognized the intruder as a friend and stuck her head under Erik's chair to grab up a small piece of bacon.

"Any news?" Detweiler stopped his partner in his tracks.

"It's her. Her husband—soon to be ex-husband—was totally

beside himself. He has an airtight alibi. Out with a girlfriend at the Ladue Country Club. All the best names saw him. He had brought the girlfriend home with him when they found...her." His recitation complete Hadcho helped himself to a big cup of coffee before pulling out the chair next to mine.

Detweiler cracked two eggs and scrambled them in a bowl. Without looking at his friend, he said, "There's sourdough bread in the refrigerator. Brawny bought it yesterday."

"The man knows how I like my food," Hadcho said with a nod of appreciation as he found the bread and popped slices in the toaster.

I was dying to know what the men were talking about. My curiosity must have shown on my face. Detweiler turned away from the burner where he was cooking the eggs and explained, "Bernice Stottlemeyer turned up late last night. Dead. Half in and half out of her car. Parked in the last row in long term parking at Lambert Field."

My eyebrows shot up to my hairline. "You have to be kidding me."

"No, he's not," Hadcho confirmed. "The call came in right before we knocked off work. Two more minutes and we would have been out of the station."

"That's what you might have heard last night when I got home," Detweiler explained. "I told Kiki we had a tentative ID. The dental records confirmed who it was."

"How'd she die?"

"Gunshot wound," Hadcho said as he buttered his toast.

"Dad-D gots shot by a gun. So did Hay-cho." Erik put a chubby hand on my arm. "I saws it. It was scary. I wetted my pants."

Although I wanted to hug him, I restrained myself. "Did you really? That must have been scary. I think I would have wet my pants, too."

"I wasn't that scared." Anya drew herself up to her full height. "I helped Mom by getting Erik to safety. We hid in Monroe's shed. The attacker came after us, but we—"

"Anya?" Detweiler interrupted her and cast a nervous eye toward his son. "Anya? Are you all ready for school?"

At first, she looked put out, but a slow realization changed her expression to one of understanding. She looked from Detweiler to Erik and back to the cop. "Uh, mainly."

"Better hop to it." Detweiler slid the eggs onto Hadcho's plate. "Brawny will drop you off. Erik? You're done there, pal. Go with your sister."

39

The kids left, and Kiki joined us. Like me, she'd bundled herself in a sweater and leggings. Under her eyes were dark circles, and her hair stuck out like dandelion seeds. I hugged her good morning and dug into my food while she made another pot of coffee. Detweiler told Kiki that the body had been confirmed as one Bernice Stottlemeyer.

"Here's what's weird," Detweiler said. "She had moved out of that house she shared with Wesley two months ago, but last week, Wesley Stottlemeyer found her inside the house. He had changed all the locks, but he forgot to get back his garage door opener. Using that, she walked in through the garage, opened the back door from the garage into the house. She was standing in the middle of the room they'd planned to use for a nursery, painting it blue."

I about choked on my coffee.

"What did he do?" Kiki's eyes were wide.

"He politely asked her to leave. She told him that she was pregnant, and they could get back together again. Everything would be fine, according to Bernice. Wesley didn't buy that.

Evidently, he was with a woman he's started dating. She wisely waited downstairs, out of sight."

Hadcho picked up the narrative. "So Wesley is arguing with Bernice, the girlfriend is downstairs listening in, and all of a sudden she hears this weird sloshing noise and a clatter. She goes running upstairs only to find Wesley covered in paint. Bernice dumped the full gallon on him."

"Can you imagine how much of a mess that made?" Hadcho laughed.

Detweiler held up a couple of eggs. "Kiki?"

She nodded and pointed to her plate. "Thanks. But now she's dead. Were there any signs she had a baby with her? In the parking lot?"

"You better hope there weren't any. Because if the crime scene investigators find diapers or whatever, that means someone grabbed the kid in the bitter cold of the night." Hadcho sighed. "So far, we haven't heard that they found any such items. But it's early. If Robbie was here, we would have known what they found immediately. But Prescott? He likes to sit on information. He's too busy giving press briefings to do his job."

"What about the journaling we found? The information on Jana Higgins? Any luck with that?" I wondered.

"Nope. Not yet," Hadcho said. "Last night Detweiler and I tried and tried to convince Prescott that we needed the Gossages to do a public appeal. Something to bring the man in those photos out of the shadows. When he realizes this Jana woman is wandering around with a kidnapped child, he'll want no part of her little scheme."

"We did our best to get Prescott to say yes last night, but he's made up his mind that a missing child might reflect badly on the department. Hadcho and I pointed out that the baby is already missing, and that a dead child would be a much, much worse outcome, but Prescott refused to budge." Detweiler slid the scrambled eggs onto Kiki's plate.

"Of course, he can't stop the Gossages if they decide to hold a press conference without him," Kiki said.

"I didn't hear that," Detweiler answered her. "You didn't either, did you, Hadcho?"

"Hear what?"

Kiki stared at her eggs as though she couldn't quite figure out what they were. Finally, she looked up at her husband. "Whether they find anything or not, mark my words: Bernice Stottlemeyer was behind all this."

"Why?" Hadcho crooked an eyebrow. "What makes you so sure?"

"It's too coincidental." Kiki sputtered and added, "Just follow the timeline. Bernice desperately wants a baby so she and Wesley contact Bonnie's firm. The album I made for them doesn't get them over the hurdle. The birth mother hates Bernice on sight and won't consider the Stottlemeyers as adoptive parents. That's so upsetting to Bernice that she has to blame someone, and so she takes after me. In retaliation, Bernice trashes my store while making hateful remarks about my pregnancy. Bonnie is pregnant, too, so it's logical that she wouldn't have escaped Bernice's wrath. That brings us to the here and now when Bonnie has her baby and is visited by a mystery woman who drugs her and takes her child. Furthermore we know someone was watching Bonnie, because they offered her a Vanilla Coke, her favorite beverage. This wasn't a random kidnapping. It was planned. Who else could have planned it but Bernice?"

"What's the connection rather than the timing?" asked Hadcho.

"There's the fact that the Stottlemeyers were told by a partner at Bonnie's firm that she'd be the perfect lawyer to help them adopt," Kiki said. "Bernice was sure they'd be wonderful birth parents. How many other couples are wandering around town feeling confident like that only to have their bubble burst?"

Detweiler rinsed out the skillet. With practiced motions, he grabbed a piece of toast before it popped up, slathered it with Brummel and Brown, and plated it for Kiki.

She was on a roll. "There's also the way Bernice went all weird and talked a lot about how I didn't deserve to have a child. She must have felt the same about Bonnie being pregnant. Stands to reason. She obviously thought this was a cosmic mistake of epic proportions. To hear Bernice tell it, she and Wesley had everything to offer a child. According to her, they'd be perfect parents, and it was simply bad luck that they'd been cheated out of having one." Kiki chewed on one edge of her toast thoughtfully.

"Was Bernice in the front seat or in the back of her car? Did she have an infant seat inside?" I asked.

"We don't know," Hadcho said and cleared his throat. "That's another problem. See, Robbie had a great relationship with all the local police chiefs but Gallaway? Not so much. Mrs. Stottlemeyer's murder occurred in Bridgeton where the long term lot is. And the police chief for that municipality there won't invite us to help out because he can't stand Prescott Gallaway. Of course, we could get involved if we could absolutely link Bernice Stottlemeyer to the kidnapping, but right now we don't have any hard evidence."

"We could go in if here's a Major Case Squad put together," Detweiler said. "But Prescott Gallaway isn't interested in that. He doesn't want to fail. That's his top priority. In his mind, that means we won't do more than we absolutely have to, since anything we're involved in could produce a negative result."

"So you can't find out more about Bernice. That's what you're saying—and we don't have a way of following any investigation into her death. I'm telling that I'm positive she's involved, and you're telling me you can't find out whether she was or wasn't. That's the size of it, right?" Kiki crossed her arms over her chest and challenged her husband with her aggressive posture.

"Right," said Detweiler. But that one word meant a lot more than, "You're correct." It carried the weight of a struggle between them, a quarrel so deep and profound their entire relationship hung in the balance.

40

After the men left, Brawny brought the older kids downstairs.

"We'll take them to school," Kiki said. "Cara and I are headed that way."

"But I'm already..." Brawny's voice tailed off. The expression on Kiki's face put an abrupt end to her complaint.

Five minutes later, we were crammed into Kiki's old red BMW convertible. Although I wondered why we weren't taking the heavier Trailblazer, I figured Kiki knew what she was doing. She'd left Ty with the nanny, so after reflection, it made sense that Brawny would have the car with a better heating system. I shivered as the warm air blowing on me quickly dissipated, leaking through the fabric roof of the Beemer.

In the back seats, which were really little more than jump seats, Anya and Erik sat stone-faced, barely awake, and miserable in the cold. Or so that's how I perceived it. Perhaps they had picked up on Kiki's unhappiness. Prior to this, both kids had seen two soul mates—Kiki and Detweiler—cruising happily through life, depending on each other, and in sync.

Now there was a barrier, as mean and as forbidding as an

iceberg, and just as difficult to scale. What had happened? How long had it been this way? And what could be done to change things?

I hopped out as we dropped Erik off. I got back in the car and Kiki swung around the corner to where the older kids were heading for classes. Once again, I climbed out. With a hand on the car door, Anya leaned her head inside, while I waited by the curb. "I don't know what's bugging you, and I don't care, but I hope you get your act together, Mom. I'm tired of this attitude."

Before Kiki could respond, her daughter flounced off. Her backpack formed a shield between the blond-haired girl and her mother.

Embarrassed by what I'd seen and heard, I said nothing, climbed back in, and snapped my seatbelt. Carefully keeping my eyes straight ahead, I fought the urge to share my opinion. It was a trick I'd learned from Honora, the older woman who came to work for me. "You don't always need to rush into the fray," she'd explained. "Most of us cannot handle ambiguity. By dwelling in the discomfort, you force the other person to make a move. It's a powerful tool."

The next half mile rolled by in silence. Out of the corner of my eye, I could see Kiki open her mouth to speak, pause, and open up again. But she didn't say a word. Not until we got to Highway 40.

There instead of going east for three exits, she got off at the second exit, which I realized was the route to the hospital. That made sense. Kiki had decided to suggest to Bonnie that she and Jeremy make a public appeal.

"This should be the happiest time in my life," Kiki said at long last. "And it isn't. Anya needs to be disciplined for talking to me that way. I can't allow it. On the other hand, how can I punish her for being truthful? Hurt feelings aside, she told me the honest truth. But how do I fix things? How do I get my life back in order?"

Taking the exit for the hospital, Kiki's mouth quivered. A tear leaked out of the corner of her eye, but she determinedly kept both hands on the steering wheel.

"Care to tell me about it?"

"Later. First, I want to talk to Bonnie."

41

The corridors echoed with the sound of our footsteps. Blessedly, the hospital seemed quiet. Since the street crews in St. Louis had gotten the chance to clear the roads, fewer car accidents left carnage in their wake. Nor were there the typical number of emergencies caused by men shoveling snow and having heart attacks, a regular occurrence after bad weather. No, for the most part, the foot traffic in the halls of Southeast was down to a quiet hum.

Stopping by the nurse's station, we learned that Bonnie was running a low grade fever. "She's listless and depressed. Of course, she has reason to be, but we're concerned nonetheless. This isn't good," said the nurse on duty.

We found Bonnie lying on her side, facing the window, but she wasn't asleep. Her fingers clutched and twisted the thin cotton blanket as she cried softly.

"Bonnie? Should we leave? It's Cara and me." Kiki put one hand on our friend's shoulder. Bonnie reached up and grabbed Kiki's glove, pinning her fingers down fiercely to her chest as she made an appeal: "Stay. I need to talk to you, to somebody who'll listen. I heard about Bernice. Kiki, what am I going to do? I'm sure she had my baby. Okay, Jana was involved, but Bernice was out to get me."

"We're here and we're with you," Kiki said. "We're on your side. We're going to do everything we can to help. Let's get you sitting up so we can talk."

I shut the door to the hallway, while Kiki helped Bonnie roll onto her back. Our friend had regular features, brown eyes and highlighted hair cut in an easy-care crop that she swept back from her forehead when in court. But the woman in the hospital bed didn't look a bit like our old friend. The lively brown eyes stared out with a dull, senseless look. Deep creases of worry marred her forehead, and her lips were chapped to the point of being bloody. Not to put too fine of a point on it, we were sitting here with the shell left behind by a competent woman who had withdrawn so completely, there was only a trace of her original self left behind.

I understood completely. If something had happened to Tommy, I would have been nuts with grief, too, but I hope I would have been able to put up a fight for my lost child. Bonnie did not look like she could cope, much less battle for her baby. The woman in the bed did not seem like the fierce courtroom advocate who'd become a bit of a legend. Other lawyers had nicknamed her Bonnie the Barracuda. "She bites you hard and won't let go." In her world, she was feared and fearless. Successful, too. In fact, our pal could have risen to the top of the heap at any law firm in the country. Hers included, except....except that she turned down several promotions because she wanted to raise a family.

A family with a missing child.

I pulled over a chair. Kiki crawled up next to Bonnie and wrapped her arms around our pal's neck. "Before you say anything, I have a suggestion."

"What?" Bonnie lifted hopeful eyes to Kiki.

"You didn't hear this from me, but there are those who think you and Jeremy should be holding a press conference. A public appeal asking that anyone with knowledge of your baby contact the authorities. See, the person who has your son is pretending to be the birth mother. She wants to show the baby off. When she does, her family is bound to have questions."

"I see." Bonnie's face lit up with the faint light of hope. "But we were told it could be dangerous. Jeremy specifically asked if we should do this. We know that a report was made to the National Center for Missing Kids. I thought that was all we needed to do. Or should do."

"I looked this up," I said. "Most of the babies recovered are the direct result of a public appeal. The media coverage works, but only if the abductor is not portrayed as a hardened criminal. If it's handled in a non-threatening way, people come forward."

"You have to get people thinking," Kiki said. "Get the wheels turning. They're bound to have questions. You need to remind them how the pieces don't fit. Tell them if there's a peculiar circumstance, they need to speak up. Sure, she might be acting like a loving mother, but that's because she's convinced herself she is."

"There've been cases when babies were returned as long as two weeks after they were taken," I said. "See? There's a lot to feel hopeful about. This woman never intended to hurt your baby. She's misguided, that's all."

"We'll do it. I'll talk to Jeremy as soon as he gets here. He's been spending the evenings with the kids. His parents didn't realize what a handful two boys can be." A sly look came over her. "Thanks for telling me what to do. I'm not thinking straight. This fever is messing with my head. I won't tell Jeremy that you suggested this. I'll say an advocate dropped by to talk with me."

Holding out my little finger, I said, "I solemnly promise to keep any and all conversations in this room a secret."

"Me, too," Kiki echoed.

"Et moi aussi," giggled Bonnie. "Finally got to use my high school French!"

We must have made a funny picture. A pale woman in a thin cotton gown and two women bundled up in winter coats all locked pinky fingers in solemn sequence. Since we were all in our mid-thirties, we were well past the age when most people would consider a pinky-swearing ceremony as a genuine commitment.

But to us it was exactly that.

"Better yet," Bonnie said as she pointed to my purse, "pay me a dollar. You, too, Kiki. That'll make you my clients. Those two bucks put me on retainer."

We laughed as we dug around for two dollar bills. Kiki produced a small notebook filled with Zentangle® designs she was working to master. Ripping out one page she wrote up an employment contract that confirmed Bonnie as our legal counsel. I even flagged down a nurse in the hall to get her to witness our solemn pact.

Oddly enough, as silly as it might have seemed, the formal document heralded a change in Bonnie's demeanor. The frightened mother stepped aside as the prudent professional took charge.

"There's a lot I shouldn't tell you, but I will," she said, after signaling me to close her door again. "You've reminded me that I'm not helpless. Even if it seems that way. How many times have I told my clients if you lie down in the grass, you're begging to be run over by a lawnmower? More than I can count. Here's the scoop: I know in my heart of hearts that Bernice Stottlemeyer is involved in this. She stalked me. She threatened me and Jeremy. When she realized I was pregnant, she went ballistic, calling the firm and screaming over the phone. Showing up at our front door and pounding on it. She swore it was my fault

—mine and yours—that she didn't have a baby. According to Bernice, Wesley wanted a divorce because she couldn't produce a child."

"Huh," Kiki snorted. "I can think of better reasons for him to want to leave her. Hello Angry Bird!"

Bonnie nodded and pulled the covers up under her arms. Whereas before she hadn't noticed the messy sheets, now she tidied up the bed. Smoothing the top sheet, adjusting her gown. "I hear you. You need to realize I had very little choice in the matter. The senior partners put pressure on me. We handle Bernice's parents' foundation, the Livesay Charitable Trust. We also handle Wesley's family's business, and on and on. Besides all that, Jeremy is doing his best to get started as a registered rep, a stock broker, and he worried that if we made Bernice or Jeremy's family into enemies, he'd never get any clients."

"But you said Jana brought you the Vanilla Coke." I was trying to figure out the connection between the women.

"Right. She has to be involved. Otherwise, where is my baby? I can imagine Bernice talking Jana into this. I can also guess that things went wrong. Kiki and I are living proof that Bernice was her own worst enemy."

Kiki took Bonnie's hand. "But whatever went wrong, your baby has to be safe. They didn't find your child with Bernice. In fact, as far as we know, they didn't find any signs of a baby in her car. So by process of elimination, Jana has your son."

"That's what I'm thinking. See, I could hold it together as long as I could console myself with the thought that Bernice wouldn't hurt him. She'd show him off to Wesley. Wesley would realize she had taken my kid—and this nightmare would be over. Jeremy called Wesley first thing when this happened, and he was horrified. He's as nice as Bernice is evil. He promised both of us that if he heard anything, even a whisper, he'd contact the authorities. I trusted him! He's not a bad man. But he's assured us he knows nothing. And I believe him. He has no reason to lie."

She paused, choking a little, so I grabbed the pitcher and handed her a glass of water. After a sip, she said, "He couldn't believe it."

"I can," Kiki said. "I can believe anything of Bernice Stottlemeyer."

42

I figured the ride back to the store would be quiet.

I was wrong. Kiki spun out, letting the wheels on her car kick up salt and sand as she backed out of her parking space. Fortunately, there was no one behind us. Although her gloves covered her hands, I could tell she was gripping the steering wheel hard because I could see how the fabric was bunched up tightly over her knuckles. At too fast of a speed, she headed for the exit ramp. We bumped over a hump intended to slow us down. And it did. The low carriage of the BMW hit the raised concrete ridge hard. My teeth clacked together.

The scraping sound of metal against concrete loosened Kiki's tongue.

"You asked me what was up and I didn't answer you. Okay, here's the deal: I'm not going to take it from him," she snarled. "I took it from George. I'm not going to let him do this to me."

I waited for more.

"Detweiler and his mother are treating me like I'm not competent of being a mother. And I'm not going to stand for it. My whole life people have underestimated me. They think I'm stupid. Or childish. They treat me like I'm an idiot. First my mother, then George, and now Detweiler and Thelma. I'm tired of it, Cara. Sick and tired of it. I'm supposed to be a good little mom and sit at home and make meals and tuck the kids in at night. Since I'm Wife #3, I'm the last in a long chorus line of other women. Oh, and might I add that I was perfectly good enough to adopt a child from another relationship that my husband had, but now there's something wrong with my mothering skills?"

She slammed her fist against the steering wheel. "Nope. Good old Kiki. Stupid old Kiki. She'll do what she's told. She'll agree to whatever her husband and his family demand of her. She's a good girl, so you can count on her to mop up your mistakes and take it, and take it, and take it. You can call her names. You can treat her like garbage, and she'll come back for more. Oh, and she's not capable of making good decisions. So why trust her to do what's right, huh? No need to respect her or her wishes! And that store of hers? It's a little hobby. A play thing. A waste of her time. A distraction that keeps her from being a good wife. That's what everyone in his family is thinking. To them, I'm a joke. A joke. Everybody is laughing..."

Fortunately, we were on a side street in a residential area. Kiki had taken the back way toward Highway 40. Now the car rolled to a stop at a four-way stop sign. Up ahead was one of the ubiquitous parks that dot St. Louis County. The entrance was clearly marked. A safe haven of parking spaces were just ahead.

"Why don't you pull in there?" I suggested softly as the sobs shook my friend's body. "I can drive."

Blubbering, she turned to me and nodded. Tears were rolling down her face. I leaned over the console with the stick shift poking me in the ribs and hugged her tightly. "I'm here, Kiki. It's going to be all right. We'll figure this out together. How about if we go to Kaldi's? Just like the old times?"

"Yes, please."

43

With an iced cookie in one hand and hot decaf in the other, Kiki settled into a booth. After a few minutes of total dedication to her treats, she was ready to talk. In a rush of words, she told me about the pressure that Thelma had been exerting on her marriage.

"It feels like I can't trust Detweiler anymore. I know that sounds insane, but it's like his mother has turned him against me. If anything goes wrong with Ty, even a bad case of diaper rash, Thelma will blame me. When she was at the house for the naming, she kept giving me these angry looks. It's like she's had a personality transplant. I've tried being a grown up and asking her what I've done. She changes the subject. Once I did manage to pin her down and she said that she was only worried about the baby, and that I was overreacting."

"But Clancy and Margit have been fielding her phone calls to check on you, right?"

Kiki nodded. "But when I mentioned that to Detweiler, he said that of course she worries about me. But that's not the way she's acting. It's not worry; it's more like gotcha! Like she's out to prove I'm an incompetent mother."

"Are you?" It was a gutsy move, I'll admit. But I figured that if I put it out there, baldly, Kiki would have to confront the question head on.

"No. I'm a good mother. I'm just having...having...having a little trouble feeling close to Ty. It's like I'm numb, you know? Rationally, he's mine and I love him. But I remember how totally gaga I was about Anya. I don't feel that sort of 'my heart is bursting with joy' feeling about him."

"Do you feel that sort of happiness about anything? Anyone?" I stuck a carrot in the hummus I'd ordered. I thought about breaking off a corner of Kiki's cookie, but I knew once I got started, I'd eat the whole pastry. So I stuck to my healthy snack.

Kiki ran a fingertip over the design in the icing. The large cookie had been painted with red buttercream, and then decorated with swirls of white and pink.

"No."

Okay, there it was. Out on the table. A moment of honesty that could finally lead to a heart-to-heart conversation, cookies not withstanding.

"Does that seem normal to you?" I probed for more information.

"No." She didn't look up.

"Have you mentioned this to your ob/gyn? Your general practitioner? Sounds to me like you've got a rollicking case of post-partum depression."

"I tried to talk to him. To tell him I didn't feel right. But Detweiler was there. I didn't want him to think..." She held up the cookie like a shield. From where I was sitting, a whiff of vanilla floated my way.

"Got it. That's understandable. Especially with Thelma on your back. Look, I'm buying myself a cookie. You want another one?"

"How about a half dozen?"

44

Besides the cookies, I bought an assortment of pastries to take back to the store. Although Kiki offered to pay, I reminded her that she and her crew had done all sorts of nice things for me over the years. I was also saving on a hotel room. Finally, she agreed to let me buy treats for her workers.

I'd gotten the coffee pot going and made Kiki a cafetière of decaf. A part of me wanted to point out that sugar wasn't going to help Kiki's depression, but I figured it also wouldn't help our relationship if I turned into a nag. Like Thelma. I did wonder what her problem was. Why had she suddenly turned against Kiki?

The back door flew open, and Margit stomped inside. Past her I could see that a fresh coating of white fluff was coming down, hard. It reminded me of the time I'd had a pillow fight with Tommy, and his broke open, scattering goose feathers all over the bedroom.

"Ach, but the streets are terrible." Margit stamped her rubber boots, trying to get the clumps of snow and ice to fall away. "More to come, they say. Did you hear the news? About that awful woman? Stottlemeyer?"

"Yup." Kiki didn't even look up from her third cookie. She'd eaten one right after another, letting the sugar buzz distract her from her sadness. Those sweets were her attempt to numb the pain, and I knew that wouldn't work. Not for long.

The front door minder rang while Margit was brushing off her coat. Kiki struggled to her feet. The weariness I'd observed in her seemed more pronounced than ever, probably as a result of her emotional state. The more she'd talked, the more I realized that Kiki was absolutely drained. Between the gloomy weather and her responsibilities, she was like a well run dry. But she certainly needed more than a good night's sleep. She needed to feel that Detweiler was in her corner. She needed help, maybe even drugs, to get over her post-partum blues. She needed someone to tell Thelma to quit nagging. And yeah, a healthy dose of sunshine was certainly in order.

I knew my way around the store, so I hopped to my feet and said, "Take your time, ladies. I've got this."

Clancy joined us. She and I worked the sales floor for the next three hours. That left Kiki and Margit to go over orders and inventory, but I did manage a call to Kiki's ob/gyn. When the receptionist heard my concerns, she scheduled Kiki for a five o'clock appointment the next day. While Kiki was handling a special order for a new customer, I asked Margit and Clancy if they could make sure the store was covered while we were gone.

"There's a crop tomorrow night. Will you be back for it?" Clancy asked. "I can cover it if necessary."

I knew that would mean she'd be driving across the river to Illinois in the dark. Illinois only has two seasons: Summer and road construction. Worst of all, they move orange cones around like a carnival barker swaps coins under cups.

"The appointment is at five. It's the last one of the day, the crop starts at seven, right? We should be back for it."

Margit adjusted her cats-eye glasses. "I will stay until you arrive."

Despite the bad weather, or perhaps because of it, we were all busy the rest of the day. At one point, I handled three customers at the same time. Kids were in school and the roads were mostly clear, but more wet stuff was on the way. Mothers came in looking for new projects, something to help them fend off the horrible cabin fever that would only get worse. In St. Louis, the bad weather hits hardest in January, keeps delivering knock-out blows in February, and only gets bearable the last week in March. If you're lucky.

For lunch we had a wild rice soup that Margit had made, plus generous chunks of sourdough bread topped with creamy butter. The meal was a solemn one, compared to other repasts I've had at Kiki's store. It was as if we were waiting for news. When would things get back to normal? Where was that tiny infant and was he still safe?

Clancy fingered her spoon. "I don't know how it is with infant abductions. When someone takes a child or an adult, every hour and every day makes it less likely that the victim is alive. Is that how it is with infants?"

"No," I said. "I did research on this last night on my iPad. Not necessarily. Most of the time the child is well-cared for. Remember, we're dealing with a woman who sees herself as a mother. Her motives are different from a child molester or a pervert."

"Margit? Would you turn on the news?" Clancy wondered. "I can't stand the silence. Thinking about the baby has me too upset."

Margit reached for the remote and turned on the little TV that Dodie had once had installed in her office, but that Kiki had since moved to the central meet and eat area. We listened with dread as the weather service warned of frostbite and other health hazards caused by another wave of cold weather.

"Ach, the bad news, it keeps coming and coming."

But all that changed when the anchor came back on the screen to take us to a live press conference at Southeast Hospital. Without asking, I turned up the volume. A somber-faced Jeremy stood with his arm around Bonnie. She'd changed out of her hospital gown and into a crewneck sweater, but the puce color did nothing for her washed out complexion. Her hair had a gummy sheen, and her eyes were raw as peeled onions. A paper in Jeremy's hands shook with nervousness as he addressed the camera.

"We know you care about our son. So do we. Please bring him back to us. We aren't angry with you, but we are worried about him. You know nothing of his medical history. His two brothers ask about him all the time. From the bottom of our hearts, we're begging you, please return our baby to us."

45

The rest of the press conference was handled by a man identified as the CEO of Southeast Hospital. Reporters pelted him with questions about how this could have happened, but we weren't interested in his answers.

"Mind if I cut this off?" Kiki stood with one hand on the dial.

"Be my guest," I said. Margit nodded in agreement.

Clancy had finished her food. She stood up and looked around, with a look of speculation on her face. "How about if I take the supplies we need for the crop next week and go home? I can kit things up on my kitchen table. I really, really don't want to get stuck behind construction crews on the other side of the river."

"Be my guest," Kiki said. "Promise to text me so I know you made it, okay?"

"You've got it."

Kiki, Margit, and I finished our food in silence. I couldn't help myself from asking Margit for the recipe for her soup. "Ja, of course, I'll give it to you," she said, as her cheeks pinked up with happiness.

The door minder rang after lunch while we were picking up. I jumped to my feet. "I'll get it."

The arrival turned out to be a very bundled up Lee Alderton. She brushed her blond hair back from her eyes and removed her tan angora cap that matched her Burberry car coat, worn over black ski pants tucked into nice leather booties.

I shouldn't have been surprised by how stylishly she was turned out. Her daughter Taylor works in a fancy boutique as a buyer.

Lee gave me a hug. "Aren't you freezing? I am. If I had my druthers, I'd be walking a beach in Florida. In fact, I'm flying back down there next week to our house in Palm Beach. If you have any free time, let's go to lunch. Or are you up here permanently?"

I explained that I'd come up to serve as godmother for Kiki's son, Ty.

"Then we're passengers on the same cruise boat. I agreed to be godmother for Bonnie Gossage's new baby," said Lee. "That's why I'm here." With a sigh, she added, "That's hoping that things get straightened out, of course. Lordy. Poor Bonnie is in a terrible state."

"When did you last see her?"

Lee shook her head sadly. "I was just there. She's crying her eyes out. Inconsolable. You heard about that surgical infection, she has? Right, well, Jeremy thinks it is because of all the stress. They're keeping her until they can bring her fever down. Who would do such a thing to them? The older kids keep asking where their new brother is. Bonnie blames herself for drinking that stupid drugged cola. I told her, 'Of course you didn't know it was drugged. Give yourself a break!' Crikey. She's so upset."

"Who wouldn't be?" I shrugged. "I think we're all feeling miserable about the kidnapping, and then there's this awful weather. Is there something you wanted in particular? Do I need to go get Kiki or Margit to help you? Are you here to pick up an order? I know where they keep those."

"No, no. I was hoping to put together a page about being godmother. I thought I'd also stop in and collect some supplies. Maybe even a page kit. Something for Bonnie to do to take her mind off things." Lee paused. "Who am I kidding? There's nothing that'll distract her, is there? I just feel so helpless. That press conference, ugh. I heard it in the car. Especially on top of the news about Bernice Stottlemeyer. You heard, didn't you? Can you imagine coming home from a two-week vacation and finding a dead body in the car next to you? That'll be the last time that family parks in the long-term lot."

"Did you know Bernice?"

"Did I know her? Yes, of course I did. I've known Bernice most of her life."

"Really?"

"Uh-huh. We belong to the same country club."

"What do you think happened to her? Any ideas?"

"Ha!" Lee frowned at me. "Like that takes any thinking at all. I'd bet good money that Wesley's girlfriend shot her."

46

"Kiki? Can you come out here a second?" I stuck my head in the back room and hollered like a mom calling to her child on the playground.

Leading her by the hand, I took Kiki to where Lee sat at the work table. As always, hugs were exchanged. Lee asked to see any new photos of Ty. I obliged, because I'd taken several since I'd arrived. Once the nice-nice formalities had been observed, I plunged right in. "Lee says that she thinks Wesley Stottlemeyer's girlfriend shot Bernice."

"Wesley's girlfriend? She might have killed Bernice?" Kiki's voice moved up a notch. I dragged over a stool for her to perch on. "Detweiler did say Wesley had an alibi. I guess he was with a woman for an event at the Ladue Country Club. But my husband didn't seem to think Wesley's girlfriend was involved in the shooting. You must know something the police don't know yet."

"Maybe. Maybe not. But everyone at the club suspects she's tangled up in it somehow," Lee said. "Her name is Lila Carola, and she's a single mom who went back to school to get her degree in graphic arts. For one of her classes, she was assigned to do a marketing project at Wesley Stottlemeyer's marketing research firm. That threw the two of them together for long stretches of time. One thing led to another. I think the contrast between Lila and Bernice really made Wesley realize what he'd been missing."

"When did all this start?" I asked.

"Last summer." Lee didn't hesitate. "Bernice had moved out temporarily. It was after she moved back that she decided they needed to adopt. I think that's when you met her, right, Kiki?"

"Wow." Kiki looked stunned. "Yes, it is. But I didn't know anything about Bernice's marital history. I was hired to make an adoption album for her. I figured everything between her and Wesley was hunky-dory. Wait. Are you suggesting that this girlfriend wasn't a recent development?"

"Depends on how you look at it. I think that Wesley and Lila were sending flirty text-messages back and forth around the Fourth of July. I remember because Bernice stomped into the club and accused him of cheating in front of everybody. Of course, we all knew that she'd moved out, and what a witch she is, so no one had much sympathy for her."

"Bernice had a breakdown, what? Three months ago?" Kiki did the calculations in her head.

"Right. Wesley felt partially responsible for that, as you might imagine. My impression was that the whole adoption idea was a last ditch effort by her to save the marriage. Frankly, I think Wesley was relieved when the birth mother wasn't interested in them. He realized that he'd done everything he could to hold the marriage together. When Bernice came in here and acted out, he demanded that she get help. He was ready to move on, but he didn't start the divorce proceedings until she had gotten a good start in therapy."

Lee sighed and rested her chin on her hands. "I've always thought that Wesley saw Bernice the way that Cesar guy on TV sees those dogs with their bad habits. Redeemable. He really, truly cared about her. No matter how messed up she was, he cared. At least he did, for a while. It took him a long, long time to decide he'd had enough."

"I wonder," said Kiki, "what makes a decent, nice-looking man keep hanging around with a woman who's seriously disturbed?"

"I have my theories." Lee unwound a silk scarf from her throat, folding it neatly into a square before stuffing it into her handbag. She wore an expensive fragrance, Light Blue by Dolce and Gabbana. The joyful scent of citron reminded me of the Treasure Coast of Florida, and just that suddenly I missed my home.

"But you think Lila shot Bernice?" Kiki pressed Lee for more details. "Since Lila and Wesley were together, why would she have bothered?"

Lee fingered a piece of paper that was sitting on the edge of the work table. After picking it up and looking at it closely, she said, "Because Bernice hounded that woman. Day and night. Lila took out restraining orders. She put motion sensitive lights around her house. She took to carrying pepper spray. It got to be too much when Bernice showed up one day at the Montessori school where Lila's kids go."

Suddenly, Lee shut up. I could see she was wrestling with herself. After a short struggle, she shrugged. "I might as well tell you the worst of it. It is public record. Bernice called the Department of Children and Family. She pretended to be one of the teachers at the Montessori school, and she reported that Wesley had molested one of Lila's daughters."

I could not even process that. At long last, I finally managed to sputter, "That's so low. Wow. Talk about messing up a man's entire life."

Lee agreed, slowly shaking her head. "It was awful. For

everyone involved. The children had to be interviewed. A nightmare. Of course, it didn't take long to figure out who was behind all that."

"What did Wesley say or do?" I wondered.

"He was more frightened than angry. He kept warning Bernice to stay out of his life. He begged her to see reason. After all, they weren't happy together! He even asked her family to talk with her. You know she has a sister who lives here, right? Her name's Janice. None of that mattered. Wesley even tried to get Bernice committed. Do you know how hard that is to do? It's almost impossible."

When it came to scaring people's kids, I had to take Lila's side and I said as much. "If a crazy woman threatened my child, I'd certainly be tempted to buy a gun and use it on her."

"But that doesn't make sense." Kiki slapped the desk top. "How could Lila have shot Bernice? She was with Wesley at the country club. At least, that's what we've been told."

"You're right. Lila was with Wesley. I saw them both. But you have to remember, they found Bernice half in and half out of the car. I have it on good authority that the car had been running with the heater going full blast. That would throw off the death examiner's best estimate of the time of death."

"Boy, oh, boy. I'm impressed," I said, looking at Lee with new respect.

"I read a lot of mysteries," she said.

Margit toddled out of the back room. In her hands, she carried the box of pastries I'd purchased from Kaldi's. "Lee? I thought I heard you. Eat these. Please. I have already had two and I cannot eat more. Oomph."

47

Shortly after Lee left, Kiki sent Margit home. "The weather is getting worse by the minute. I don't want you driving in this. Promise that you'll call and hang up to let me know you've made it home."

I walked the older woman to her car.

"She is not herself these days," Margit said as she slid behind the steering wheel. You see Kiki is not right, ja?"

"Yes. Don't forget that I am planning to take her to see her doctor tomorrow."

"Of course. She is depressed I think. She loves her new little boy, but her body is not good. Hormones."

"I think so too. Now let me scrape off the windows for you. Go ahead and warm up the car, okay?"

That left me definitely missing the Sunshine State. How on earth did I ever live here? My fingers felt like blocks of wood. My nose ran. The soft snow had turned into a mean pelting mess as tiny balls of ice hurled themselves at my skin.

Kiki decided to close early. She sent out an email blast, warning customers that she was closing up shop in a half an hour. While the time ticked past, I helped Kiki cut out hearts for a Valentine's Day project. Usually she's pretty chatty, coming up with ideas for future promotions. Catching me up on the latest about her customers. Before Christmas, she had bubbled over with excitement about the new baby. But as we cut and packaged pieces, she had nothing much to say. I realized she hadn't even bothered to call Brawny and ask about her baby. That hit me hard.

She definitely was not her normal self. To keep from dwelling on her mood, I chattered like a chipmunk, telling Kiki what we were doing at the store.

"You're able to source all your merchandise by buying through estate sales and consignment shops?"

"Sixty percent. Of course, we don't turn around and sell those raw materials we buy. We recycle, upcycle, and repurpose everything. Most of what we get doesn't look like much. It's our job to see the treasure in the trash."

"Give me an example."

"We pick up bottles that wash up on the beach. We even offer people a small amount for bringing them in. Then we decorate the outside of the bottles and sell them as vases."

"That's pretty iffy. I mean, what if no one brings in any bottles? Then what do you sell?"

"That's the best part. Skye is always coming up with new ideas. I make regular runs to consignment shops and buy raw materials. Oh, and we're not opposed to stopping by a curb and picking up junk. Right before I left, I saw one of those pressed wood computer desks. I borrowed Poppy's truck and we picked it up. The whole unit didn't weigh much. Because the pressed wood warps easily, the piece looked pretty rough. Poppy glued portions back together and sanded them flat. Skye decoupaged most of the piece with maps of Florida. We put it on the floor and it sold in an hour."

"But that's a big piece. You wouldn't get those very often."

"No. However, Skye has been turning stray drawers from dressers into cool under-bed storage containers. We find those all the time."

"Could we run by and see Bonnie on our way back to the house?" she asked. "I want her to know we're here for her."

"I was going to suggest that myself."

By the time we arrived at the parking lot of the hospital, I was talked out. By contrast, my friend was curiously quiet. The weight of the conversation had tired me out. "I could use a bottle of water. Let's hit the gift shop and get more magazines for Bonnie," I said, checking the time on a big black-rimmed institutional clock. "If we hurry, we can get there before it closes."

The volunteer in the pink jacket counted change, as a prelude to finishing her workday. "We're closed," she said, looking incredibly pleased with herself.

Small rant: Why on earth do people who hate people volunteer for jobs that put them face-to-face with people? In particular, why go into retail, if you hate the public? Hello? Isn't that asking for a string of one bad day after another? End of rant.

"That's a shame," I said, pointing to the clock on an adjoining wall. That's one thing about hospitals, they are big believers in honking huge clocks. "Because it's four fifty and your sign on the door says you won't be closing for another ten minutes."

"All right, all right. Make it snappy," she said. Narrowing her eyes, she added, "And you'd better make it worth my while to recount this change. Did you know that the United States pays 1.7 cents to make one penny? No wonder we have such a large national debt! We need to do away with this nonsense. Heard someone talking about it on NPR. All these coins? A huge waste of resources. In fact, we'd probably have done away with them by now if not for the folks who make those silly coin counting machines you see at the grocery stores."

I had to admire her patriotism.

"Couldn't agree with you more." From the floral case, I grabbed a nice bouquet in a vase. In a second cooler, I found bottled water. Kiki dumped a stack of magazines onto the counter.

Speaking to the clerk, I said, "I'll pay you in cash, or credit card, or by check. Whatever is easiest."

"Credit card." Her mouth settled into a flat line. Her eyes were beady behind glasses smeared with fingerprints. I tried not to stare at her as she shuffled through the items, ringing them up, but there was an unsettling aspect to her appearance. My brain struggled to process the disparity, but it eluded me. As I watched her do the work of tallying up our purchases, I gave up trying to understand what was wrong. I'd learned from crafting with Skye that answers come unbidden when you quit chasing them around a bush.

Kiki wandered around a bit, getting ideas for Valentine's Day. She picked up a box of chocolates in a cute cardstock container fashioned to look like a woman's purse. I could see that her creative wheels were turning a mile a minute. I signed the bill and waited patiently for the volunteer to decide which of the slips would go into the drawer and which would be returned to me.

"Oh, my heavens! Cara! Cara, look!"

The volunteer and I both swiveled our heads to follow Kiki's directional finger-pointing. My friend stood in front of a glass display case mounted on the wall, with her attention directed to a set of fat plastic letters spelling out, "We LOVE our volunteers!"

But I had no idea why the sign mattered.

"Cara? Is your phone charged? Mine's dead." Kiki came over and opened her palm in a demand for my device.

"Sure." I handed over my iPhone. "What are you looking at?"

Kiki pointed at a photo. A glare from the overhead lights obscured the image. I shifted my stance and stared into the smarmy countenance of Bernice Stottlemeyer.

48

"If that doesn't tie Bernice to the disappearance of Bonnie's baby, I don't know what would. I'm sending this to Detweiler and Hadcho." When Kiki was finished pushing buttons, she approached the strange woman behind the cash register.

"Who's in charge of the volunteers? What's the name of your supervisor?"

In response, the clerk folded her arms over her chest and stuck out her jaw. Given that her wig was now crooked, the effect struck me as more comical than authoritative. I covered my mouth so as not to laugh.

"Why do you want to know those things? How about you leave your name and phone number with me? I'll give it to my boss. She can call you."

I'd had about enough. "See, that woman? Your volunteer of the week? She was murdered in the parking lot at Lambert Field."

"Whoa. That was Marie? She's the dead person at the airport?"

"Marie?" Kiki and I shrugged at each other.

I pointed to the picture on my phone, which was still in Kiki's hand. "What's the name of this woman? What did you call her?"

"Marie Livesay."

"Really?" Kiki's eyes widened. "You have to be kidding. I've met her attorney, been to her house, and talked to her husband. When I did, she went by the name Bernice Stottlemeyer."

Okay, the woman in the photo wore her hair in a crop that was totally different from the style preferred by the Bernice who frequented our restaurant, and those big glasses with the over-sized frames changed her look, too, but Kiki had been right. The volunteer was Bernice Stottlemeyer.

The clerk dialed down the attitude considerably. Chewing on her bottom lip, she stared at the photo on the phone, glanced up at the picture on the wall and nodded. "We all knew her as Denise. She wasn't nice or friendly. Our boss said she was shy. I thought she was stuck up. I was right. She was full of herself."

"Sounds like the Bernice we all knew and hated. By the way, my name is Kiki Lowenstein-Detweiler, and this is my friend Cara Mia Delgatto."

"I'm Midge Wonderlick." After a furtive glance around, she said, "Marie only got the job here because her brother-in-law, Douglas Livesay, is a big shot. On the hospital board or something. See, we didn't really need more volunteers, especially not here in the gift shop. As for being 'Volunteer of the Week,' that's a crock. Once a month, they pull a name out of the hat because the CEO of the hospital went to a stupid motivational program where they taught him that giving praise makes people happy. That might work if the praise was sincere, but not when it's totally random."

No kidding. I bit back a chuckle.

"Was she working here when the Gossage baby was stolen?" Kiki asked in a hushed voice.

"I think so. In fact, I'm sure of it. Would it help if I got the schedule so you could see it? Better yet, I'll make a copy of it for you. That way you'll have it."

With that Midge disappeared into the office.

"I can't believe how that woman went from our worst enemy to our best ally in nothing flat. What're the odds of that?" I shook my head.

"Hey, nothing like a nasty villain to bring people together. The odds are good that people will turn against you when you're as awful as Bernice Stottlemeyer. If she had treated other folks like they were human beings, we would have never gotten all this help. It never occurred to Bernice that her own behavior was the trigger for her problems. No, this is a perfect example of how being a jerk will come back and bite you on the butt."

"Posthumously," I added.

Kiki laughed. The sound reminded me that my old friend was in there, somewhere, just struggling with all the changes life was dealing her. "Necrophiliac butt-biting. What will they think of next?"

Midge returned with a sheet of paper still warm from the copier. "Marie is on the schedule for the same time that the baby was abducted. I remember because I was here in the gift shop when all the cop cars pulled up outside. Marie was really weird that day. Stranger than usual. She asked if she could do my job for me."

"Do your job?" I repeated.

"Yes. We all take turns dropping off flowers. She offered me twenty bucks if I'd let her do the rounds and drop off the florals. We've got this really nice cart. The person in charge puts a damask tablecloth over the top, so it looks really fancy. Then she or he loads the cart by checking the names against the floral deliveries. It's definitely the fun part of this position, delivering a little joy like that. Ringing up purchases is...a drag. Customers who come in are stressed because they've got a sick loved one here. I get that. It's just, hey, don't take it out on me!"

I could see where she was going, and I hesitated long enough to be respectful. "Could we see the cart?"

"Why?" She fisted her hands on her hips. Miss Huffy was back, and Midge, the nice clerk, had taken a hike.

"Someone managed to sneak a baby out of here. The police can't figure out how it was done. We don't know either. If we could put two and two together, that might move the investigation along," I explained. "We're really worried now that Bernice is dead. What if the baby is out there somewhere in the cold?"

"On top of that," Kiki said, "if it's happened once, it could happen again. Especially if the police can't work out the way it was done. You'd hate to see that, wouldn't you? Maybe Bernice—or Marie—was part of a ring of people who are stealing babies. I know she wanted a child, and she wanted it badly. Maybe she got in contact with a bunch of crooks who steal kids from their mothers. It's possible that they killed her just to keep her quiet."

Kiki's theory was certainly news to me, but it made about as much sense as anything else I'd heard. Clearly, she'd been thinking this over.

"Be right back," Midge said. She turned on her heel and walked away.

Kiki and I waited for what seemed like hours. I glanced at the clock. "I sure hope that after all this, we'll still get to see Bonnie."

"Even if we don't, we're doing her a favor. I have a hunch this cart is how Bernice got the baby out of the room. Look, there it is!"

Midge came out of a back room. She was pushing a metal cart on rubber casters. "We keep this in a storage closet. I grabbed a tablecloth, too, so you could see how it looks when it's in use."

"What do you want to bet that's the same storage closet where the janitor found the device to disable a RFID? The one that Detweiler told us was found on the premises?"

"Good thinking," Kiki said. I squatted down on my haunches to inspect the lower shelf. You forget how little babies are when they're just born. Holding Ty had reminded me that I buy a turkey for Thanksgiving that weighs more than he did at birth. Shoot, I decorate pumpkins that are his size for Halloween. Sure enough, a baby could very easily be hidden on the lower shelf of this cart. The draped white cloth would be the perfect camouflage.

"My phone?" I held out my hand, and she passed it to me. I took a couple of pictures of the bottom shelf, before stepping away from the cart to get a photo of the whole thing. An idea began to form, the pieces coalesced into a coherent plan. "Here's what I'm thinking. Bernice was in this all along with Jana Higgins. Jana attended your baby album crop looking for Bonnie. After all, Bernice knew that you and Bonnie were friends, and that you both had approximately the same due date. She had to figure that Bonnie would attend the class on baby albums at your store. That's how they came up with the idea of taking Bonnie a Vanilla Coke laced with Valium. Jana brings by the cola, sees that Bonnie drinks a little, and remember Bonnie is already taking pain killers because of her C-section. All she needed was a small extra dose to knock her out. Jana text-messages Bernice when she's leaving the room. Then Bernice comes up with the cart, rolls it into Bonnie's room, puts the baby on the bottom shelf, and goes down the hall to a storage closet. Once she's there, she removes the RFID from the baby's ankle."

"RFID?" Midge frowned at me.

"Radio Frequency Identification. It's that do-jobby that sets off an alarm if you try to leave the premises with an infant," I said.

"But who actually walked out of the hospital with Bonnie's little boy?" asked Kiki. "Someone had to carry the baby out the front door."

"That was Marie, I bet. Bernice. Whatever her name is. Was," said Midge with a nod of her head. "See, after she did the rounds with the flower cart, she complained she had a migraine and left early that day. I remember because she looked perfectly fine to me. I had a friend who used to get migraines, and you could tell when one was coming on. She'd just look terrible. But Marie seemed fine. Perfectly all right. And I know how she carried the baby out of the hospital past security."

"You do?" Kiki and I asked in chorus.

"Uh-huh," said Midge. "She had this big black bag that looked like a gym bag. She brought it in a week before the abduction. I remember because she didn't seem like the type who'd want to break a sweat, so I asked her, 'When did you join a fitness center?' She told me it was none of my business and that I wouldn't know a gym bag if it bit me."

49

Kiki sent the photos of the cart to Detweiler. She took down Midge's full name, address, and phone number. Then she extended a slender hand to our new friend. I did the same and said, "Midge? You've been invaluable. Thanks ever so much. We're going to run upstairs and try to see our friend, Bonnie Gossage. As you can imagine, she's miserable."

Midge's skin was dry and papery to the touch. The cloying scent of hand sanitizer came away on my palm. I resisted the urge to wipe it on my pants' leg. The stuff was so pungent that my nose started to run. Midge reached under the counter and found a box of tissues that she pushed toward me.

"I lost my own baby when he was a year and a half old. There's no grief like a mother's grief." Midge pulled out a tissue and dabbed her eyes. "My husband, Charlie, couldn't take it. We went to counselors. Talked to our priest. Fat lot of help that was. He told us that we had to accept God's will. Charlie wanted to know what kind of a God takes a child from his mother. Eventually it got to be too much for my husband and he left me. Mailed me a letter, that coward. Said that he wanted to start over, and he couldn't if he had to look at me because he'd always remember our son. Last I heard, he was married with three kids, two grandkids, all in Wyoming with a new wife. She used to be my best friend. Lived not two houses down from us."

My eyes bugged out of my head. "He told you? About the kids and grandkids? He had the nerve to share that with you? After he left you high and dry?"

"Goodness no. I found all that out on Facebook. Went snooping around one day, and there he was grinning into the camera, bouncing a grandkid on each knee. So then I went to his wife's Facebook page and asked her if we could be friends."

"And she accepted you?" Kiki asked. Her eyes were big as tea saucers in her head.

"Yes, ma'am. She never was very bright. People are really gratified to have 'friends' on Facebook. It's pathetic, really. That's how I got them back."

Kiki's eyes sparkled with interest. "What did you do?"

"I used a piece of stationery from the hospital to send both of them certified letters that they'd been exposed to an STD. But the way I wrote it, each of them had a different diagnosis! Their status on Facebook went from 'married' to 'it's complicated' overnight."

50

Kiki couldn't walk away from Midge without handing her a gift certificate for ten bucks from Time in a Bottle. "I keep these in my purse just for occasions like this," my friend explained.

Midge was over the moon with happiness. "I'll hop right over there tomorrow and use this, for sure. I've been working on a goodbye album."

"If you're planning a big trip, we have lots of cool paper with destinations, names of cities, and stuff like that," said Kiki.

Midge snickered. "I suppose you could call it a big trip. A really, really big trip. Or even the trip of a lifetime. See, I've got cancer of the brain. It's terminal. Before I check out I'd like to put together an album. I think one of my sister's kids might like it."

I felt a lump in my throat, because I'd been judging this woman from the first. I'd thought her poorly suited for retail, which she was. I'd found her abrasive, which she had been. Worst of all, I'd inwardly cringed at her ill-fitting wig. The sour taste of regret filled my mouth. What right did I have to judge

Midge Wonderlick? That woman was much more alive than I, because she was fully cognizant that her time here was brief.

I vowed to be more generous in the future. I could well afford to be. I had my health, my own son, and a long life ahead of me. Impulsively, I reached over the counter and gave the woman a hug. At first, she stiffened. Then I felt her body sag, as if the starch had been rinsed out of her skeleton. When I let go of Midge, Kiki followed my lead. "Midge? We'll keep you in our prayers."

"Yes, please do that." She pulled free. "Pray that I go easy, okay? Not too much pain? Not too much lingering? I've got a stockpile of pills, but you never know. Could be one day I'll be feeling fine and then it'll hit me, and I won't have any say in the matter, see? But I'm hoping I can time this just right. I live alone, and there's no one to come take care of me, so I don't want to be at the mercy of a nurse. Or an orderly. I've seen too much of that, working here. It's not that they aren't good people. They are. But they're overworked and underpaid."

What was there to say?

Nothing.

So we thanked her again, picked up the bouquet, the bag full of magazines, and the bottled water.

Kiki and I paused on our way out to give Midge one last word of farewell.

"You two are doing a good thing, trying to help your friend. I wish I'd had girlfriends like you. Now go on and get out of here before I get in hot water for keeping this shop open so long."

51

Bonnie had been moved from the maternity ward to another unit.

That alone made me sad. I hadn't thought about what it must have been like for her on the floor with all those mothers and their babies. But as Kiki and I walked from the nurses' station to the elevator, it struck me how the natural noises of babies crying would be incredibly hard for Bonnie to take.

We nearly bumped into a nurse coming out of our friend's room. "You can drop off the flowers, but please turn right around and come back, okay? She needs her rest. Still has a fever."

We found Bonnie curled into a fetal position, facing the wall.

"Bonnie?" Kiki sang out. "We're here, sweetie, and I think we've made some progress."

Bonnie lifted her head, and I nearly gasped. She had always been a bit chunky, but now her face was drawn and sallow, except for her eyes. They were bright red and puffy. No one had washed her hair. Limp strands hung down in her face.

"Progress?" She repeated. "Did that woman call? The one who took my baby?"

"No." Kiki pulled up a chair and explained what we'd learned about Bernice Stottlemeyer.

"You definitely found her," Bonnie said. "That's her full name, Bernice Marie Livesay Stottlemeyer. Remember, I have her legal documents."

"We think she might have been working with Jana Higgins. Is that possible?"

Bonnie struggled to sit up, so I helped her, putting a couple of pillows behind her back. Then I took a seat on the edge of her bed. The quieter we were about our visit, the longer we might be able to talk.

"Yes." Bonnie covered her mouth with her hand. "Yes! Remember how Jana glommed onto me at the album class? She followed me out to my car and asked to keep in touch. I figured she was nervous about having her first child, so I gave her my number. Aye-yay-aye, was that ever stupid. She called me six times a day asking if I'd felt any contractions yet. Jeremy finally blocked her for me. That's one reason I was surprised and relieved to see her here at the hospital. I figured once she had her own child, she'd move on."

"What we need is a connection, a nexus," I said. "Can you think of a way that they might have met? Some intersection? If we can prove that they knew each other, we might be closer to finding your baby."

"Connection?" Bonnie sounded foggy. But she pushed herself to a seated position. "Bernice and...Jana Higgins? I have no idea."

"Let's go at this another way," suggested Kiki. "What can you tell us about Bernice? Her activities? Start with what happened after she threw the fit in my store."

"Okay. After she got out of jail on bond for busting up your store, she drove over to the adoption center and threw a brick through the window. Unfortunately, she chose a really bad time to pull that stunt, because a janitor was there cleaning the building. He suffered minor cuts from the flying glass. While we were working to get a court-ordered involuntary admission set up, Bernice pretended to be a teacher at a Montessori school and reported Wesley for molesting a child. As you might guess, it took a while to get that ironed out."

"Geez Louise. She was on a rampage," I said.

"Right. You can't be recommended for involuntary commitment by a family member. Not in Missouri. Has to be a mental health coordinator or the head of a facility. As you can imagine, that makes it much, much more complicated. How do you get someone who has a problem to submit to evaluation? Good luck with that. Since her brother is on the board here, he brought in a psychiatrist who testified that she was not herself. The doctor didn't use the term schizophrenic, because her family didn't want her stigmatized—"

"Would that be Douglas Livesay, her brother?" Kiki asked for clarification. "The woman in the gift shop mentioned him."

"Right. Douglas didn't want her stigmatized. The psychiatrist said that Bernice had been treated for infertility and that the combination of hormones and so on had caused her to have a chemical unbalance. We offered to pay a fine and of course, Bernice's family paid for all the damage she did to your store. The judge asked her to do one hundred hours of community service. That was that." Bonnie paused.

Kiki poured a glass of water for Bonnie and handed it over.

"Wait," Bonnie said. "That's not all. I remember now! Judge Riddenbacher also wanted her to attend counseling sessions. The psychiatrist wanted to see her once a day for the next few months, but Douglas Livesay protested. He pointed out that there are a lot of good group counseling sessions held here at the hospital. If Bernice was coming here for community service, Douglas would be a way to keep an eye on his sister. Judge

Riddenbacher is a soft touch. I think he's known the Livesay family for years. You know how it is with these Old St. Louis families. Douglas got exactly what he wanted."

"But the Livesays knew Bernice had a problem, right?" I wanted clarification.

"Cara, have you ever tried to deal with a family member who has mental illness issues? As a society, we aren't set up to handle these problems adequately. Most people with mental illness wind up dead, homeless, or in prison. That's how we cope. We aren't much better than the Victorians, who locked them away in insane asylums. In fact, in 2010 the number of beds in psychiatric facilities in the US plunged to match the number of beds we had in 1850. Can you believe that? And 1850 was the start of civilized, humane care for the mentally ill. Thirteen states closed 25% of their total beds in the years between 2005 and 2010, and yet our population has grown by nearly 10% during that same time period.

"How bad is it? It's bedlam. Know where that term came from?"

Kiki nodded. "It's a nickname for the Bethlehem Hospital in London. We say that a chaotic situation is 'bedlam,' because that's what it was like inside. People chained to the walls and locked inside cages, screaming."

Bonnie snorted. "Here we are, centuries later, and have we made progress? I don't think so. Case in point, Bernice Stottlemeyer. Wesley was at the end of his rope. When he married Bernice, she was stable and on meds. Then she decided she didn't like the way they made her feel. Couldn't cope with the weight gain. She went off the deep end faster than Michael Phelps hitting the water at the Olympics. Wesley tried and tried to get Bernice help, but her family blocked him at every turn. Then her sister had a baby and suddenly Bernice is convinced that's all she needs. Yeah, a baby would make everything A-okay." Bonnie shook her head. "Right. A baby will make you crazy if you aren't already. Between hormones and no sleep, you'll go nuts. I tried to tell Wesley he was making a big mistake by agreeing to adopt, but he was desperate."

Although I didn't like the picture Bonnie was painting, I appreciated the fact that this was the Bonnie Gossage I'd known before her baby was stolen. Putting her mind to the task of helping us solve this mystery had awakened the intelligent professional within. Maybe, just maybe, we could figure this out. The three of us were certainly making progress.

"To recap," said Kiki. "We've got a couple of points where the two women might have met. Community service. Group therapy. What about a gym? The woman down in the gift shop told us that Bernice was carrying around a big gym bag. She asked Bernice if she'd joined a fitness program, and Bernice told her that it wasn't any of her business. Could the two women have met in a gym?"

"I doubt it," said Bonnie. "As far as I know, Bernice was resistant to working out. I say that because I mentioned to Wesley that one of my clients improved her erratic moods dramatically by visiting a holistic doctor and lifting weights on a regular basis. I even offered to take Bernice with me to a yoga class. Wesley told me that Bernice had no intention of touching equipment that other people had dripped their body fluids all over. I suppose it's possible that she changed her mind, but it's not very likely."

52

The elevator door had nearly rolled shut when Kiki pushed the OPEN DOOR button and held it for us.

The navy blue wool cape that Brawny had sewn reminded me of Superman's famous garb. In many ways, there was a similarity. Kiki rarely stood up for herself, but she'd risk everything to help a friend. Getting involved with Bonnie's problem had revived Kiki's natural sense of protectiveness. But would it be enough to lift her out of her depression?

When we got back to her house, Kiki went immediately upstairs to feed Ty. As simple as that act seemed, I thought it a good sign. I also learned that she had expressed milk while we were at the store and stored it in a small thermal bag in her purse. Realizing she hadn't totally forgotten about her infant son lifted a huge weight from my heart.

While she took care of her little man, I helped Brawny set the table for dinner in the formal dining room. A rich, robust fragrance had greeted us at the door. "That smells terrific," I told the Scot, as I put out place mats and cutlery. I loved the idea of Kiki's family having a sit-down dinner. I remembered doing the same with Tommy, and I felt this ritual would pay lasting dividends for our relationship.

"Coffee braised pot roast." She'd picked up a bouquet of evergreens and carnations at the grocery store. The pink and green brightened up the room considerably.

"You have to be kidding me!"

"No. Uses a tablespoon of espresso powder. Gets the wee ones to eat their vegetables. I put in pineapple, sweet potatoes, green beans, an onion, garlic, and green peppers."

"I want that recipe. I only use espresso powder for making tiramisu. Sounds fabulous."

Erik and Anya couldn't wait to tell us about the day they'd had at school. I snapped a few photos of them to send back to my pals in Florida. Anya already has a terrific sense of style. She wore a long-sleeved black and white striped turtle neck dress over black leggings that tucked into a pair of adorable chunky booties. Her platinum blond hair was pulled up into a cute ponytail and tied with a black ribbon. Erik wore adorable green corduroy pants and a matching green and brown sweater that I was sure Brawny had knit for him.

Because Tommy is eighteen, I'd forgotten about all the teenaged drama that played such a big part in Anya's life. Who "liked" who. Who was going with who. What teacher assigned a stupid project that would take half of Anya's life to complete—and that would not ever, ever be useful. No way.

Erik wiggled with excitement as he told us about the guinea pig that had been given to his teacher as a new pet for the classroom. "You know his teacher," Kiki said as she smiled at me. "Maggie Earhardt. Aren't we lucky? Erik did Miss Maggie want a guinea pig? I didn't know she was looking for a new pet for you guys."

He thought about that. "Aubrey Whitehall's daddy was gonna gived it to da dog pound. Or put it outside in the snow. He dinna like the guinea pig. He said it was stinky and it squealed like a pig."

All that was probably true. I bit back a smile.

"So Miss Maggie sayed she find room for Giggles. That's his name. I gots to pat him a little. Then he squeaked and that scared me."

"I'm glad to hear that," Kiki said. "It's awfully cold outside, isn't it? Even with a fur coat, that guinea pig would be miserable. Speaking of which, Anya? Please take an apple out to Monroe. That poor donkey hates this miserable weather."

We'd finished eating when Detweiler and Hadcho arrived. Cold air clung to them like a moving blanket of frosty weather. They took their places at the table while Brawny dished out two large helpings of the pot roast. I assembled salads while Kiki heated more sourdough bread. Both men ate with gusto, pausing long enough to explain they'd skipped lunch. After Anya and Erik told their father how the day had gone, Kiki excused both kids from the table. When Anya hesitated, Kiki firmly said, "I'm counting on you to set a good example for your brother. This is homework time."

That brought on an impassioned, "Aw, Mom!" But Anya took her younger brother by the hand and led him into the family room.

"Ballistics came back," Detweiler said. "This'll be all over the news tonight, so there's no harm in sharing it. Bernice Marie Livesay Stottlemeyer was shot at close range with a gun registered to her husband. A Glock."

53

"What?" Kiki couldn't contain her surprise. "You don't seriously think that Wesley killed her, do you?"

"Nope. Not for a second. The Bridgeton police hauled him in for questioning. He lawyered up, which was a smart thing to do. Especially since his lawyer was able to tell them that Bernice had broken into the Stottlemeyers' house a month ago."

Hadcho got up to pour himself a glass of milk. "Not exactly correct, buddy. She didn't break in. Seems that Wesley had changed the locks after she moved out, but he forgot to get back the spare garage door opener. So Bernice let herself in, through the door from the garage to the kitchen. Then she helped herself to the contents of the safe in his office. Took ten grand in cash and the gun. Wesley didn't report it to the police because he felt like a dope for not thinking about the garage door gizmo."

"Her brother promised to pay Wesley back," Detweiler said. "Since the divorce hadn't been finalized, Wesley told his lawyer to deduct the cash from his part of their joint bank account."

"From what we've heard, Douglas Livesay had a full-time job mopping up after his sister." I noted with appreciation that

Brawny had gotten up to serve us decaf or regular coffee after our meal. A plate of shortbread cookies and lemon curd tempted me to sin. "Recipe," I said, pointing to my plate.

Brawny laughed.

"And what exactly did you hear?" Hadcho asked.

Kiki and I repeated everything we'd learned from Midge about Bernice (AKA Marie) Stottlemeyer. We passed around photos of the flower cart. We shared our analysis of what might have happened. The fact that Bernice had used her middle name rather than her given name while working at the hospital gave credence to the idea that she'd been planning something all along. As for hiding a baby in a gym bag, the men were dubious about that. Hadcho seemed to think there'd been a hand off, and Jana had walked out with the child. I wasn't so sure, but I felt like the gym bag was an odd accessory for a woman who didn't like the intimacy of a fitness center.

"Even if she was averse to working out in a gym, Bernice could have hired a personal trainer," I suggested.

Hadcho didn't respond to my idea. He simply listened. Finally, I couldn't take it any longer.

"Well? What are you thinking?" I asked, looking up at him. I was seated at the table, and he'd had his third or fourth cup of regular coffee. Since I was in a questioning mode, I added, "How can you sleep after all that caffeine?"

He grinned at me. "Like a baby. Doesn't stop me at all. The minute my head hits the pillow, I'm out like a light bulb that's been shot with by a BB gun."

Lucky guy.

Detweiler stroked his chin thoughtfully. "We've got two mysteries here. Who shot Bernice? Wesley? His girlfriend Lila? Bernice's brother? Her sister? Jana Higgins? Jeremy Gossage? Or an outsider?"

"Given the fingerprint smudges on the gun, I'd guess that

Bernice had it with her when she arrived at the long-term lot," Hadcho said. "I figure she pulled it on the wrong person."

"But if she walked out with the baby—if she's the one who took the baby from the hospital—she had no reason to meet anyone in the parking lot," Kiki said. "Think about it. Bernice was not a woman who put herself out or did favors for other people. And she'd been raised with money. People like that don't save money by parking their cars in the cheap lot. They take a nice warm cab or even a limo—"

"That's a good point," Hadcho said. "We need to ask all the local limo services if they've given any rides to women with infants over the past few days. You're right, Kiki. Bernice would have called a service to pick her up."

"Let's back up. Okay, say you're right. Jana drugs Bonnie and calls Bernice down in the gift shop. Bernice takes the floral delivery cart from floor to floor. When she gets to Bonnie's room, she puts the baby in her gym bag—"

"Wait a minute. Here's a thought. Maybe it wasn't a gym bag. Let me show you what she used," and I thumbed through images on my cell phone. "Remember? Midge, the clerk at the gift shop, called it a gym bag and Bernice corrected her. She even said that Midge wouldn't know a gym bag if it bit her. It wasn't a gym bag. It was a Sherpa travel bag. You use them to transport a pet when you fly with them. See? They have this lamb's wool fleece on the bottom. If she used a gym bag, the baby couldn't breathe and would get cold. But if she put the baby in this, the fleece would help keep him warm."

"So Bernice Stottlemeyer was planning to fly out of town with the kid in tow," Hadcho said, after he'd looked over the photos I'd pulled up of the Sherpa bags.

"No. That wouldn't have worked. They make you open up your bag at the airport and take out your pet. Bernice never intended to fly with the baby. At least, I don't think she did. Do you know if she bought a plane ticket?"

Detweiler punched in a text message. In a minute, he had an answer. "No. My contact in Bridgeton says there's no record of her buying a plane ticket."

"That proves it," Kiki slapped her palm against the table. "Bernice Stottlemeyer wasn't there because she was flying out of town. Bonnie told us she figured Bernice was there because she had to meet someone, probably Jana Higgins. I think she's right. There's only one reason that Bernice would agree to meet with Jana, especially in a parking lot in bad weather."

I agreed. "It's because Jana promised to sell her the baby."

54

"Bernice was totally convinced that she was the smartest person in the room," I said. "I remember once she lectured a server on the translation of pasta e fagioli. According to Bernice, it's Italian for bean and bacon soup. Of course, that's wrong. It's just pasta and beans, but she was sure we'd prepared the food incorrectly. Given her history, I would imagine she had decided to double-cross Jana. That's why she brought along the gun to their meeting."

"Makes perfect sense to me," Kiki said. "Bernice had this rollicking sense of entitlement. No way was she going to pay ten grand for a baby. Huh-uh. Instead, she took the gun with her thinking that she would pull it on her accomplice. That way she'd get to keep both the baby and the money. I bet if they dust for fingerprints, they'll find them on the seat belt buckle in the back seat of Bernice's car," Kiki said.

"Why?" Hadcho frowned at her.

"Because infant car seats buckle into the back seat, facing the rear of the car, for safety," Detweiler explained. "As a godfather, that's news you can use."

The men gave each other a high-five.

"Bernice could not have gone out and bought a car seat. That would be too obvious. And no one reported finding an infant seat in her car. She must have been meeting another person who was bringing the baby—and that person brought along a car seat. That would have fit Bernice's plans to a tee. See, she would plead ignorance and ask the other person for help transferring the infant seat into her car. While that other person—Jana probably— was futzing around with the seat belt, Bernice could pull a gun on her."

"That makes sense," Detweiler said. "Why else would Bernice steal all that cash and a gun from the safe in Wesley's office? We know she had access to money of her own. Bernice was a trust fund baby. She couldn't withdraw ten grand cash from a bank quietly, because they'd be obligated to report that amount to the IRS. Rather than go through that hassle, she took the money out of Wesley's safe."

"And she probably felt justified taking the cash," Kiki said. "After all, she wanted a baby. She thought it would fix their faltering marriage. Why not make Wesley pay for the baby? It would serve him right. Of course Bernice couldn't steal the infant all by herself. Too many eyes were watching her because of her bad girl behavior. She had to have help getting close to Bonnie Gossage."

"That's why there were all those attempts at stealing infants," Hadcho said. "What we were seeing was Bernice working out how to get the job done."

"But she couldn't manage it by herself," Detweiler warmed to the idea. "There was no easy way to slip a baby past security. Even if you disabled the RFID alarm, like she did, the hospital's CCTV cameras would catch you in the act of taking the child off the premises."

"She needed to hide the baby twice," Hadcho said. "Once while taking it from Bonnie and then when sneaking it out of the building. Having two people passing a baby back and forth really complicated the crime. We didn't know to look for Bernice. We kept scrolling through the CCTV footage trying to find Jana Higgins."

"This Jana woman fits the profile of an infant abductor," explained Detweiler. "She's overweight, so she was able to convince people she was pregnant. She tends to be unsure of herself and have poor self-esteem. Usually there's a man in her life who wants a child. Or at least who expects one. The most common scenario is one where she winds up backed into a corner. She's been lying about her pregnancy, but she can only lie for so long. When the time comes to produce a baby, she sees no other option but to steal a child."

"That makes perfect sense." Kiki ticked off the points on her fingers. "Jana said that she was expecting, but she couldn't give me a due date. Every woman knows her due date! She couldn't tell me where she planned to deliver. There's definitely a man in her life. He has two children by a previous relationship, and she mentioned what a good dad he is. But if Jana Higgins fits the profile of an infant abductor, how'd she get hooked up with Bernice Stottlemeyer?"

"Better yet," I said, "why did she work with Bernice? Bernice wanted a child, too. What was the plan? They couldn't split the baby in half."

"Maybe that's how things went wrong. Maybe they fought over who got to keep the baby," said Detweiler. He buttered a shortbread cookie with more lemon curd. My mouth watered as the tangy scent of citrus came my way. "That would explain why Bernice was murdered. She thought she was buying a baby, even though she hoped she would be able to cheat Jana out of the money. Jana wasn't about to give up the baby."

"But don't forget Jana needed Bernice, too," Hadcho said. "Bernice was the brains of the outfit. She's probably the one who figured out how to get the job done. Bernice must have bought the RFID blocking device. It wasn't cheap. Bernice was able to get a job at the hospital so she could keep tabs on Bonnie's pregnancy."

"And Bernice 'found' Bonnie," I said, putting the quotation marks around the word 'found.' "She was able to point Jana in the right direction. Give her all the particulars like the fact that Bonnie spent a lot of her free time at the scrapbook store."

Kiki rubbed her eyes. "I am suddenly, very, very tired."

"It's this case," Detweiler said. "It's so emotional. She's a friend, and we can imagine ourselves in her position. Believe me, we're doing everything we can to work this abduction. I even put in a call to Robbie. I was that fed up with how Prescott is stonewalling our efforts."

"I need to get the kids to bed and hit the sheets myself." Kiki pushed her chair away from the table. "Tomorrow evening there's a crop at the store. I've got a full day of kit prep to get done, and I need to go over the plans for the baptism ceremony this Sunday."

"And we need to schedule time together. You and me," I said. That was code for, "We're going to pay a quick visit to your ob/gyn."

Blinking at me slowly, Kiki gave a tiny shrug. "I don't know where we'll find any free time, Cara. Really I don't. Maybe we can talk while I assemble kits."

Well, rats. And here I'd thought the matter was settled.

55

I got up before dawn the next morning and crept downstairs, hoping to catch Detweiler so I could tell him my concerns. At first it looked like I was the only person awake, but then I realized there was coffee in the automatic coffee maker and pancake mix in a container with a pour spout. In the air was the heavenly fragrance of vanilla and hazelnut coffee. Totally worth getting up for. After pouring myself a cup, I listened carefully to the sounds of metal clanking down in the basement. Detweiler and Brawny were lifting weights. She spotted him, encouraging him and keeping him from hurting himself with a cautioning word or two.

Not wishing to interrupt them, I waited and sipped my brew. A few minutes later, I was rewarded by the appearance of two sweat-soaked people as they trudged up the stairs.

"Morning!" Brawny's face was flushed. Her track suit was soaked, and a few gray hairs had escaped from the tight ponytail she always wore. Not for the first time did I notice how solidly she was built. Her shoulders were broad, and her biceps large for a woman.

"Cara! You're up early." Detweiler went to hug me but pulled back. "Wait a minute. I'm pretty stinky. I need a shower," and he turned toward the staircase leading to the bedrooms.

"Don't go. Not yet. I need to talk to you. Maybe even to both of you."

That stopped both of them in their tracks. Brawny gripped the mug in her hands and frowned. "Aye, something wrong? Are the children all right?"

"Fine. They're fine. At least as far as I know. The problem isn't with them. It's with Kiki. Have either of you noticed how down she is? Maybe not because she lives with you and you see her every day, but I'm shocked. I've seen her go through all sorts of tough times, but she usually picks herself up and forges ahead. Not this time. She's barely holding on by her fingernails."

Detweiler pulled up the chair next to mine. His green eyes had darkened, the way the ocean does before a storm rolls in. "What do you mean? Is she unhappy? Have I done something wrong?"

"I suspect she has a bad case of post-partum depression. You do realize that she sits in the shower and cries every morning?"

Detweiler looked horrified, as did Brawny. They exchanged worried glances. Brawny spoke first. "Are ye sure about that? Couldn't she be fretting over my wee lad? He misses his mother something fierce, ye know. Taken to wetting the bed now and again."

"I'm positive this isn't about Erik. She and I had a long talk about how she's feeling."

"What did she say?" Detweiler's jaw flexed, and he'd knotted up his hands.

"She's scared to death that she can't be a good mother to all three kids. She blames herself because Erik is regressing—"

"But—" Brawny tried to interrupt.

"Yes, she knows that's normal. That's not the point. Kiki is like a house divided. Her logical self knows Erik's bedwetting is temporary. That it's a predictable response to a new baby. She even recognizes that Anya's sassy mouth is her own sort of regression as well. But deeper than that is her fear that she's inadequate.

"I've done a little reading up on this. Usually any propensity for post-partum depression is exacerbated by a trauma during pregnancy. I would guess that having your husband nearly die of gunshot wounds, and being in the middle of a gun fight yourself, would definitely qualify."

"But Kiki hasn't said anything to me about feeling blue." Detweiler opened the water and gulped it down.

"That's the point. She wouldn't, would she? I'm certain she's depressed. Usually she gets excited about what's happening at the store, but have you noticed that she doesn't seem to care anymore? As I recall, she always loved spending time with her kids. Although I left shortly after Erik arrived, she used to tell me all the cool things she'd done with him. She put aside Sundays and always spent them with Anya. But I haven't heard one thing about doing things with the family. Not any projects. Not any plans to go to the zoo or the City Museum or the Magic House. That's not like her. Added to all this, the weather up here has been drearier than usual. You've had more precipitation. She and I used to joke about having Seasonal Affective Disorder, but it's not really a laughing matter. Especially now, when I see her and she's dragging her hindquarters like a dog that's been hit by a car."

For the longest time, neither Brawny nor Detweiler said anything. That didn't really bother me. I've come to realize that silence isn't a rejection. In the right circumstances, it can indicate that your message is being mulled over. Detweiler rolled the end of his water bottle around in a small circle on the table.

"This is my fault. I haven't been paying attention to her. Did she tell you I was upset about Ty not being born in the hospital?"

Tread carefully, Cara, I told myself. "Yes. I also know that she and your mother aren't getting along as well as they once did. Your mother seems to be concerned that Kiki isn't up to the task of being a mom."

A look of horror crossed Detweiler's face. Quickly that was replaced by anger. "What are you talking about, Cara? Where is this coming from? Are you exaggerating a bad situation just to prove your point?"

"Excuse me?" My famous temper flared.

"Cara is telling you the truth," Brawny hurriedly interjected. "Mrs. Detweiler has said as much to me. Before the young master was born, your ma called me to see what Kiki was doing and how long she was working at the store. I know she called the store a couple of times a day, too. Finally I told her politely her bum was oot the windae."

"Huh?" I couldn't understand what Brawny was saying, but I knew she was upset because she'd reverted to her native tongue. Or a version thereof.

"I respectfully told Mrs. Detweiler that she was wrong. She meant well, but she didna have no cause to be fretting about Kiki's mothering skills. But your mother has a thistle stuck under her blanket. She'll no listen to me, and she's brought it up to me at least twice since."

Detweiler sank down into a kitchen chair. After running his hands through his hair several times, he said, "Brawny, you should have told me about this."

"I tried. You were not hearing me."

"Time out." I used my hands to make the universal sports signal. "This isn't about blame. It's about helping Kiki."

Detweiler nodded, but I could see the frustration in his face. "She's my whole world, Cara. This injury and the situation with

Prescott, well, I've been distracted. I figured we were making an adjustment. As a family. I know she pushes herself. I told myself to give it time. I guess I messed up."

I reached for his hand. "Look, buddy, you did not mess up. You're adjusting, too. You guys have been through more in the short time you've know each other than most couples go through in a lifetime. Be kind to yourself. Now, here's my plan..."

We'd agreed that they'd support me in taking Kiki to the doctor's office when the back door flew open. Hadcho blew in on a gust of frigid air, greatly at odds with the fury in his flint hard eyes. After the door slammed shut behind him, he kicked the side of the nearest kitchen cabinet.

"Temper, temper." I wagged a finger at him.

Detweiler got to his feet. "Decaf coffee? Chamomile tea? Obviously, you don't need anything to get you more cranked up."

With a complicated shrug, Hadcho slipped off his beautiful coat. I'd never seen him drape it over a chair. Instead he always walked to the coat closet and neatly lined up the shoulder seams as he hung it on a wooden hanger. But not today. Today, he didn't seem to care.

"Prescott is steaming mad about the Gossages appealing to the public. Calls are flooding in, and he's angry about having to pay to have the phones covered."

56

Okay, I'd gotten Detweiler and Brawny on board. Detweiler was going to do everything possible to meet us at the doctor's office, but I decided we shouldn't count on it. He agreed. "It would be better to surprise her, than to disappoint her."

But how was I going to handle my friend? Kiki had suggested last night that she wouldn't have time for "girl talk." Had that been a subtle code for, "I don't want to visit my ob/gyn"?

I wasn't sure, but I would not take no for an answer. My greatest liability in life has been my horrible temper. My second biggest problem is my stubborn streak. I come by that naturally. Poppy, my mother's father, could make Monroe, the donkey, seem like a well-trained dog. My grandfather would dig his heels in, drag himself through the mud, and fight you tooth and nail, if he didn't want to go along with you. The mixed metaphors were wholly appropriate because my grandfather defied all attempts to characterize his willful nature. When it came to stubborn, Poppy was in a league of his own.

And I was his granddaughter, so being tenacious came naturally to me.

Rather than fight with Kiki over breakfast, I said nothing about her alterations to our agenda. While Brawny made waffles, Kiki poured orange juice, and I encouraged Erik and Anya to eat. While they finished up, the nanny took a quick shower. On the pretext of getting dressed myself, I went upstairs with the kids. Erik wanted to show me his room, and that gave me a good reason to help him get his clothes on. I was encouraging Erik to pick out a pair of socks when Brawny came in and asked for my iPhone. In hushed tones, she programmed in her phone number. "Call me if the appointment runs late. I will pick up the children from school, but I can go by the store and start the crop. Or help Margit if need be."

She took the kids to CALA, the Charles and Anne Lindbergh Academy. Considering that Kiki had concerns about working a doctor's appointment into her busy schedule, she seemed strangely unhurried. She took her time getting dressed. Kiki nursed Ty, changed him, and settled him in a baby play pen. Gracie was stretched out on the floor, right next to her young master, with her blocky head resting on her paws.

"She is totally smitten by that baby," said Kiki.

That baby? This did not sound like my old friend Kiki Lowenstein. Or my newly married pal, Kiki Lowenstein-Detweiler for that matter.

Kiki went on talking about her son. "He makes a sound and she's right there by his cradle. He cries and she howls. Honest to Pete, that dog has fallen hard for the baby."

That baby and now the baby? Wow. Her lack of attachment scared me. I felt sick with worry, but I couldn't let her see how concerned I was. I couldn't risk making a tough situation worse.

"That's good, isn't it? My Chihuahua Jack raises a ruckus when anyone comes up my drive. I like having a doggy alarm system. Makes it highly unlikely that some creep can sneak into your house."

"Highly unlikely? I'd say it's darn near impossible. Gracie would tear him limb from limb. She's even been known to growl at the plumber. That's a new trick for her. Usually, once I let a workman in, she'd do everything but dance on her hind legs to get his affection. But now? Since the baby has arrived? She actually snarled at a pizza delivery guy. I had to take her into Anya's bedroom and lock her up. She had that guy shaking like a kite in a strong wind."

Around ten, Brawny returned from dropping off the older kids. "I guess I'd better get to work," Kiki said.

I offered to drive. We were in my car and I was pulling onto the street when Thelma Detweiler turned onto my empty spot. I politely rolled down my window. "Hi, Thelma," I said with the cheeriest voice I could muster."

Her normally pleasant face pinched with worry. A woven wool scarf in shades of brown was tucked into her tan car coat. She wasn't wearing a hat. I was surprised to see that an inch of her gray roots showed. Usually she gets her hair colored regularly. "Where's Ty?"

I sucked in air. This was not going to be pretty. I felt like an umpire officiating the deciding game in the World Series. "Ty is inside with Brawny. Kiki fed him, changed him, and he's ready for his nap."

Thelma wasn't buying any of that. She stuck her head inside my window, forcing me to lean back in my seat. "Kiki? You are coming back soon, right?"

"There's both milk and formula for him in the refrigerator. He'll be fine."

"That baby needs his mother." Thelma grabbed the handle on my car door.

Again with the "that baby" stuff!

"She'll be home soon. I promise." I smiled. Or at least, I tried to smile.

Thelma didn't move.

"We're going now."

She still didn't move.

I rolled up my window. Thelma glared at me and reluctantly let loose of the handle. I tapped the accelerator so that we moved forward, out of her grasp.

57

"I cannot believe that woman," I said, as we followed a stream of traffic onto Highway 40. "That was totally inappropriate."

"You think?" Kiki huffed. "I've been dealing with that attitude ever since I went back to work after New Year's Day. She went from being my best friend to hating me. I tell you, Cara, I've been through this before with Sheila. I've got the tee shirt. Not going there again."

My head was still reeling from Thelma's aggressive behavior. "I can't blame you."

"At least Sheila loved Anya so much that she'd always consider how her behavior might impact my daughter. Since Ty's so young, Thelma has no reason to chill. She doesn't care how she makes me look. I swear to you, I have no idea what her problem is. None."

I thought about that. Turned it over and over in my head. "You know, I went to a therapist after my husband and I broke up. She once told me that when a person's reaction is totally disproportionate with the situation at hand, it's a tell. Like in poker. That tell is a signal that there's something going on inside the person. I suspect that Ty's birth triggered a reaction in Thelma."

"Yeah. Too bad it wasn't an IUD."

"Um, I think you mean an IED."

"What did I say?"

I got to giggling. "IUD, as in birth control. You meant an IED as in an explosive device."

Once we got to laughing, the day got marginally better. We stopped again at Kaldi's for coffee and more cookies. If it took sugar and butter to keep Kiki on an even keel, that was fine by me.

This evening's crop would have a Valentine's Day theme. Participants would bring photos that represented people, places, or objects they loved. I helped my friend package up paper, butcher's twine, and lace. In between making progress on that, we waited on customers.

At noon, we turned on the news. The reporter interviewed Prescott, a man whose evolutionary tree includes weasels and other small rodent-like creatures. He did his best to look sincere, but that's hard when you have a face like a badger. Over and over, he assured the public that he was "on top" of the infant abduction suffered by the Gossages.

"But are you making any progress? Do you have a suspect? A person of interest?" The reporter pushed her microphone closer to the acting police chief.

"I can't comment on that," he snapped. "This is an ongoing investigation. A child's life is hanging in the balance here."

"No thanks to you," Kiki said.

I agreed.

At four-thirty, I tapped Kiki on the shoulder. "Time for us to head to Dr. Gretski's office."

"Cara! I told you we don't have time for this!" Kiki narrowed her eyes and glared at me. The effect was ruined by the gooey cookie in her hand.

"Yes, we do."

"I'm fine. Honest I am! There's tons of work that needs to be done here. This can definitely wait."

I sent up a prayer. "No, it can't. You are not yourself. We both know it. If the doctor thinks you're fine, then I'll apologize and let it go. But I don't think that's the case. You don't either."

She folded her arms over her chest. A pink heart waved in my face dangerously. Rather than let the subject drop, I added, "Let me ask you one thing. One thing only. What are you looking forward to?"

"Plenty of stuff."

"Such as?"

Her mouth puckered and then trembled. "I, uh..."

"Go on."

"Valentine's Day?" Her voice nearly cracked with emotion.

"Pretty weak, girlfriend. Come on. If we hustle, this shouldn't take long. The office closes in thirty minutes."

58

All waiting rooms look alike. I don't know who does the bulk of interior decorating for doctors, but it would be a mercy if someone lined them all up and shot them. Seriously. Most waiting rooms are populated with terribly uncomfortable seating, nasty looking magazines, and battered coffee tables. In this one, shelving units were packed with handfuls of garish brochures, most of which were not suitable for a PG audience.

A tired silk flower arrangement covered dust on one of the side tables. The palette was an objectionable tired mishmash of pastels. The peach colored wallpaper looked faded. The peach and aqua chairs were wholly out of place here in St. Louis. They might work in Florida, but really only in a pinch. My fingers itched with the desire to take photos and send them to my friend and co-worker, Skye Blue. Together we could refurbish this tacky room and make it much more welcoming.

"I'm fine," said Kiki to the receptionist.

Four other women in various stages of pregnancy struggled to get comfortable on the unyielding chairs.

"No, she's not," I shot back.

"Do you have an appointment?" A woman with a zebra-striped pair of cheater readers asked Kiki in a quarrelsome voice. What was it with the attitude? I began to wonder if there was a nasty demeanor virus running rampant through the streets of St. Louis.

"No," said Kiki.

"Yes," I said. "I called in yesterday. It's at five. She definitely needs to see Dr. Gretski. Right now. Today. Can't wait."

"He's very busy. You might need to re-schedule," said the receptionist, and she actually put one hand on the sliding glass window in preparation for slamming it shut in our faces.

Instead, I reached up and grabbed it. "I'm afraid that's not good enough. My friend here has a serious case of post-partum depression. She needs to be looked after right now."

"I wasn't the one who made the appointment. She didn't log it in correctly, I'm sorry but—"

"No, that won't cut it. She needs to see the doctor. Today. I don't think you heard me correctly." I levered myself on my toes so that most of my torso was stuck inside the window. This caused the rest of the support staff to turn and stare at me, but I didn't care. I had a job to do, and I wasn't leaving until it was done. "My friend needs to see the doctor right now. Today. Cannot wait. We're not going anywhere. This is a dangerous situation."

"Cara, don't—" Kiki tugged at my sleeve, but my direct appeal had caught the attention of one of the other support staff members. A tall, angular woman with intelligent eyes. She'd been tucking folders in the file cabinet, but now she stopped to listen. Whereas the receptionist had simply been put out with me, this woman showed genuine concern. I knew I had her attention, and being the granddaughter of a car mechanic, I understood the basic principles of leverage. That's how you could raise a two-ton car off the ground with nothing but your body weight and relatively tiny jack.

"I am worried about my friend's safety and the safety of her children. Is a silly little appointment mix-up more important than getting my friend the help she needs?"

That did it for the tall woman by the file cabinet. Without preamble, she leaned over the receptionist's shoulder. "Bring her on back. You can come with."

"But—" The receptionist drew herself up, puffing up with anger. "I make those decisions."

"No, you don't," said the tall woman with intelligent eyes. "I'm the head nurse. This is a medical decision, not a clerical one."

That left the receptionist sputtering and fuming, but I didn't much care. Instead, I grabbed Kiki by the hand and dragged her toward the door as it swung open. Kiki protested, but her complaints were half-hearted. The other women stared after us, not that I cared.

"I'm Jacey," said Miss Intelligent Eyes. "Let's put you right here. This is Dr. Gretski's office. He's with another patient, but I'll get him right away. It's Lowenstein, right? Lowenstein-Detweiler, right? Let me go pull your chart. Won't be but a second. Can I bring you any coffee? Decaf? Green tea? Good. I'll have Marcy get it for you. Just ignore her frowny face."

With that, she closed the door firmly behind her.

"I can't believe you did that," Kiki said. "I'm not really in any distress. You're a dear friend, but you've gone overboard, Cara."

"Maybe."

"There's nothing wrong with me. Nothing serious. I just need to buck up and accept my responsibilities. I've just been a little weepy lately. That's all."

Time for a good distraction. Or two. Or three. A photo of the good doctor holding a sailfish prompted me to tell Kiki about my new hometown. "Look at that fish! Did I ever tell you that Stuart, Florida, is the Sailfish Capital of the World? It sure is. Wait until you come and visit, Kiki. You'll love the cool old cottage I've moved into on Jupiter Island. You'll never guess who I saw yesterday when I was out walking my dog."

"Who?" she sounded mildly interested, but at least she wasn't complaining.

"Celine Dion. She was jogging. Wearing these great big sunglasses, little running shorts with the waistband rolled down and a matching top. So cute. Of course, her hair was in a ponytail as always, and some dude was riding his bike alongside of her. For protection, I guess. But she waved, and that's how I knew it was her because most joggers give you just this little head nod and keep on going, but it was like she was accustomed to—"

The door flew open. In walked a man with a full head of gray hair and a stylish pair of round tortoiseshell glasses. The harried expression on his face told me he wasn't really happy about us being shoehorned into his schedule.

Big whoop.

"What seems to be the problem, Kiki? I just saw you, what? Ten days ago? Everything going all right?" As he slid into his oversized brown leather chair, Jacey opened the door and handed him a thick file with colored letter tabs on the edge.

"I'm fine." Kiki's tone was flatter than a piece of paper.

"She is not fine," I said. "She's crying in the shower every morning. She shared with me her concerns that she won't be able to take care of all three children. I'm her best friend, Cara Mia Delgatto. I've known Kiki for years, and I've never seen her this way. Usually she gets all excited about crafting projects, but not now. And do you know what she calls Ty? She calls him 'that baby.' Just ask her what she's looking forward to, would you? I did, and she couldn't think of anything.

Finally, she came up with Valentine's Day and then she started to cry."

Gretski looked from me to Kiki to Jacey, who gave him a subtle nod of the head. His eyes widened and his hands shook as he fingered the papers in the file jacket.

Grabbing a pen from his desk, he said, "Kiki, I'm going to ask you a couple of questions. I need you to answer honestly. I want you to talk and you alone. Is that clear, Ms. Delgatto?"

"Perfectly. Fire away, pal."

"All right," he said, as he took a long, deep inhale. "Since the baby was born, have you been bothered by feeling down, depressed or hopeless?"

The room drowned in silence. It was thick and heavy, a worrisome weight on my shoulders. Had I been right about my friend's condition? Or was I practicing medicine without a license? Instead of looking over at Kiki, I simply reached for her hand and held it. That simple gesture broke open the dam of pent-up feelings. Big tears welled up, spilled over and ran down her face. With her free hand, she flicked them away until Jacey handed her a fresh box of tissues.

"I, um, I'm not sure I can cope, you see. I wonder how I'll do it. I mean, how I'll do everything. Take care of the kids, my husband, my mother, my sisters, and the store. See, it's all a bit much. M-m-my mother probably needs to go into a care facility, but my sisters are waiting until I can discuss it with them. I know she'll think she should come live with me. Sheila, that's my mother-in-law, she's in rehab for alcoholism, and she's not getting better, and I miss her. A lot. Cara's down in Florida, except now. Detweiler loves me, but he's had two bad marriages already, and I disappointed him when I had Ty at home and his mother, Thelma, I thought she liked me but..." with that she dissolved completely into noisy, shuddering sobs. I leaned out from my chair so I could wrap my arms around her. Softly I patted her back and murmured comforting sounds.

The door flew open, nearly hitting Jacey. Detweiler came racing in. He dropped to his knees in front of Kiki. "Sweetheart? You okay? Shhh. It's going to be all right."

"I see," said Dr. Gretski. "Well, it's a good thing that you stopped in today, Kiki. I think we can get you back on track."

PART IV

59

~Cara Mia Delgatto~

Dr. Wade Gretski wrote Kiki a prescription for an antidepressant, a generic drug called fluoxetine, otherwise known as Prozac. "This won't kick in for a couple of weeks."

"What does she do until then?" Detweiler was standing over his wife, rubbing her shoulders.

"Uh, she takes it easy," said Gretski.

"That's all you have to offer?" I was almost amused. How could he send her back out into the world knowing that she wouldn't get relief for two weeks?

"Jacey? Any ideas?" Gretski seemed eager to bug out, and frankly, I wasn't very impressed with the man. "Jacey knows a lot about this. She did a paper on it. I'll let her take over, if you don't mind. Kiki? Make another appointment with me so I can see you in two weeks."

With that he was gone.

Jacey slipped into his chair. Steepling her fingers, she leaned closer to us and spoke in a calm, authoritative way. "Actually, there's a lot you can do. This isn't Dr. Gretski's forte. You have to understand that in med school, if it can't be cut or fixed with a pill, they try to ignore the problem. But I'm going to give you the name of a good friend of mine, an acupuncturist. Believe it or not, there are many studies that show a faster relief from depression, a more long lasting relief, and a more profound relief when acupuncture is used. Especially in conjunction with fluoxetine. In fact, while I wouldn't tell you to toss Dr. Gretski's prescription away. I'm thinking you won't need another script. The acupuncture will give you dramatic results, fast."

"Needles?" Detweiler rubbed his chin. "How can they help?"

"In Chinese medicine, the practitioner concentrates on helping the body heal itself. Depression is a problem caused by stagnation of energy. The needles act as conductors, helping the electric pathways of the body reconnect and recharge."

"But will they hurt?" I wondered.

"Not much. Have you ever plucked a hair? That's what it feels like. Once in a while, the doctor will place a needle in a sensitive spot and that can sting, but it goes away pretty quickly. In fact, most people fall asleep during treatments. Even with the needles waving in the air."

Detweiler didn't look totally convinced. He asked, "What else can Kiki do? Or can we do for her?"

"I can suggest a great vitamin supplement. Lifting weights has proven extremely beneficial. Doing tai chi is incredibly helpful because it works to harmonize the body's energy, too. Getting good sleep is a must. I suggest you take a hot bath in Epsom salts with a touch of lavender oil added to them. That lowers the body's temperature, which in turn, promotes good sound sleep."

She wrote all this down for Kiki. We got up and thanked Jacey.

"Why didn't you become a doctor?" Kiki asked, after the nurse gave her a big hug.

"My parents explained to me that women don't go to medical school. Silly, right? But back then, I didn't think it was an option. I'm a licensed nurse practitioner, and believe it or not, I love working with Wade. That's why I married him."

"Oh!" I laughed, and so did Kiki and Detweiler.

"He's a good guy, but he's still a guy. He might not know a lot about alternative medicine, but he's always willing to listen. Did I mention you might want to take yoga classes? Those are helpful, too. Tell you what. Here's my phone number. If you have any questions, send me a text-message. I'll get back to you as soon as possible."

Kiki took the business card and studied it. "How do you know all this?"

Jacey's face changed. "My older sister had postpartum depression. Twenty years ago. It didn't end well. I vowed then and there to do as much research as I could into the problem. That's why I'm totally serious about you calling me. It's my way of reconnecting with my sister, even though she's gone. Every time I help another woman through a postpartum depression, I'm doing for that person what I couldn't do for her."

60

Kiki and I waited in the prescription drop-off line at the local CVS pharmacy. Once we'd gotten Jacey involved, the entire visit to Dr. Gretski had taken less than twenty minutes. On our way out, she'd hugged both Kiki and me, saying, "I'll have a talk with our receptionist. She's well-meaning but over-zealous. Cara? I'm glad you stood up to her."

Kiki sent me a smile. "You forgive me for being nasty with you? For fighting you about going to see Gretski?"

"Of course I do. I'll probably be even more forgiving and more thankful when you feel better. Needles? Can you believe that? Who would guess that being poked with needles would raise your spirits? Doesn't make a bit of sense to me."

"Yup. Thanks heaps, Cara, for turning me into a human pincushion." To that, she added a playful punch to my bicep. Although we hadn't walked out of the doctor's office with a solution, we'd been given a more powerful medicine: hope. Kiki's whole demeanor seemed buoyant.

"I bet you'll find a way to scrapbook this, and the needles."

"I'll certainly do my best." We got to the counter and Kiki handed over the slip of paper.

"We're backed up. This is going to take at least twenty minutes." The young man wore a badge that claimed he was a pharmacy tech. To me, he looked about the same age as my son, Tommy. That's life. You get older and the rest of the world gets younger. But then, what's the alternative?

"Okay." Kiki turned to me. "How about if we grab a cart and cruise the aisles? We might as well enjoy ourselves because once we get my pills, we need to hurry back to the store. I'm feeling the need to express myself, if you get my drift."

We combed the sale shelves and scored two half-price, cinnamon scented candles, Anya's favorite. That gave Kiki the idea to run up front and grab a sales circular. From that, we ripped out a coupon for two-for-one nail polish. It took us a while to decide but we chose a sunrise orange and a cool, cobalt blue. Next we hit the snacks display. The Blue Diamond almonds were on sale, so we grabbed four bags. Two were for the store, and two for her house. A circular rack nearby was loaded with postcards. I chose a colorful collage featuring the famous Clydesdales. That would go to Skye Blue, who loves horses. For MJ, I found a picture of the historic Old Cathedral, because she's a history buff. For Honora, I hoped to get a postcard that showed photos from the St. Louis Miniature Museum, one of my favorite places in the whole world. Instead, I settled for one of the Robert Campbell House, detailing the interior of a home built by a fur trapper. Last but not least, I found two postcards cut in the shape of beer steins. One would go to Sid, my young computer guru, and the other would go to Tommy.

By the time Kiki's prescription was ready, we'd loaded up the cart.

After we pushed it toward the front counter and stood in yet another line, Kiki turned to me. "This is how you know someone is a true friend. You took a risk. I could have gotten so angry at you that it ruined our relationship, but you dared to stay the course. You cared more about me and my health than about me getting mad at you. When that receptionist didn't want to let me see Dr. Gretski, you had a perfect opportunity to turn tail and run. But you didn't."

"That's because my idea of fun is running up and down the rows of a CVS drugstore. Do we know how to have a good time or what?"

"Fun is when friendship collides with the mundane. You mean the world to me, Cara."

I hugged her. "Promise you'll come visit me in Florida?"

"I promise."

61

~ Kiki ~

I'll be honest: I had done everything possible to avoid going back to see Dr. Gretski. I could just imagine the word LOSER written on my forehead in neon lights. HYPOCRITE wouldn't fit because there were too many letters.

Here I was, bad-mouthing Bernice Stottlemeyer, saying what a horrible mother she would be, and why she was totally unsuited for parenthood. All the while, I was feeling no affection for my baby. Sure, I wouldn't have hurt him, but wasn't it as bad or worse to be missing that gushing, overwhelming love that would cause a mother to walk in front of a train for her child?

To top it off, I spent most of my waking moments puzzling over what had happened to Bonnie Gossage's baby. Me! The woman who left her infant in the hands of a nanny. The irony wasn't lost on me.

Maybe that was one reason that Thelma Detweiler's comments stung as badly as a hornet sting. See, a bee stings you once and dies. But a hornet can stab you over and over and over. Thelma had found my soft spot. I couldn't defend myself because she had a point. (No pun intended.)

But on my way back to the store with Cara, this sense of calm came over me. No, I wasn't myself. True, I needed help. But it was on the horizon, beckoning me to keep struggling toward the light.

Just saying out loud how bummed I felt took a huge pressure off. Holding it all inside had been difficult. While I hated seeing the hurt look in Detweiler's eyes, and hearing him blame himself, I knew I'd done the right thing by explaining how frightened and alone I was. His hug had always made me feel loved and cherished, but never more than when I was sitting in front of Wade Gretski's desk and admitting that I couldn't cope. The fact that Detweiler hugged me harder meant we'd tackle the problem together, as I'd once hoped we'd face anything that life threw me.

Yeah, I got my mojo back.

This crop was going to be fun!

62

We had two separate projects planned for our evening at Time in a Bottle. Participants could dedicate pages to anyone or anything or any place that they loved. For this, Cara and I had rounded up a ton of die cut shapes, printed embellishments, and stickers. We'd also cut lengths of red and white butcher string, similarly colored ribbons, and lace into smaller amounts and packaged it in baggies. Of course, Margit had ordered a stunning assortment of papers.

The second aspect had come to me in a flash as we walked through the CVS. We made a quick detour and ran by the nearest Dollar Store. There I swept all the heart-shaped boxes of chocolates into our cart. Thirty dollars-worth.

"You are welcome to use any of these containers as a vault," I explained. "By that I mean, you can create those "I love" pages, but cut them into a heart-shape and bind them together to make a miniature album that'll fit inside an empty chocolate box."

The oooohhs and aaaaahs rose to an almost deafening pitch as women sorted through the boxes. "Of course, I would never,

ever waste chocolate," I said. "My beautiful assistant is here to share the spoils with you."

Cara took a slow turn around the table, offering every attendee a chance to pick out a wrapped candy or two from a large plastic bowl we'd found. By dumping out all the chocolates and collecting them in one place, we'd emptied the cardboard shells so everyone could see how to fit their mini-album inside. We'd also made sure there wasn't any fighting over type of candy.

Lee Alderton carefully chose a milk chocolate covered caramel. "Kiki, I have to say, you really know how to throw a party. As I was leaving the house, Jeff wondered why on earth I'd go out in the cold on a night like this. I told him that you'd make it worthwhile. The ideas you come up with are super, but it's the little extras that really, really make us love you."

I blushed with happiness. Lee's one of the nicest people I know, and I've been to dinner parties at her house where she has a printed out menu card and a place card for her guests. Not to mention, stunning low flower arrangements so you can see across the table. She's into details herself, so this was high praise.

A blast of cold air caused the papers on the table to levitate. Margit had left. Clancy wasn't around. Cara had checked in our attendees. I craned my neck around the shelf units we roll to one side to give us more room when we crop. Deena Edmonds strode in, flicking snow off her heavy coat. With a tug of her cap, more snow went flying off in all directions.

"Deena! Come join us."

"I didn't sign up," she admitted. "Do you have room?"

"Another person canceled at the last minute," Cara said. "Here's a spot for you."

As Deena got settled, she explained, "My husband told me to leave so he could bond with our munchkin. At first, I thought about staying home, what with the weather and all, but he insisted. It's probably good for him, right? A chance to be the parent in charge of Emma."

"Absolutely," Kiki agreed. "When you're there, you're the default key. The men tend to holler for help rather than figure out what to do. It's best to get out of their way and let them see that they're capable."

"Easy for you to say," Lee teased. "You've got Brawny. You know that Jeff and I lived in the UK for a year. They consider child care a profession there and take it seriously. You hire a child minder there, and you know you're getting a person who's been thoroughly vetted and trained."

"That must be a relief," Amy Romanov said, letting a hand curve protectively over her growing belly. "After what happened with Bonnie Gossage's baby, I think I'll be too afraid to leave my child with anybody but family. Has anybody heard any more? I saw the appeal the Gossages made on TV."

No one had. That put a damper on the conversation temporarily.

"Cara, when are you going back?" Deena asked. "You must miss Florida and the nice weather." "The baptism ceremony is Sunday and I'm leaving Monday," Cara said.

A lump formed in my throat. I grabbed a bottle of water and swallowed hard. I would miss Cara, and all she'd done for me. But I reminded myself that I'd promised to fly down and visit her. With that cheery prospect in mind, I unwrapped a caramel and popped it into my mouth.

The hours flew by. I passed around photos of Ty. Cara shared pictures of her new home on Jupiter Island. Most of my guests shared pictures of beloved grandkids or pets. Lee Alderton had a terrific photo of her family visiting France. Deena's snapshots of Emma delighted all of us. The tiny pink bows taped to the wispy gold curls proved too cute for words.

The evening proceeded with nary a hiccup, and with a nod to my friend, I'd encouraged the participants to, "Finish up, ladies. We need to call it a night." While Cara rang up purchases and tallied open tabs, I went from woman to woman, as a subtle reminder for each to put away her supplies.

Deena carefully slipped photos of Emma back inside a plastic pouch.

"Deena, do you remember Jana? From your class?"

"Uh-huh. I bumped into her at the Kids R Us store two days ago when we had that one warm afternoon. For all of two hours the temp got above freezing. Some of the ice and snow even melted. She was carrying her baby in one of those car seats. All bundled up. She said she hated to take the baby outside, because of how cold it was, and she wouldn't have done so except she'd run out of diapers."

63

Saturday I worked only a half day, so I'd have plenty of time to get ready for the baptism on Sunday.

Detweiler had been raised a Methodist. I'd been raised Episcopalian. Anya was a Jew, and she'd been working hard to get ready for her bat mitzvah later in the summer. Erik had been baptized in an unaffiliated church out in California, where he'd lived with his mother and stepfather at the time.

Obviously, deciding how to raise Ty could be an ecumenical challenge.

Over the years, since I first married George Lowenstein, I'd spent many hours in temple. Whenever our family had needed spiritual counseling or plain old good sense, we'd turned to Rabbi Sarah. As a leader of a Reform Judaism congregation, Rabbi Sarah was the most accepting religious leader I'd ever known until Laurel brought Father Joe into our lives.

Calling Joseph Riley by the title of "Father," totally upset Erik's apple cart. After losing Van Lauber, the only father he'd known, and coming to accept Detweiler as his new daddy, hearing Anya call Laurel's boyfriend "Father Joe" freaked our son out. Erik was convinced that he was going to be shifted to yet another household—and torn away from another loving dad.

Nor was my mother-in-law Sheila thrilled about welcoming an Episcopal priest into our midst and according him a religious title.

But Joe was the embodiment of the man he followed, Jesus Christ. As such, he was more concerned with calming the restless waters of a storm than sticking to dogma and watching a boat sink. "Call me Joe," he'd suggested, getting down on his knees so that he and Erik were face to face. "Is that all right with you?"

Those teary brown eyes that had seen so much sadness and loss already blinked back emotion. Mulling it over, Erik studied Joe's face and considered the offer. We held our collective breath until the boy said, "Okay. Fine." A pairing of words he'd copied from his older sister.

In planning the baptism, I did a data-dump on Joe. "We aren't members of your congregation, I want Rabbi Sarah there, please be respectful of the Jewish portion of our family, the Detweilers are eager to see this child baptized, Cara Mia and Hadcho will be godparents, but Hadcho is Native American and for all I know he worships the gods of his tribe, and..."

"Relax." Joe slipped his arm through mine. "It's all good. We'll hold it after the regular church service on Sunday afternoon. A small gathering. I'll say a few prayers and bless the baby, welcoming him. Rabbi Sarah and I will coordinate our efforts, because I'm particularly fond of the prayer where the Jews say every Sabbath exhorting their sons, 'May you be like Abraham and Isaac.'"

"But they don't. I hate to correct you, but it's, 'May God make you like Ephraim and Manasseh,'" I said. "Anyway, Rabbi Sarah will say the priestly blessing and include Anya and Erik, too. I've already asked her."

"Hmm," Joe said.

That's when it dawned on me that I'd corrected a priest. My stomach turned a flip. How totally disrespectful could I get? Oh, golly!

He peered at me curiously. "I forget sometimes what a truly extraordinary woman you are, Kiki Lowenstein Detweiler. You bring people together under a tent of love. That's remarkable." With that, he gave me a hug and added, "Don't forget that Laurel and I have the paperwork you gave us so that we can be your children's legal guardians should anything ever happen. Not that it will, but it was the most wonderful responsibility anyone ever invested in us. But you need to take a copy and keep it in a safe place. Ours will go in a lock box."

"I will."

64

Pancakes are a tradition in our family on Sunday mornings. This particular morning, Cara and Detweiler took turns pouring batter into funny shapes. She's a big fan of Mickey Mouse's silhouette and her efforts to replicate the three interlocking circles were spot on.

"Wow! That's great!" Erik was tickled by her artistic efforts.

"Y'all need a family vacation in Orlando. We've got to get this child to Disney World," Cara said.

"I took my wee master there frequently," Brawny answered with a huff. In honor of the upcoming ceremony, she was dressed in her clan's best dress tartans, a darker version of her normal attire. "Are ye thinking I failed in my responsibilities as a child minder? Miss Cara, keep it up and you'll be feeling the sharp end of my stick."

"Oh, no! Not the sharp end of her stick," wailed Erik in mock distress.

That sent everyone into gales of laughter.

After eating our fill, the rest of us hurriedly got ready for church. Brawny had sewn a new dress for me, a simple navy A-line that buttoned down the front so I could easily nurse Ty.

Anya had a navy skirt, crisp white blouse and short gray sweater. Erik matched her in navy slacks, a white polo shirt, and a gray sweater. Detweiler looked dashing in a new navy suit. And the baby? He outshone us all.

Shortly after Ty was born, Leighton had brought over an elaborate christening gown that had been in the Haversham family for centuries. "I'll understand if you have no interest in it, but Lorraine insisted that I at least be courageous enough to offer."

Although I'd half expected Detweiler to guffaw and send the man on his way, instead he tenderly lifted the fine fabric and held it to the light. "To think that generations of good people before Ty have worn this makes it a real honor, Leighton. Thank you."

We'd agreed to pack in the diaper bag an adorable little boy's suit in navy and white that Laurel and Joe had given us as well. That way, we could change Ty out of the keepsake after the ceremony and put the gown away for the future.

"Who knows," Deweiler said. "Maybe one day, Anya's babies will wear it, too."

The idea of one family being connected to another through the ages brought a tender smile to my husband's face. But it also brought up a tender subject.

"Who all will be coming? From your side?" I asked as I waited for him to hook my single strand of pearls behind my neck. I knew my sisters would bring my mother if they could manage to slip her a Xanax first. She'd grown increasingly unpredictable, emotionally up and down, oscillating between cheerful and distraught in the course of hours. Soon we'd have to find a new home for her, as leaving her by herself grew increasingly more dangerous. Of course, Leighton and Lorraine would join us, but because her MS had recently flared up, we'd pointed out they could simply join us at Cara Mia's, the restaurant that the Delgattos owned for years. There we'd have a celebratory family meal. Not that we didn't want Lorraine there for the service, but there was no need for her to brave the cold twice. The group from my store—Clancy, Margit, Rebekkah and her father, Horace Goldfader—had all been invited and were expected to come. As I fingered the pearl necklace that George Lowenstein had given me after Anya was born, I wondered if there was a pearl for each person who brought luster to my life. When I put it away, I'd have to name each creamy bead, and see if the number predicted that I had more friends yet to add.

"My sisters and their husbands, Emily, Hadcho," he paused. "And yes, my parents, too. Kiki, I know what happened with my mother on Friday. How she acted toward you."

I didn't turn around. Instead, I fiddled with my earrings. "Oh?"

"After you left, she came in and gave Brawny a piece of her mind."

"Really?" I took my time rather than meet his eyes. Being careful not to squirt him, I sprayed myself with the Bulgari scent he'd gotten me for Christmas. Crystalline was delicate, floral, and woodsy, but the spray container was intricately shaped. Half the time I splurted the perfume in my face. I'd learned to study the bottle carefully before spraying.

"You'll be pleased to know that Brawny stood up for you. In fact, she phoned me and suggested I get here right away. She was having problems getting my mother to calm down. Hadcho gave me a ride. I've never seen him so put out with my mother. He's definitely Team Kiki."

"That's too bad. About your mother." I didn't mean a word of it. After the visit to the doctor, I'd decided to put my problems with Thelma Detweiler on hold, indefinitely. Sure, I knew she'd come to the ceremony today, and probably join us afterward at

Cara Mia's, but I'd intended to put as much physical distance as possible between Thelma and myself.

She'd been right, in that I wasn't as motherly toward Ty as I should be. But she'd been wrong in hurling accusations. If she had broached the subject with me, treated me with respect, maybe I would have stuck up for myself and been more forceful when I talked to Dr. Gretski. She could have been my ally rather than my enemy. I had needed her, and she'd failed me.

No, it was more than failing me. Thelma had turned on me, the way a trusted dog does when it abandons its loyalty and bites its owner in the face.

That shamed me and my cheeks warmed with embarrassment. Thelma wasn't a dog. The analogy might be apt, but I'd gone too far, even if it was nothing more than a thought that occurred to me.

"After that happened, Hadcho and I went back to work," Detweiler continued. "If you recall, that's the day we visited Dr. Gretski. Good old Hadcho dropped me off. I owe that dude meals for a year to thank him for his service as a cabbie. Yesterday, Dad and I met for breakfast. You won't have any problems with my mother today. I wanted you to know that because I didn't want you worrying through the ceremony. They will be coming, but Dad's promised she won't be upsetting you. Just so you know."

With that, I turned to face him. My husband opened his arms and gathered me up. After kissing the tender spot on my throat right below my ear, he said, "I've got your back. Now and forever."

I responded in a husky tone that came from a place I thought had gone out of business, "And I've got yours."

65

Father Joe and Rabbi Sarah performed the most amazing ceremony ever. Sure, it had been a challenge for her, because Jews don't believe in original sin and that's the basis for baptism. But Joe went easy on the sin and heavy on the Welcome to this wonderful world and people who love you. And so the two clerics, both wearing somber black robes, represented both the old and new faiths we were combining.

Poor Anya missed Sheila terribly, especially at times like this. Visiting the church reminded my daughter that she was the last Lowenstein standing, thanks to Sheila's marriage to Robbie Holmes. Detweiler seemed totally absorbed in the miracle of our son—but bless his heart, he still noticed Anya's hunched shoulders and watched as she covered her mouth rather than let a sob escape. With a quick and graceful movement, he passed Ty to Laurel. Then he beckoned to my daughter and she hurried to find a place under his sheltering arm. I didn't leave my spot from beside Rabbi Sarah, as moving would have put me too close to Thelma. She'd done an admirable job of avoiding my eyes, and I'd extended the courtesy back to her in equal measure.

Cara and Hadcho had bookended Detweiler and me,

fulfilling a silent pact that I was to be protected. Laurel stood between her fiancé Joe and Detweiler, her lovely features rendered even more other-worldly than usual because she adores all children, and mine in particular. She and Joe seemed usually dialed in to each other. I could only assume they were anticipating their upcoming marriage and the start of their own family.

My sisters held onto my mother, the way a nervous dog owner clutches the choke chain, keeping her away from anything she could pee on, bite into, or otherwise destroy.

Leighton held Lorraine's left hand and Brawny managed to hold her old employer's elbow, while Erik burrowed close to his aunt by wrapping his arms around her waist. This whole business of making room in his world for a baby brought out the good and the bad aspects of being a five year old. Saturday afternoon when Ty threw a wonky (as described by Brawny), Erik suggested we send Ty back and get a new baby that didn't fuss so much. "Or a guinea pig. Like Giggles. He don't make lots of noise. Just squeaks." Horace Goldfader wiped his eyes as he rested one hand on his daughter's shoulder. At times like this, we all missed Dodie Goldfader, but we also recognized what a blessing she had been, because it had been Dodie, through her love of scrapbooking, who'd brought us all together. Margit and Clancy stood next to Detweiler's sisters and brothers-in-law. Emily, his niece, stood quietly to one side and waited for Anya, a thoughtful gesture from a thirteen-year-old.

Colored sunlight filtered through the stained glass windows and dimly lit the nave of the church. As a girl, I'd been told that a church was designed to look like a ship turned upside down. Certainly, from my vantage point, I could stare up at the ribs and imagine us floating on a sea of tears. Sorrow for George Lowenstein, who'd done so much wrong in his life but also so much right, and who'd fathered my fabulous daughter. Sadness for

Sheila who'd initially seemed as tough as a fieldstone wall, but who'd turned out to be a crumbling surface worn down by regrets. Bitter tears for Brenda, Detweiler's second wife, a drug addict, mingled with real regret for Gina, his first wife and Erik's mother, whose love affair with a black policeman brought our adorable five-year-old boy into this world. The soaring lines of the roof. What was a life but a complex orchestration of loss and adaptation with a few crystalline moments of pure joy sprinkled in?

And what was a family except a tribe committed to sharing those times together?

66

"You've got everything? Photos? Chargers? Cords?" I asked as I opened the driver's side door of my car. I managed to avoid a chunk of melting ice as it fell off the gutter of the garage and landed at my feet. The Monday of Cara's departure had rolled around far too quickly. I couldn't believe she was heading back down to Florida today.

"Sure do." Cara nodded as she climbed into the passenger side seat of my BMW. A drip of wet snow splattered her shoulder before she closed the door. "Finally, you're getting a break in the weather. Might even warm up enough to melt off the snow later in the week."

"I sure hope so. I'm sick of this. It's pretty at first, but the sand and exhaust turns it gray and yucky. I'm also tired of being cold, even though I'm not as cold as I was before I got pregnant. That's hormones for you." Watching the view behind me, I backed out slowly. "We're going to be early."

"It was nice of Detweiler to take my rental car back for me. That meant we could spend more time together before my plane takes off."

"How about if we get your bag checked and then grab a

coffee from Starbucks in the terminal. It isn't Kaldi's, but it'll do, right?"

"Absolutely."

I'd forgotten the sound of tires on dry pavement. In the convertible, it's louder than in a hard-top. "Remember how there are all those yellow daffodils planted along Highway 40? To me that's always the best sign of spring."

"You'll have to send me pictures of it," Cara said. "Speaking of spring, plan to come down for Easter or Spring Break, okay? You'll be able to get a good dose of sunshine. Anya and Erik will love the beach outside my house. You and Detweiler and Ty can have my room. Brawny can sleep upstairs. I have a pull out bed in my office. The kids can have the guest room and I'll sleep on the sofa in my living room. We'll have a blast."

"We'll figure something out." I couldn't help but smile. The ocean right outside your door? How cool was that? And the thought of collecting shells? Doing projects with Cara and her pal, Skye Blue? My mouth watered at the thought. "Lee Alderton made me promise we'd come visit her and Jeff, too. We might bring Emily Volker along too. Give the cousins a bit of a chance to build memories. If we do that, you'll have a house full."

I pulled onto 40, speeding up to match the rest of the traffic. From there to Lambert, Cara and I discussed the different places we could see when we visited. Her list was extensive, forcing me to realize that Orlando might get the bulk lot of publicity, but there's a Florida beyond the rides, movie tie-ins, and touristy traps. Our discussion kept us busy until after I parked the car. Cara had packed lightly, but I'd loaded her up with scrapbook supplies to take home. Paper is heavy. It tends to get tattered edges if you don't ship it properly. I'd rolled sheets tightly and stuffed them into empty paper towel tubes to protect them. A few papers with tiny patterns on them would be perfect for

Honora, the miniaturist who worked out of Cara's store, to use in tiny projects.

"How do you come up with all those ideas for recycling and reusing what you find?" I asked, as we passed a sign for a furniture store on our way to the airport. "I like to think I'm creative, but what you all do is amazing."

Cara gave a hoot of a laugh and tugged on her purple scarf. Her bright knit cap set off the reddish highlights in her dark hair. "Remember how I didn't think I was creative or crafty? You might say I was a closeted crafter. Seriously, though, I've learned so much from Skye. She always studies an object and asks, 'What if?' While she does, she'll turn the piece upside down or on its side.

"That works?"

"Sure does."

"I can't imagine it working for me." I wagged my head back and forth. "No way."

We were both quiet as I took the airport exit. "No long term parking for me!"

"No way!" Cara agreed, as we found a space and unloaded her gear.

"You need silence to be creative," she said as we walked toward the terminal entrance. "The quiet seems to incubate ideas. I get my best "A-ha!" moments when I'm all alone walking the beach. Or in the shower. Did you know that Agatha Christie said the best time to plot a book was while you're washing dishes? Water helps. If there's too much noise, you can't hear the creative ideas bubble up. They're like soap bubbles, floating just out of reach, and you have to grab them fast before they sail away."

"There isn't much silence in my life," but even as I said that, I knew I wasn't complaining. I was simply stating a fact. "I'll really have to plan to find it."

"Yes, you will. Especially with three kids in the house. It was a beautiful christening. Absolutely perfect. I'm so glad you invited me to be Ty's godmother. Did you get things straightened out with Thelma? I know I'm being nosy, but I had to ask." Cara stepped onto the moving sidewalk with her rolling bag behind her. She was careful to move so I could take my place behind her and not block other patrons. They could pass us on the left if they wanted to.

I sighed. "Louis took her by the arm and escorted her to a seat at the far end of the table. We didn't talk. That was fine by me."

"And your mother? How'd she do?" Cara asked after we'd ordered our coffees and settled into a booth so we wouldn't spill them. She'd decided to leave her boots with me. I'd bring them to her when we came down to Florida. Instead, she wore the cutest Keds designed by Taylor Swift. The black and gray leopard pattern played off her oversized gray sweater and black yoga pants. In Florida, she'd told me that she mainly wore Lily Pulitzer florals, but for up here, she'd dug out her dark colors again.

"She flirted with Leighton the whole meal." I laughed, thinking back on how embarrassed her behavior had made Anya. "No matter how many times she's been told that Leighton and Lorraine live together, Mom doesn't get it. My sisters and I are going to visit various assisted living facilities next week. Mom can't be left alone any more. Last week, Amanda was cleaning in Mom's room. She decided to vacuum behind the bed. When she pulled it away from the wall, she heard this ca-chink, ca-chink noise rattling in the hose. Turns out, Mom's been dumping her medications behind her headboard. When Amanda emptied the canister of the vacuum cleaner, she poured out an entire cup full of pills!"

67

I choked up as I waved goodbye to my friend, and Cara disappeared through the airport security check point. The coffee had gone through me, so a quick pit stop was in order. Coming out of a stall, I bumped into Amy and we exchanged hugs. "I can't wait to see your baby," she said. "I'd like to see Deena's too. Maybe when the weather's better, right? I'm so glad mine isn't coming until early May. This cold is wicked, right? Only an idiot would take a baby out in the cold when it's like this."

I agreed. "So you aren't due until May?"

"That's right. I'll take maternity leave then. You're still planning to do another 'A Star Is Born' album class, aren't you? I thought about attending the one you're having on Friday, but I figured if you were repeating it, I'd come after my baby's born so I can use the photos."

She talked so fast I could barely keep up, especially since an emotional fog had descended on me after saying goodbye to Cara.

"Dan, my husband, works for the airlines. He'll stay home, too. I'm so glad I didn't marry a pilot. I almost did. They would have to try and change their flight schedules if they wanted to stay home for a while. That would be so hard, right? Sure, it would mean more money, but I'm glad that when Dan came home he decided to work as an air traffic controller and stay in the same town."

We agreed to stay in touch, and she walked me part-way to the parking garage. Once outside, I noticed the signs for long-term parking. The directions to get there seemed convoluted. Not surprising. After they lay out an airport, they ought to force all the head honchos to drive around. They'd quickly see that their signage stinks. For example, the terminal signs to Lambert are mainly hidden by metal crossbeams. You can't figure out what it's telling you until the very last minute. And the route to the long-term area? Totally counter-intuitive.

Just following it in my head sent a shiver up my spine, as I thought about Bernice and the fate that had awaited her. Whatever possessed that silly woman to agree to meet someone—anyone!—in such a remote and secluded place.

To keep my mind busy, I decided to play her "What if?" as I tooled along I-270.

A few miles later, my car came to a standstill. The scent of exhaust wafted through my air vents as I joined a long line of cars. An accident must have blocked the south-bound lanes. Unfortunately, the nearest exit was behind me. I had no choice but to poke along at the pace of a limping snail, leaving more space between me and the next car so I didn't have to inhale the fumes. I found myself thinking about Thelma. She had underestimated her son's loyalty to me. She'd also underestimated me. Sure, I was having a tough time, but I'd still been a good mother.

Then it hit me. "She'd underestimated me." I repeated it, feeling the words in my mouth. Letting the meaning soak in.

What if...we'd underestimated Jana and overestimated Bernice?

What if...Jana was smarter than we thought? Maybe Jana had set Bernice up, instead of the other way around? What if Jana knew the long-term parking area like the back of her hand? And Bernice didn't? Wouldn't it make sense for the killer to choose somewhere familiar? That was exactly how organized killers worked. They planned, they plotted, and they came prepared.

What if ...Jana had taken maternity leave? That day when she came to the store, when Lee was there, Jana had said she needed to get back to work. Maybe no one reported the baby because Jana had been appropriately cautious about exposing the child to bad weather?

The temperature on the day of the abduction had been sub-zero with wind chill warnings. What did we know about women who abducted infants? They considered themselves to be good mothers.

What would a good mother of a newborn do when faced with such inclement weather?

A good mother would make sure the baby wasn't out in the cold for longer than absolutely necessary.

I called Detweiler. He listened carefully to what I had to say. "You make a lot of good points. If you're right, it's possible that Jana is home on maternity leave. That's why no one has reported a suspicious birth. It's also possible that she works for an airline or a business connected to the airport. Either way, there's a lot to follow up on."

68

After running home and nursing Ty, I left him in Brawny's capable care. But not before thanking her for taking my side when Thelma Detweiler had come to call.

"*Aye,* she was in a right bad state. Worked herself up something fierce. But she behaved herself at the christening. Leads me to wonder what's twirling around in her head," Brawny said. "Detweiler told me about your visit to the doctor. I am kicking myself all the way down the football field and back for not noticing how ye were struggling. But dinna fash yourself, lassie. I'm here for ye." Her strong hand on my shoulder provided comfort.

"I know that, and I appreciate you, Brawny. I kept telling myself that I shouldn't feel overwhelmed. After all, I have you!"

"'Tis not a matter of logic. 'Tis a physical adjustment and more. Ye'll be fine. But ye need to tell me if I can do more for you."

Bolstered by her kindness and a hearty lunch of stew that she'd tucked into a Thermos for me, I drove to the store. Cara's suggestion about the quiet got me thinking. Instead of listening to the radio, I drove in the silence. She'd been right. The ambient noises of life had blocked the powerful voice of creativity in my head. I came up with all sorts of nifty ideas for new crops.

But it wasn't until I ran into Kaldi's and treated myself to tall cup of decaf that the real brainstorm hit me hard. Sure I'd been asking myself a lot of questions about Jana. But I hadn't asked myself the right question, the one that would open Door #1. In fact, I wouldn't have come up with it except that the adorable barista who handed me my hot drink also pointed to a sign-up sheet. "If you'll share your email address with us, we'll send you coupons and tell you about our specials."

"Oh, my word!" I stood there with my mouth open. "That's it!"

69

Once inside my car, I called Lee Alderton to ask a question. She answered on the first ring. "Lee, do you remember that young woman in the baby album class? You took her over to the sign-up sheets at my request. She did sign up for the 'A Star Is Born' class didn't she? I think she did, but I can't remember."

"She did. I told her she wouldn't want to miss any of your classes, especially one that was new. I saw her grab the pen and write down her email address. Then we took it to Margit so the girl could get her twenty-five percent discount. Why?"

"I'll tell you later, if I can. For now, thanks a million."

"Toodles!" and Lee disconnected the call.

Back at the store, I hurried to find Margit, who was teaching a class on how to knit socks using double needles. "Sorry, folks," I said, but I have to borrow Margit for a bit. I'll bring her back."

Seeing the dark look from a woman who was pulling out wrong stitches, I added, "This is an emergency. Honest."

Rather than talk in front of our guests, I hustled Margit to the back room. "Remember how we had that sign-up sheet for people who wanted the twenty-five percent discount? If they signed up in advance for my new class 'A Star is Born,' they got the discount right then?"

"Ja." Margit frowned at me. "What is the point of this? I have students waiting."

"The woman who stole Bonnie's baby signed up. Remember? Jana Higgins was the name she used. Lee Alderton took her over to the sign-up sheet. Lee saw her put down an email address and take the sheet to you so she'd get her discount."

"Ja, this is correct."

"Where is that email address?"

"In the computer. In the Constant Contact list. I do my job, Kiki." She drew herself up in a huffy stance.

"I know you do, dear heart. I'm simply trying to figure out a way we can get back in touch with her. Did you save the sign-up sheet?"

"Ach, nein." She shook her head sadly. "I am sorry."

"Is there any way we can find that address in the list? Does it put a date next to the addresses as you add them?"

"I do not know. But even so, that would be difficult. I add many, many addresses at once. I do this every month, two times."

"Rats. Okay, thanks. Go on back to your class."

70

I didn't want to call Detweiler again. I don't want to be one of those wives who phones her husband ten times a day, interrupting his work and making a general nuisance out of herself. Instead, I studied our upcoming class calendar. "A Star Is Born" was scheduled for this coming Friday. One reminder had already gone out, thanks to the ever-so conscientious Clancy.

She'd noted we had fifteen people signed up and paid in advance. That did me little good, because Jana Higgins had used cash again.

"Clancy?" I called her at home. "Do you have the email addresses for the people signed up to take the 'A Star Is Born' class?"

"Sure I do. Why?"

I explained what I wanted and she promised to send over a file.

I spent the next two hours trying and failing to concentrate on upcoming class projects. Although I checked my email repeatedly, the file did not come. I text-message Clancy again, she sent it again, but for whatever reason, it didn't load.

That shouldn't have surprised me. Because she was in Illinois and I was in Missouri, we had two different digital access carriers. Often they didn't play nicely with each other. This was one of those days.

I reminded myself that Jana had plans for coming back. At the very least, Detweiler and Hadcho could nab her when she did. But would she bring the baby? That was more of a question in my mind.

Monday dragged on and on, but still no email from Clancy. Finally, I suggested that she simply forward her file to Detweiler. I gave up on being "coy" and called him, explaining that Jana's address had to be one of the fifteen listed.

"Unless she lied," he said.

I sighed. "Yeah, you're right. Unless she lied. She might have signed up and given us a bogus email address so we can't track her."

"She still might show up for your class on Friday. Don't give up hope. We're following up on all the business connected to the airport. There's more of them than you would think. We're asking if they have women employees who are taking maternity leave."

"Sounds redundant to me. Who else takes maternity leave except for women?"

Detweiler's laugh warmed me through and through. "Babe, get with the program. Fathers take parental leave. I sure wish I could!"

"I do, too."

71

Tuesday morning dawned with the promise of temperatures soaring to the 40s. They didn't make it. Wednesday was a little better, and we nearly got up to freezing. First thing Thursday I had my first visit to the acupuncturist.

After we had left Dr. Gretski's office, Detweiler had remembered Leighton saying that Lorraine was seeing a Chinese medicine specialist. "There's also an acupuncturist and an herbalist who share the office with the specialist. I guess Western medicine has its limitations when it comes to treating MS. this Oriental wisdom seems to be helping Lorraine."

Cara immediately volunteered to phone the doctor's office and make an appointment for me. After the situation was explained to her, the acupuncturist was able to get me in quickly.

"What did she sound like? Asian?" Cara asked when I called her on the way back from my treatment.

"Actually, she's from Oklahoma."

"Come again?"

"Her married name is Rhonda Lee. Her husband is ABC, American Born Chinese, but she hails from a town on the border of Texas and Oklahoma. Wait until you hear her thick southern drawl. Nice as could be. Called me 'sugar.'"

"Did it hurt?"

"Like a mosquito sting."

"That's manageable."

"I agree," I said, as I pulled into a parking space at the side of my store.

"There has to be a story behind this," Cara said. "Tell me everything."

"Rhonda's grandmother was a Native American Indian. A healer. As soon as Brenda could walk, her grandmother was teaching her how to gather herbs and use them. High school and Brenda did not mix together well. After fighting with all the teachers and her mother, she took off hitchhiking until she landed in San Francisco. There she worked in a tiny herbalist shop, saving her money and getting her GED. After that, she applied to a college in California and got in. In addition to biology, she took Chinese and when the chance came up to study abroad, she went to Guangzhou. Took a semester off to study Chinese medicine. It was a good fit. She took a second and third semester off. Four years later, she met her husband. Her mother was dying of cancer, so she came back to the US, and there you go."

"Did it help?"

I laughed. "She warned me the results wouldn't be immediate."

"Have you heard anything from Bonnie? Jeremy? How're they doing?"

Through the phone came the soft roar of the ocean. I closed my eyes and tried to picture Cara standing there, her feet in the water.

"Oh, Cara. I called but Jeremy didn't want to talk. As for the baby, well, nothing has happened. Not yet. That woman who calls herself Jana Higgins gave me a fake email address. They've got cops checking out women on maternity leave. It just seems hopeless, but I've got my fingers crossed. If this warm weather continues, maybe she'll come to the crop on Friday night. It's not much, but..."

"I'll light a candle," she said.

72

Being "puncted" left me a little tired, so I went directly home and took what I planned as a short nap. Instead, I slept until dinner. Over spaghetti and meatballs, Detweiler asked me if it would be convenient for his sister Ginny to swing by the house right after lunch.

"Emily has been having growing pains. The pediatrician in Illinois says it's normal, but Ginny wants a second opinion, so she's bringing her here. To get her in to see someone, she's taking Emily out of school at noon." He paused and chuckled. "I guess Emily has been begging and begging Ginny to see her new cousin. I hope that's okay with you. I know you have that crop, and we're hoping that woman will show up, but my sister and Emily should be on their way home by then."

"No problem," I said as I helped myself to Brawny's fabulous roasted garlic paste. A dollop of that on toasted sourdough bread and my taste buds went to heaven. "It's great that Emily is so excited about Ty."

I didn't want Detweiler's family to feel awkward around me because I wasn't getting along with Thelma. The fact that Ginny had called in advance rather than simply calling on her way here signaled an attempt to be extra-considerate.

"I get out at one fifteen," Anya said. "But all I've got before that is lunch and study hall. Mom, could I leave school early? I won't miss anything. Could Brawny give me a ride home so I can see Emily when she's here?"

"Of course."

Friday morning set butterflies fluttering in my chest. After the kids had gone to sleep, Detweiler told me that Bonnie Gossage was not doing well. "She blames herself. I updated Jeremy on our progress, or lack thereof, and he was grateful. Your ideas were good ones, but as you know, this is the plodding type of work the public never realizes is happening. Banging on the doors of companies, explaining to their HR people that we don't need to invade anyone's privacy. We've got that Indenti-Kit image of the woman who calls herself Jana Higgins. We're simply trying to match up a person on maternity leave with our abductor."

"When you say Bonnie Gossage is not doing well, what exactly do you mean?"

He spoke to the light fixture overhead. I watched the sharply cut silhouette of his mouth and chin as he found the right words. "She's deeply, deeply depressed. They might need to move her into a hospital and get her psychiatric care. This has really hit her hard. Jeremy explained that Bonnie has always seen herself as an extremely capable woman, which she is, and this has rocked her foundation."

Even after his breathing became deep and regular, I couldn't get to sleep. Tiptoeing out of bed, I crept into the nursery. Ty's lips puckered and trembled in his sleep as he dreamed of nursing at my breast. A warm tingling told me my milk had let down. Pulling over the padded rocking chair, I sat in the narrow band of moonlight streaming through the space between the blinds and the sill. There was only enough dim light for me to see my son's fuzzy hair. I thought about touching him, but it's best to let sleeping babies lie. Especially when they've got a good routine going, like Ty has. So instead, I watched him and counted my blessings. I rocked my way around the world and back, saying prayers for Bonnie and her baby.

73

Rather than go into work only to turn around and come back home, I sent Brawny to take my place at the store. Before she dropped off Erik and Anya at school, I made an executive decision that Erik might as well come home early, too. Seeing his cousin Emily would be good for him. It wasn't like I would ruin his chances of going to college by letting him skip out a half-day of kindergarten. He and I could cuddle up on the sofa and watch movies until I went in to teach my crop.

With Brawny gone, I had the chance to spend a bit of Mommy and me time with Ty. I marveled over his perfect fingers and adorable toes. Gracie wandered over and sniffed his head while I fed him. When she licked his crown with that huge, wet tongue of hers, his eyes grew wide and I could have sworn he smiled.

At noon, the doorbell rang and I opened it to Ginny and Emily, both carrying brown paper bags with food from Panera. "I figured it was easier than having you make something," she said after giving me a hug.

Each time I saw Ginny, she looked more and more like her

brother. At first, I couldn't see the resemblance, but her mannerisms and the cadence of her speech patterns matched his. Emily has Ginny's eyes and her father Jeff's round face, but she loves animals and moves with a speed and strength that's surprising for a thirteen-year-old. "Can I see the baby, huh?"

"Manners, young lady," her mother admonished her.

"Of course you can," I said. "He's sleeping in his play pen on the floor in the family room."

"Don't you dare wake him up." Ginny shook a finger in Emily's face. "Did you hear me? He'll be up soon enough. I'm sure Kiki's got him on a schedule."

With that stern warning, Emily flounced off into the family room while Ginny and I went into the kitchen. As I got down plates, I said, "Anya, Erik, and Brawny will be back soon. I decided to let them take a half day off. It's been pretty hectic around here."

"Um, I've been meaning to talk to you about that." Ginny knew where I keep the cutlery, so she opened the drawer and retrieved eating utensils. Without looking at me, she said, "Mom's been really tough on you, and I think you deserve to know the reason why."

I arched an eyebrow. "I know why. She's been very clear. According to her I work too much. I'm not home enough. I've endangered my baby."

Ginny turned around and leaned against the counter, a pose so like her brother's that the resemblance was uncanny. "No. That's what you think is bothering her. It's the proverbial tip of the iceberg. Possibly the same chunk of frozen water that sank the Titanic. It's that big expanse under the water that you need to be aware of. See, I figured no one told you, so it was up to me."

"Told me what?"

"Mom lost three babies. All late term. One before Chad and one before and after she had me."

A swift punch to the gut wouldn't have knocked more air out of me. I struggled to catch my breath. "What? How?"

"Whew," Ginny exhaled. "I figured you didn't know. I'm not sure Chad does, either. Patty has had problems carrying a baby to term, too. Paul doesn't want her to try again, but she's got the fever now. Seeing little Ty."

"Back up. Tell me about your mother." I sank down onto one of my kitchen chairs. Ginny took one, too, facing me. As per usual, she wore an Oxford cloth button-collar shirt, a cardigan, and jeans. Patty was more of a girly-girl. How odd it was that the more feminine of the two sisters was the one who didn't have a child.

Ginny pushed a green tea toward me. "I remember Chad saying you like these. Here's the deal: Mom had problems with her first pregnancy. When there wasn't a heartbeat, the doctor told Dad, but didn't tell her. He insisted to Dad that Mom should carry the baby until her body expelled it. Some nonsense about how it would train her womb to get it right the next time. As you can imagine, the result was horrifying. When Mom found out that Dad knew, and kept it from her, it nearly destroyed their marriage. Chad came along. That helped a lot. But when she got pregnant again and started spotting, the doctor blamed her. Said she'd been on her feet too much. She delivered a stillborn girl. I was her way of making it up to Dad for 'killing his daughter.' Those are her words."

I could not believe what I was hearing. "She actually believed that hooey?"

"Yeah," Ginny blew out a long gust of pent up air. "Yeah, she did. You have to remember, we're talking about a country doctor. People didn't go get a second opinion back then. Mom never planned on having Patty. She was an accident. Patty's a bit of a stinker because Mom carries this awful guilt about the babies she lost."

I didn't unwrap my turkey sandwich. I couldn't. My stomach had tied itself into a knot. Instead, I contented myself with sipping at my tea. Ginny's story struck me as unspeakably sad. A doctor's ignorance had infected Thelma Detweiler's psyche, sickening her. He had twisted her natural sense of responsibility into an irrational way of thinking. As a result, she'd panicked when she saw me working up until the time of Ty's delivery.

"I don't know what to say." I lifted my eyes to Ginny's. I'd expected her to demand that I forgive her mother. Maybe even call Thelma on the spot and tell her that I understood.

"I don't expect you to say anything. Or do anything." Ginny gave me a lopsided grin. "That's not why I told you. I wanted you to know this isn't about you. You're doing a wonderful job raising three terrific kids. Don't let Mom's burden weigh you down."

74

Brawny had wisely foreseen that Erik would be the odd man out, figuratively speaking. Rather than chance him getting in the way of his older cousins, she'd taken the precaution of asking if Chase Lutz could come over and play. Chase was another kindergartener, a boy that Miss Maggie heartily approved of. Brawny had even phoned Chase's mother to see if she could pick him up early. Nancy Lutz was more than willing to comply because she had tons of errands to run.

The three kids hit the back door in a flurry of excitement, promptly waking up Ty. That was fine, because while Brawny took care of coats and lunches, I was able to show off the baby. Ginny and I helped Emily, Erik, and even Chase as they took turns holding Ty. Chase wrinkled his nose in disgust after we heard a gurgling splat. "This baby stinks."

While I took Ty upstairs to fresh him up, Anya shared the photos she'd taken of Ty's birth. I was none too pleased about this, but I decided we'd discuss the matter later. "See?" I heard my daughter's eager voice. "It was really, really gross and messy. Like when that barn cat had her babies only a lot more yuck."

"Anya?" I heard Ginny's mildly reproachful tone. "Would you

want your daughter to share photos like that? Those seem very personal and private to me. I suggest you put your phone away before your mother comes downstairs and sees what you're doing."

A grin spread across my face.

I hadn't been entirely sure what to think of Ginny Volker. She had always been nice enough. Pleasant, although distant. I actually knew Emily better than her mother, especially after Emily and Anya had become good friends.

Ginny had taken a chance by telling me about her mom. She'd also made a stand and come down on my side, rather than leaving me floundering around in the dark. I hadn't expected to have a baby and gain a sister. But maybe that's exactly what had happened.

If so, I was one heck of a lucky mom.

75

At four o'clock, I figured I'd better get going. It was hard for me to leave the house, but I was obligated to teach the "A Star Is Born" class. Besides, there was always the chance that Jana Higgins might turn up. I doubted it. After so many days and nights of wondering and worrying about Bonnie's baby, I'd reached a point where my emotions were worn out. None of our ideas for tracking the child down had worked. Jana had proven herself to be a cagy adversary—and lest I forget, a murderer as well. I tended to focus on the baby, but Detweiler had reminded me over breakfast, "She's also a cold-blooded killer. Shooting a person at close range takes an emotional detachment that even police officers have trouble with. If she does show up at your store, don't kid yourself. She's gone to extraordinary measures to abduct that baby, and as time passes, and she sees herself as his mother, she's liable to resort to even more violence to keep her little boy."

While the little boys played with a Star Wars set of action figures and the girls dabbled in makeup that Laurel had given Anya, Ginny and I had relaxed on the sofa taking turns holding Ty. All in all, it had been a very pleasant visit. One that I was loath to see end. But there was no help for it. While I put on my coat, I asked Ginny if Emily might like to come with us to Florida. She cocked her head and considered the invitation. "How about if we meet you down there? Jeff and I have been talking about taking a family vacation. That way the girls could stay with us so you'd have more room at your friend Cara's house." That sounded pretty terrific and I said as much.

Then I gritted my teeth and told my kids, Emily, Ginny, and Brawny goodbye.

Because I'd taken most of the day off, I knew I needed to arrive back at Time in a Bottle early for the class. I doubted that Jana Higgins would show up, but it could happen. The session would begin at six, and the page kits had been prepped for a while, but I wanted to go over my notes again. There were always a dozen small chores to perform. I use a small wipe board as a visual aid, and I like to make sure it's cleaned thoroughly before each class. Erasable pens have a habit of drying up easily. Checking them is a good idea. I like to print the first page of my handouts on colorful paper, because that makes them more memorable. That also means I need to collate and staple together the plain pages that follow.

Margit was working the sales floor when I arrived. I told her to go put her feet up and have dinner. She'd baked homemade gingerbread cookies for our guests. I had planned to order pizza rather than fuss around with a slow cooker meal as we usually did.

Clancy had taken a dinner break, but Margit assured me she would be back soon. I took my notes to the front counter where I could look them over and greet any customers who arrived super early. That's where I was when the front door flew open and Jana Higgins came in. A scarf shielded her features as she glanced around furtively. "I paid for this class," she said.

"Yes, I know you did. It starts at six." An electricity in the air buzzed around us.

"I can't stick around. I left the car running with my baby in it."

"Oh." I half expected her to pull a gun on me, right then and there. "Okay, so I guess you want to take the kit and leave? Is that it? You could always turn off the car and bring—"

"No."

Out of the corner of my eyes, I noticed Margit pop her head out of the back room. Please, oh, please don't come out here and say anything, I sent her a wordless message. She must have understood, because she disappeared.

"All right. The kits are on the worktable. Let's go see them. You've got several choices." As I walked past her, every hair on my body stood at attention. Would she follow? Would she stab me in the back? Shoot me?

But I heard her feet shuffle behind me. When we got to the table, I spread the layouts in front of us. "Take your pick."

After going through them, she said, "Who all are coming tonight?"

"I don't remember. The list is up at the counter. Want me to get it? Or was there anyone in particular you were hoping to see?"

"That lawyer lady." She turned to stare at me, her eyes gleaming with intensity.

"Bonnie?"

"Yes. Did she have her baby?"

I swallowed. Was this a test? How was I supposed to answer? If I lied, wouldn't she realize I was onto her? I had no choice but to tell the truth. "Yes, she did."

Jana slid one hand deep into a coat pocket. I tried to ignore her gesture. With the other, she picked up a packet. "This one."

I did my best to smile. "I like that one. You get an album with it. They're behind the counter."

Once again, I turned my back on her. I could feel sweat breaking out along my upper lip. How on earth was I going to help Detweiler find this woman? No way would she give me any information he could use. I couldn't walk out to her car. That would be too obvious. I couldn't tackle her, because she was bigger than I, and what if she ran off? We'd never find the baby.

"You'll want a bag," I said. "Especially since you'll be carrying the baby into the house. It's still cold out, isn't it?"

"I have a heated garage," her words seemed eerily flat. "So is Bonnie bringing her baby tonight?"

Another test. I concentrated on opened one of the paper shopping bags we keep under the counter. "No."

"Why not?"

I didn't dare look at her. Instead, I fumbled around with tissue paper. "Something happened. She doesn't have her baby. I don't know much about it."

"Probably for the best, don't you think? Her husband didn't want a boy. Remember? She said he didn't. You shouldn't be allowed to have kids if you don't want them. Because then you don't treat them right, do you?" Her whole person leaned into the counter with an urgency I wanted to draw back from. And yet, I knew I couldn't. This was how Jana Higgins had justified what she'd done. She'd pick up on Bonnie's casual comment about Jeremy wanting a girl, and she'd extrapolated it. In that simple statement of preference, Jana had found an excuse for abduction...and murder.

"You're right," I said, hoping against hope that I wouldn't give my true feelings away. "They didn't want a boy. They didn't deserve to have a child. Someone else should have it. Someone who's going to love it with all her heart."

With a quick move, Jana grabbed the bag out of my hand. "You've got that right."

76

Three hours later

There had never been a longer class in the history of my store. Ever. I thought I was going to jump out of my skin before it was over. Each time a customer made a mundane statement I wanted to yell, "Do you realize what's happening out there? My husband is trying to track down a murderer! A killer who snatched Bonnie Gossage's baby! And you're griping because you can't get your letters straight on your page? Gimme a break!"

But I didn't. Probably because Clancy handed me half a Xanax. "You're going to need this to get through the evening. I'll drive you home."

She was right. When I wasn't drumming my fingers on the work tables or stuffing my face with pizza, I was picking at my scalp, a bad habit that surfaces when I'm upset.

"Do you have lice?" asked one of my customers.

"Not that I know of," I said. "It's anxiety."

"Over what?" asked a middle-aged woman who used scissors the way a jungle guide whacks vines with a machete. She'd totally destroyed two sets of embellishments, and she was whittling down a third when I yanked the pieces out of her hand. (By the way, that's something I never do, which only shows you how frustrated I felt. First of all, it's rude. Second, it's counterproductive because people learn by doing. Last of all, it's dangerous because certain people, like this woman, have been known to stab instructors in the hand with craft knives. This is a dangerous hobby, under adverse circumstances.)

"My mother-in-law," I blurted. "She's driving me nuts."

As an excuse, it proved superb. The rest of the evening women one-upped each other talking about the horrible treatment they'd endured at the hands of their dear MILs. On a more cheery note, the class ended with a comparison of common poisons and how to administer them.

Once Clancy locked the door behind everyone, she planted herself in the middle of the store and lectured me. "Do not ever, ever share with our customers again your personal favorite methods for knocking off family members. Okay? I could have lived the whole life without hearing how anti-freeze mixed in Gatorade is practically undetectable. Or that cutting a slit in a nicotine patch and slapping it into someone's skin will do them in. What's gotten into you? Next time, I'm dosing you with the whole Xanax. See if I don't."

She grumbled most of the way to my house. Taking me by the arm, she marched me into the kitchen and plunked me down in a chair. "Brawny? She's your problem now."

But before she could get back into her car, Hadcho pulled up with Detweiler in the passenger seat. "Dudley Do Right and his sidekick have arrived," Clancy said as she came back into the kitchen. "Okay, boys, spill it so I can hit the road. It's been a long, long night and I'm eager to crack open a bottle of wine."

"We got her." Detweiler pulled me into an embrace. I shivered at the cold feel of his jacket. "It's over," he said to my hair. "The baby is fine. That woman put up a bit of a howl, but nothing we couldn't handle."

Hadcho clapped me on the back. "Way to go, Kiki. Your idea of slipping your cell phone into that shopping bag was genius. Pure genius. Detweiler was able to turn on the 'Find my iPhone' app and we were golden."

Brawny clapped her hands together. "Aye, what a spot of good news!"

But we didn't have the chance to celebrate for long, because we were interrupted by a loud knocking at the front door. Anya yelled, "I'll get it," from the living room, where she'd been watching a movie with Erik. The sounds of the song "Let It Go" seemed oddly incongruous given the news that the Gossages' baby had been recovered.

Detweiler let loose of me and followed our daughter to the foyer. "Anya? What have I told you about answering the door?"

"But you're here, and so is Hadcho," I heard her sass him.

"We'll discuss this later," Detweiler said, over the sound of the dead bolt turning.

A hushed murmur of men's voices followed.

"You don't suppose that's the news media, do you?" Clancy wondered.

Her question hung in the air for only a tick as Detweiler came back into the kitchen. Behind him were two men with short cropped haircuts. Both carried themselves with military bearing, and they wore identical long topcoats. The man in the front opened a leather wallet and flashed a badge. "I'm Special Agent in Charge Bret Sanders. This is Special Agent Phillip Montana. We're here to speak to Bruce Macavity."

"Bruce Macavity?" I repeated his request. "You must have the wrong house. We don't have anyone by that name here. There's

Brawny, and she's a Macavity, but you must have gotten your wires crossed."

But Brawny moved me gently to one side and stepped forward to face Agent Sanders. Squaring her shoulders, she said, "I am—I was—Bruce Macavity."

***

KIKI'S STORY CONTINUES WITH...

Fatal, Family, Album: Book #13 in the Kiki Lowenstein Mystery Series

A SPECIAL GIFT FOR YOU

I am deeply appreciative of all my readers, and so I have a special gift for you. It's a full-length digital book called ***Bad, Memory, Album.*** Just go here and tell me where to send your digital book https://dl.bookfunnel.com/jwu6iipe1g.

All best always,

Joanna

For any book to succeed, reviews are essential. If you enjoyed this book please leave a review on Amazon. A sentence or two can make all the difference! Please leave a review of ***Glue, Baby, Gone*** here – here http://www.Amazon.com/review/create-review?&asin=B01F9YGX91

THE KIKI LOWENSTEIN MYSTERY SERIES

BY JOANNA CAMPBELL SLAN

Every scrapbook tells a story. Memories of friends, family and ... murder? You'll want to read the Kiki Lowenstein books in order: Kiki Lowenstein Mystery Series - https://amzn.to/38VkBjW

~

Looking for more enjoyable reads? Joanna has a series just for you!

Cara Mia Delgatto Mystery Series, a traditional cozy mystery series with witty heroines, and former flames reconnecting, set in Florida's beautiful Treasure Coast - https://amzn.to/3oz9urN

The Jane Eyre Chronicles, Charlotte Bronte's Classic Strong-Willed Heroine Lives On. – **https://amzn.to/3r3Ybmd**

The Confidential Files of John H. Watson, a new series featuring Sherlock Holmes and John Watson. - https://amzn.to/3bDnSWo

About the author...
Joanna Campbell Slan

Joanna is a *New York Times* and a *USA Today* bestselling author who has written more than 40 books, including both fiction and non-fiction works. She was one of the early Chicken Soup for the Soul authors, and her stories appear in five of those *New York Times* bestselling books. Her first non-fiction book, ***Using Stories and Humor: Grab Your Audience*** (Simon & Schuster/Pearson), was endorsed by Toastmasters International, and lauded by Benjamin Netanyahu's speechwriter. She's the author of four mystery series. Her first novel—***Paper, Scissors, Death: Book #1 in the Kiki Lowenstein Mystery Series***—was shortlisted for the Agatha Award. Her first historical mystery—***Death of a Schoolgirl: Book #1 in the Jane Eyre Chronicles***—won the Daphne du Maurier Award of Excellence. Her contemporary series set in Florida continues this year with ***Ruff Justice Book #5 in the Cara Mia Delgatto Mystery Series***. Her fantasy thriller series starts with ***Sherlock Holmes and the Giant Sumatran Rat***.

In addition to writing fiction, Joanna edits the Happy Homicides Anthologies and has begun the Dollhouse Décor & More series of "how to" books for dollhouse miniaturists.

Joanna independently published ***I'm Too Blessed to be Depressed*** back in 2004 when she was working as a motivational speaker. She sold more than 34,000 copies of that title. Since then she's gone on to independently publish a full-color book, ***The Best of British Scrapbooking,*** numerous digital books, and coloring books. Her book ***Scrapbook Storytelling*** sold 120,000 copies.

She's been an Amazon Bestselling Author too many times to count and has been included in the ranks of Amazon's Top 100 Mystery Authors.

A former talk show host and sought-after motivational speaker, Joanna has spoken to small and large (1000+) groups on four continents. *Sharing Ideas Magazines* named her "one of the top 25 speakers in the world."

When she isn't banging away at the keyboard, Joanna keeps busy walking her Havanese puppy Jax. An award-winning miniaturist, Joanna builds dollhouses, dolls, and furniture from scratch. She's also an accredited teacher of Zentangle®. Her husband, David, owns Steinway Piano Gallery-DC and five other Steinway piano showrooms.

Contact Joanna at JCSlan@JoannaSlan.com.

Follow her on social media by going here
https://www.linktr.ee/JCSlan